MUCHO RAVES
FOR
MU

"A SPRINGLOADED tlesnake of a novel tha into you when you lea expect it. Readers already familiar with Lansdale's work won't want to miss this one, and as for those who aren't—where the hell have you been?"

—F. Paul Wilson, author of *The Select*

)

"IT'S THE SNAPPY, FREQUENTLY RAUNCHY DIALOGUE that widens the eyes and provides the burst of humor. . . . When you read a novel starring Leonard Pine and Hap Collins, you spend a lot of time laughing and shaking your head. Emulating an early hero, Mark Twain, he uses crisp dialogue and humor to leaven serious topics."

—*Rocky Mountain News*

)

"I've never read anything like it. Not just a fine mystery full of unexpected moves, but a better novel about black-white friendship and rural life than anything I've ever read. I LOVED IT, MAN, THOUGHT IT WAS A HOWL FROM BEGINNING TO END."

—James Crumley, author of *The Mexican Tree Duck*

)

more . . .

"JOE LANSDALE IS ONE OF PUBLISHING'S BEST-KEPT SECRETS."　　　　*—Dallas Morning News*

)

"SAVAGELY ENTERTAINING . . . TAP DANCES THROUGH TWIN MINEFIELDS OF RACE AND OFF-BEAT SEX. . . . To read this novel is to live in that terrible and exhilarating moment between the knife-cut and the pain, between the gush of blood and the deadly onset of shock."

　　　　　　　—Joe Gores, author of *Menaced Assassin*

)

"THOUGHTFUL AND WITTY . . . Lansdale sneaks over philosophic points cleverly. I can't remember a more entertaining blueprint for the way blacks and whites, gays and straights can live in friendship."

　　　　　　　　　　　—*Charlotte Observer*

)

"JOE R. LANSDALE IS A BORN STORYTELLER, AND *MUCHO MOJO* is the story he was born to tell. This is the kind of mystery that would make Agatha Christie hide under the bed."

　　　　　　　—Robert Bloch, author of *Psycho*

)

"SATISFYING . . . EXTRAORDINARILY MEMORABLE. The friendship and smart-ass patter between Hap and Leonard is so real it's palpable. The plot is compelling. And one can practically hear the wind and taste the dust of an East Texas summer. Damn, this is good."　　　　　　**—*Booklist* (starred review)**

"A GRIPPING PLOT lays bare the East Texas mindset, unexplained murders, and raw truth about ugly secrets. A GREAT READ."

—*Los Angeles Features Syndicate*

)

"A CROSS BETWEEN ROBERT B. PARKER AND STEPHEN KING. . . . It gets your attention, that's for sure."

—*San Jose Mercury News*

)

"JOE R. LANSDALE HAS STAKED HIS CLAIM AND STRUCK PAYDIRT with his macabre tale of a serial killer in MUCHO MOJO. . . . I often found myself grinning like an idiot while reading MUCHO MOJO, thanks to Lansdale's strange, often ribald humor."

—*Mostly Murder*

)

"THE PROSE IS HARD-BITTEN, THE TONE DARKLY HUMOROUS."

—*Houston Chronicle*

)

"NOT ONLY A TOP-DRAWER THRILLER, BUT A SOCIAL PORTRAIT OF A SOCIETY IN PAINFUL EVOLUTION. . . . There's a touch of Harry Crews in him, a streak of Cormac McCarthy . . . Joe R. Lansdale keeps his own voice, and it's one well worth listening to and enjoying. . . . MUCHO MOJO will make you both laugh and wince, and keep on turning the pages."

—*Locus*

"*MUCHO MOJO* IS SOME MAJOR MAGIC . . . as funny as all get-out . . . a story of richness of character and setting. . . . It's not inappropriate to place it in the tradition of cross-cultural buddy novels that goes back through *Huckleberry Finn*. It's that good."

—*Ft. Lauderdale Sun-Sentinal*

)

"A REAL NAIL-BITING PAGE TURNER . . . [with] truly memorable characters . . . a superbly crafted and compelling murder mystery . . . a worthwhile addition to the category of the gay mystery." —*In Step*

)

"LANSDALE COULD EASILY SWEEP THE AWARDS. . . . The hypnotic otherworldly setting alone is worth the read, but the lead characters are wonderfully charming. Readers can only hope the author will bring them back." —*Texas Monthly*

)

"MORE THAN A MYSTERY, *MUCHO MOJO* is about friendship, family loyalty, and pride. . . . Lansdale is one of the best regional novelists around."

—*Killing Time*

BRILLIANTLY EXECUTED. . . . One thing about Lansdale, he's always exploring new directions. He's one of America's most gifted writers, and MUCHO MOJO proves why."

—*Time Tunnel*

)

"A SUPERB WORK. . . . embraces the mystery field while transcending its every convention. . . . One of the best novels of the year. . . . READ IT AS SOON AS POSSIBLE—YOU WON'T BE DISAPPOINTED."

—*BookLovers*

)

"Hunting Joe R. Lansdale novels has provided me with many of my most delicious moments as a book collector. . . . He is this generation's one and only answer to Frederic Brown, Seabury Quinn, Manly Wade Wellman, H. P. Lovecraft, all those gleeful pulp gods of the 1940s. . . . He's got a wicked streak the size of the Rio Grande and a compassionate streak at least as long. HE'S ALREADY PRODUCED THREE FLAT-OUT CLASSICS, AND HE'LL WRITE MORE."

—*Creative Loafing*

BY JOE R. LANSDALE

Novels

ACT OF LOVE

THE MAGIC WAGON

DEAD IN THE WEST

THE NIGHTRUNNERS

THE DRIVE-IN: A B-Movie with Blood and Popcorn, Made in Texas

THE DRIVE-IN II: Not Just One of Them Sequels

COLD IN JULY

SAVAGE SEASON

CAPTURED BY THE ENGINES

MUCHO MOJO

THE TWO-BEAR MAMBO

Juvenile

TERROR ON THE HIGH SKIES

Short Story Collections

BY BIZARRE HANDS

STORIES BY MAMA LANSDALE'S YOUNGEST BOY

BESTSELLERS GUARANTEED

WRITER OF THE PURPLE RAGE

ELECTRIC GUMBO

Anthologies (as Editor)

BEST OF THE WEST

NEW FRONTIERS

RAZORED SADDLES (with Pat LoBrutto)

DARK AT HEART (with Karen Lansdale)

WIERD BUSINESS (with Rick Klaw)

Nonfiction

THE WEST THAT WAS (with Thomas W. Knowles)

THE WILD WEST SHOW (with Thomas W. Knowles)

ATTENTION: SCHOOLS AND CORPORATIONS

MYSTERIOUS PRESS books are available at quantity discounts with bulk purchase for educational, business, or sales promotional use. For information, please write to: SPECIAL SALES DEPARTMENT, MYSTE-RIOUS PRESS, 1271 AVENUE OF THE AMERICAS, NEW YORK, N.Y. 10020

**ARE THERE MYSTERIOUS PRESS BOOKS
YOU WANT BUT CANNOT FIND IN YOUR LOCAL STORES?**

You can get any MYSTERIOUS PRESS title in print. Simply send title and retail price, plus 95¢ per order and 95¢ per copy to cover mailing and handling costs for each book desired. New York State and California residents add applicable sales tax. Enclose check or money order only, no cash please, to: MYSTERIOUS PRESS, P.O. BOX 690, NEW YORK, N.Y. 10019

JOE R. LANSDALE

Mucho Mojo

THE MYSTERIOUS PRESS

Published by Warner Books

A Time Warner Company

If you purchase this book without a cover you should be aware that this book may have been stolen property and reported as "unsold and destroyed" to the publisher. In such case neither the author nor the publisher has received any payment for this "stripped book."

MYSTERIOUS PRESS EDITION

Copyright © 1994 by Joe R. Lansdale
All rights reserved.

Cover design and illustration by Matt Tepper

The Mysterious Press name and logo are registered trademarks of Warner Books, Inc.

 Mysterious Press books are published by
Warner Books, Inc.
1271 Avenue of the Americas
New York, NY 10020

Ⓦ A Time Warner Company

Printed in the United States of America

Originally published in hardcover by The Mysterious Press.
First Printed in Paperback: September, 1995

10 9 8 7 6 5 4 3 2 1

This book is dedicated with love and respect and the deepest devotion to the most imortant person in my life. My wife, Karen.

Thanks are in order for some folks who helped see this project through: Barbara Puechner; Andrew Vachss; Neal Barrett, Jr.; David Webb; and of course, Jeff Banks. I'd also like to give a nod toward my old rose-field buddies, Sam Griffith and Larry Walters, and thank my "Aunt" Ardath as well as my karate instructor, Richard Metteauer.

It doesn't matter whom you are paired against; your opponent is always yourself.

—*Nakamura*

1.

It was July and hot and I was putting out sticks and not thinking one whit about murder.

All the other rose-field jobs are bad, the budding, the digging, but putting out sticks, that's the job they give sinners in Hell.

You do sticks come dead of summer. Way it works is they give you this fistful of bud wood, and you take that and sigh and turn and look down the length of the field, which goes on from where you are to some place east of China, and you gird your loins, bend over, and poke those sticks in the rows a bit apart. You don't lift up if you don't have to, 'cause otherwise you'll never finish. You keep your back bent and you keep on poking, right on down that dusty row, hoping eventually it'll play out, though it never seems to, and of course that East Texas sun, which by 10:30 A.M. is like an infected blister leaking molten pus, doesn't help matters.

So I was out there playing with my sticks, thinking the usual thoughts about ice tea and sweet, willing women, when the Walking Boss came up and tapped me on the shoulder.

I thought maybe it was water break, but when I looked up he jerked a thumb toward the end of the field, said, "Hap, Leonard's here."

"He can't come to work," I said. "Not unless he can put out sticks with his cane."

"Just wants to see you," the Walking Boss said, and moved away.

I poked in the last stick from my bundle, eased my back straight, and started down the center of the long dusty row, passing the bent, sweaty backs of the others as I went.

I could see Leonard at the far end of the field, leaning on his cane. From that distance, he looked as if he were made of pipe cleaners and doll clothes. His raisin-black face was turned in my direction and a heat wave jumped off of it and vibrated in the bright light and dust from the field swirled momentarily in the wave and settled slowly.

When Leonard saw I was looking in his direction, his hand flew up like a grackle taking flight.

Vernon Lacy, my field boss, known affectionately to me as the Old Bastard though he was my age, decked out in starched white shirt, white pants, and tan pith helmet, saw me coming too. He came alongside Leonard and looked at me and made a slow and deliberate mark in his little composition book. Docking my time, of course.

When I got to the end of the row, which only took a little less time than a trek across Egypt on a dead camel, I was dust covered and tired from trudging in the soft dirt. Leonard grinned, said, "Just wanted to know if you could loan me fifty cents."

"You made me walk all the way here for fifty cents, I'm gonna see I can fit that cane up your ass."

"Let me grease up first, will you?"

Lacy looked over and said, "You're docked, Collins."

"Go to hell," I said.

Lacy swallowed and walked away and didn't look back.

"Smooth," Leonard said.

"I pride myself on diplomacy. Now tell me it isn't fifty cents you want."

"It isn't fifty cents I want."

Leonard was still grinning, but the grin shifted slightly to one side, like a boat about to take water and sink.

"What's wrong, buddy?"

"My Uncle Chester," Leonard said. "He passed."

I followed Leonard's old Buick in my pickup, stopping long enough along the way to buy some beer and ice. When we arrived at Leonard's place, we got an ice chest and filled it with the ice and the beer and carried it out to the front porch.

Leonard, like myself, didn't have air-conditioning, and the front porch was as cool a spot as we could find, unless we went down to the creek and laid in it.

We eased into the rickety porch swing and sat the ice chest between us. While Leonard moved the swing with his good leg, I popped us a couple.

"Happen today?" I asked.

"They found him today. Been dead two or three days. Heart attack. They got him at the LaBorde Funeral Home, pumped full of juice."

Leonard sipped his beer and studied the barbed-wire fence on the opposite side of the road. "See that mockingbird on the fence post, Hap?"

"Why? Is he trying to get my attention?"

"He's a fat one. You don't see many that fat."

"I wonder about that all the time, Leonard. How come mockingbirds don't normally get fat. Thought I might write a paper on it."

"My uncle's favorite bird. I always thought they were ugly, but he thought they were the grandest things in the world. He used to call me his little mockingbird when I was a kid because I mocked him and everybody else. I see one, I think of him. Hokey, huh?"

I didn't say anything. I focused my eyes on the floorboards at the edge of the porch, watched as a hot horsefly staggered on its disease-laden legs, trying to make the little bit of shade the porch roof provided. The fly faltered and stopped. Heatstroke, I figured.

"I want to go to Uncle Chester's funeral tomorrow," Leonard said. "But I don't know. I feel funny about it. He probably wouldn't want me there."

"From what you've told me about Uncle Chester, spite of the fact he disowned you when he found out you were queer—"

"Gay. We say gay now, Hap. You straights need to learn that. When we're real drunk, we call each other fags or faggots."

"Whatever. I'm sure, in his own way, Chester was a good guy. You loved him. It doesn't matter what he would have wanted. What matters is what you want. He's dead. He's not making decisions anymore. You want to go to the funeral and tell him 'bye because of the good things you remember about him, go on."

"Come with me."

"Hey, I'm sorry for Uncle Chester on account of what he meant to you, but I don't know him from brown rice. Fact is, him dying, you coming around upset, and me leaving the rose fields like that, I figure I don't have a job anymore. He

4

screwed up my income, so why the hell would I want to go to his funeral?"

"Because I want you to and you're my friend and you don't want to hurt my teeny-weeny feelings."

This was true.

I didn't like it, but I agreed. Going to a funeral seemed harmless enough.

2.

Funeral was the next day at three in the afternoon, so early next morning we drove to LaBorde in Leonard's car and over to J. C. Penney's.

We went there to buy suits, something neither Leonard or I had owned in years. My last suit had had a Nehru collar and a peace symbol about the size of an El Dorado hubcap on a chain a little smaller than you might need to tow a butane truck.

Leonard's last suit had been designed by the military.

Suits from Penney's didn't come with a vest and two pairs of pants anymore, least not the decent ones, and the prices were higher than I remembered. I thought perhaps we ought to go over to Kmart, see if they had something in sheen green. Something we got tired of wearing, we could use to upholster a chair.

I ended up with a dark blue suit and a light blue shirt and a dark blue tie. I bought black shoes, socks, and a belt. I tried the stuff on and looked at myself in the mirror. I thought I looked silly. Like a tall, biped pit bull in mourning.

Leonard bought a dark green Western-cut suit, a canary-yellow shirt, and a tie striped up in orange and green and yellow. Shoes he got were black with pointy toes and zippers down the side. Kind of shoes you hoped they stopped making about the time the Dave Clark Five quit making records.

"You're gonna bury Uncle Chester," I said. "Not take him on a Caribbean cruise. Show up in that, he might jump out of the box and throw a blanket over you."

"Jealousy is an ugly thing, Hap."

"You're right. I wish I looked like a head-on collision between Dolly Parton and Peter Max."

We changed back into our clothes, and I paid up because I was the only one working these days, even if it was sporadically, and because Leonard never let me forget it was my fault his leg was messed up. He'd say stuff like, "You know I got this leg messed up on account of you," then he'd pick something he wanted and I'd pay for it, because what he said was true. Wasn't for him, my funeral would have come before Uncle Chester's.

The services were in a little community on the outskirts of LaBorde, and after we went home and hung out awhile, we put the suits on and drove over in Leonard's wreck with no air-conditioning.

Time we got to the Baptist church where the funeral was being held, we had sweated up good in our new suits, and the hot wind blowing on me made my hair look as if it had been combed with a bush hog. My overall appearance was of someone who had been in a fight and lost.

I got out of the car and Leonard came around and said, "You still got the fucking tag hanging on you."

I lifted an arm and there was the tag, dangling from the suit sleeve. I felt like Minnie Pearl. Leonard got out his pocket knife and cut it off and we went inside the church.

We paraded by the open coffin, and of course, Uncle Chester hadn't missed his chance to be guest of honor. He was one ugly sonofabitch, and I figured alive he hadn't looked much better. He wasn't very tall, but he was wide, and being dead a few days before they found him hadn't helped his looks any. The mortician had only succeeded in making him look a bit like a swollen Cabbage Patch Doll.

After the eulogies and prayers and singing and people falling over the coffin and crying whether they wanted to or not, we drove out to a little cemetery in the woods and the coffin was unloaded from an ancient black hearse with a sticker on the back bumper that read BINGO FOR GOD.

Underneath a striped tent, with the hot wind blowing, we stood next to an open grave and the ceremony went on. There was a kind of thespian quality about the whole thing. The only one who seemed to be truly upset was Leonard. He wasn't saying anything, and he's too macho to cry in public, but I knew him. I saw the way his hands shook, the tilt of his mouth, the hooding of his eyes.

"It's a nice enough place to get put down," I whispered to Leonard.

"You're dead, you're dead," Leonard said. "You told me that. It's a thing takes the edge off how you feel about your surroundings."

"Right. Fuck Uncle Chester. Let's talk fashion. You'll note no one else here looks like a black fag Roy Rogers but you."

That got a smile out of him.

During the preacher's generic marathon tribute to Uncle Chester, I spent some time looking at a pretty black woman in a short, tight black dress standing near us. She, like Leonard, was one of the few not trying out for the Academy Awards. She didn't look particularly sad, but she was solemn. Now and then she turned and looked at Leonard. I couldn't tell if he noticed. A heterosexual would have noticed if there was anything romantic in her attitude or not. It can't be helped. A heterosexual dick senses a pretty woman, no matter what the cultural and social training of its owner, and it'll always point true north. Or maybe it's south, now that I think about it.

The preacher finished up a prayer slightly longer than the complete set of the *Encyclopedia Britannica* and signaled to lower the coffin.

A long lean guy with his hand on the device that lowers the coffin pushed the lever and the coffin started down, wobbled, righted itself. Someone in the audience let out a sob and went quiet. A woman in front of me, wearing a hat with everything on it but fresh fruit and a strand of barbed wire, shook and let out a wail and waved a hanky.

A moment later it was all over except for the grave diggers throwing dirt in the hole.

There was some hand-shaking and talking, and most of the crowd came over and spoke to Leonard and said how sorry they were, looked at me out of the corners of their eyes, suspicious because I was white, or maybe because they assumed I was Leonard's lover. It was bad enough they had a relative or acquaintance who was queer, but shit, looked like he was fucking a white guy.

We were invited, not with great enthusiasm, to a gathering of friends and family, but Leonard passed, and the crowd faded out. The pretty woman in black came over and smiled at Leonard and shook his hand and said she was sorry.

"I'm Florida Grange. I was your uncle's lawyer, Mr. Pine," she said. "Guess I still am. You're in the will. I'll make it official if you'll come by my office tomorrow. Here's my card. And here's the key to his house. You get that and some money."

Leonard took the key and card and stood there looking stunned. I said, "Hello, Miss Grange, my name's Hap Collins."

"Hello," she said, and shook my hand.

"You know my uncle well?" Leonard asked.

"No. Not really," Florida Grange said, and she went away, and so did we.

3.

Uncle Chester's house was in that part of LaBorde called the black section of town by some, nigger town by others, and the East Side by all the rest.

It was a run-down section that ten years ago had been in pretty good shape because it was on the edge of the white community before the white community moved farther west and the streets were abandoned here in favor of putting maintenance where the real money and power were, amongst the fat-cat honkies.

We drove down Comanche Street and bounced in some potholes deep enough a parachute would have been appropriate, and Leonard pulled up in a driveway spotted with pea gravel and several days' worth of newspapers.

The house in front of the drive was one story, but large and formerly fine, gone to seed with peeling paint and a roof that had been cheaply repaired with tin and tar. The tin patches caught the sunlight and played hot beams over it and reflected them back against the crumbly bricks of a chimney and the limbs of a great oak that hung over one side of the roof and scratched it and gave the yard below an umbrella of dark shade. There was more tin around the bottom of the house, concealing a crawlspace.

A ten-foot, wisteria-covered post was driven in the ground on the other side of the house, and sticking out from the post were long nails, and the mouths of beer and soft drink bottles engulfed the nails, and many of the bottles looked to have been shot apart or banged apart by rocks and clubs. Glass was heaped at the bottom of the pole like discarded costume jewelry.

I'd seen a rig like that years ago in the yard of an old black carpenter. I didn't know what it was then, and I didn't know what it was now. All I could think to call it was a bottle tree.

Front of the long porch some hedges grew wild and ungroomed, like old-fashioned, Afro-style haircuts, and between the hedges some slanting stone steps met the graying boards of the porch, and standing on the boards were two black men and a young black boy.

Before we got out of the car, I said, "Relatives of yours?"

"Not that I recognize," Leonard said.

We got out and walked up to the porch. The boy looked at us, but the men hardly noticed. The kid popped a thin rubber hose off his arm and tossed it aside, started rubbing his arm. The boy appeared confused but pleasant, as if awakening from a long, relaxed sleep.

One of the black men, a tall, muscular guy in T-shirt and slacks with a wedge of hair cut like a thin Mohawk and a hypodermic needle in his hand, said to the boy, "More candy where that come from, you got the price."

The boy went down the steps, between me and Leonard, and out into the street. Mohawk dropped the needle onto the porch. There were a couple other needles there, along with the rubber hose.

The other black guy was wearing a light blue shower cap, an orange T-shirt and jeans, and was about the size of a Rose Parade float. He looked down from the porch at us like it tired him out. He said to Leonard, "Shit, if you ain't the fucking bird of paradise."

"And propped on a stick," said Mohawk. "Who dresses you, brother? And you, white boy. You preachin' somewhere?"

"I'm selling insurance," I said. "You want some? Got a feeling you might need a little, come a few minutes."

Mohawk smiled at me like I was one funny guy.

"What are you doing here?" Leonard asked.

"We're standing on the motherfucking porch," Parade Float said. "Whatchoo doin' here?"

"I own the place."

"Ah," said Mohawk. "You must be that nutty Uncle Tom's boy?"

"I'm Chester Pine's nephew, that's what you mean."

"Well, hey, we was just doing a little business," said Mohawk. "Don't let your balls swell up."

"This ain't your office," Leonard said.

Mohawk smiled. "You know, you're right, but we was thinking of making it kind of an extension." He came out to the edge of the porch and pointed next door. "We live over there. That's our main office, Captain Sunshine."

I looked. It was a large run-down house on the lot next to Chester's place. A number of young black men came out on the long porch, stood and stared.

"That wasn't any measles vaccination you gave that kid," Leonard said. "How old was he? Twelve?"

"Don't know," said Parade Float. "We don't send him no birthday presents. Shit, all you know, we're free-lance doctors."

"I think you're free-lance assholes," Leonard said.

"Fuck you," Parade Float said.

"Do-gooders," Mohawk said. "Like in the movies. That's what you fucks are. Right?"

Leonard gave Mohawk a studied look. "Get off my property. Now. Otherwise, your friends next door'll be wiping you out of your big friend's ass here. Provided they can get what's left of him out of that shower cap."

"Fuck you," Parade Float said.

"I was wondering about that cap," I said. "You leave the water running? Go looking for a towel?"

"Fuck you," Parade Float said again.

"You run out of your daily word allotment," I said, "how you gonna beg us for mercy?"

"Wooo," Mohawk said. "This little talk could lead to something."

"Don't make me happy prematurely," Leonard said.

And then Leonard moved. His cane went out between Mohawk's legs, and he popped it forward, locking one of Mohawk's knees, and the move tossed Mohawk face-forward off the porch.

Leonard stepped aside and Mohawk hit the ground on his head. Sounded like it hurt.

That was my cue. As Parade Float stepped off the porch to get involved, I shot out a side kick and hit him on his stepping leg, square on the kneecap. He came down on his head too.

He got both hands under him, started to rise, and I kicked him in the throat with about a third of what I had.

He rolled over on his back holding his throat, gurgling. The shower cap stayed in place. I never realized how tight those little buddies fit. Maybe it was just the light blue ones.

Leonard had Mohawk up now and had dropped his cane and was working Mohawk with a series of lefts and rights and knee lifts, and he wouldn't let him fall. Mohawk's body was jumping all over the yard, like he had a pogo stick up his ass.

"That's enough, Leonard," I said. "Your knuckles will swell."

Leonard hit Mohawk a couple more under the short ribs and didn't move in close enough to support him this time. Mohawk crumpled on the grass, made a noise like gas escaping.

Parade Float had gotten to his knees. He was still holding his throat, sputtering. I checked out the folks on the porch next door. They were just standing there. In tough postures, of course.

Leonard yelled at them. "You retards want some, come on over."

Nobody wanted any. Which made me happy. I didn't want to tear up my brand new J. C. Penney's suit.

Leonard picked up his cane and looked at Parade Float, said, "I see you or your buddy here again, even see someone reminds me of you two, we're gonna kill you."

"Couldn't we just mess up their hair instead?" I said.

"No," Leonard said. "I want to kill them."

"There you are, guys," I said. "Death or nothing."

Mohawk had casually crawled to the edge of the yard near the bottle tree and was trying to get up. Parade Float had it together enough now that he could get up and go over and help

Mohawk to his feet. They limped and wheezed toward the house next door.

A tall black man on the porch over there yelled, "Your times are comin', you two. It's comin'."

"Nice meeting you, neighbors," Leonard said, and he got out his key and we went inside.

4.

The house was hot and filthy, the fireplace was full of trash, and there were great skeins of cobwebs all about. As we moved, dust puffed and floated in the sunlight that bled through thickly curtained windows and the place smelled sour and the smell came from a variety of things. One of them I felt certain was Uncle Chester himself. You die in a house and lay there for two days in the heat, you get a little ripe, and so do your surroundings.

I left the front door open. Not that it helped much. There wasn't any wind stirring.

"Damn," Leonard said. "It's like he didn't live here."

Considering the aroma he'd left behind, I felt that was debatable, but I said, "He was old, Leonard. Maybe he didn't move around much."

"He wasn't that old."

"You hadn't seen or heard from him in years. He could have been in a bad way."

"Maybe him giving me this place was some kind of final jab in the heart. I loved this house when I was a kid. He knew that. Shit, look at it now."

"Final days he maybe got his shit together. Decided to let bygones be bygones. Ms. Grange said he left you some money too."

"Confederate, most likely."

We moved on through the house. The kitchen was squalid with dirty dishes stacked in the sink and paper plates and TV dinner receptacles stuffed in the trash can. There was a pile of debris around the can, as if Chester had finally given up taking out the garbage and had started merely throwing stuff in that general direction.

Flies buzzed on patrol. On the counter, in a TV dinner tray, squirming in something green and fuzzy that might have been a partial enchilada, were maggots.

"Well," I said. "He damn sure lived in here."

"Shit," Leonard said. "This ain't no recent mess."

"No. He worked on this one."

Off the kitchen was a bedroom. We went in there. It was relatively neat. On the nightstand by the bed was a worn hardback copy of Thoreau's *Walden*. That was Leonard's favorite book, especially the chapter titled "Self Reliance."

I looked around the room. One wall was mostly bookshelf. The books were behind sliding glass.

Leonard went over to the closed curtain and opened it. The window glass was dusty yellow and tracked with fly specks. The frame had bars mounted on the outside of it, and you could see the house where Mohawk, Parade Float, and the assholes stayed.

"Old man was scared," I said.

"He wasn't never scared of nothing," Leonard said.

"You get older, you got to get scared. Courage is in proportion to your size and physical condition and what caliber weapon you carry. Some cases how much liquor, crack, or heroin you got in you."

"Man, this neighborhood hadn't never been ritzy, but it's really gone to the fucking dogs."

"Dogs wouldn't have it."

"This shit next door. I don't get it. Crack house and anyone with a glass eye in their head could tell that's what it is, but what're the cops doing? Kid was getting a jolt of horse on the porch, man. Right out in front of God and everybody."

"That's probably a free jolt," I said. "Horse doesn't come cheap. Later on, they get him needing a little, they'll tell him to try some rock. He takes that and he comes back 'cause it's got him and it's cheap. A kid can get rock for five dollars, even if he's got to steal trinkets to sell."

Leonard closed the curtain and we went out into the hallway and past the bathroom into the room next door.

"Jesus," Leonard said.

The room was full of ceiling-high stacks of yellowed newspapers. There was a little path between the stuff. We went down that, and the path turned left and opened up. There was a chair and table in the opening with a small rotating fan and papers on it.

If you sat in the chair and looked across the table, you could see the window opposite it, and provided the curtains hadn't been drawn shut, I figured I'd have been able to see bars and a dusty view of the crack house.

There was a ballpoint pen and a composition notebook on the desk. The notebook was open and I looked at the page.

Uncle Chester had been doodling. There were a number of little rectangles and the rectangles were numbered. There were some lines drawn at the top and bottom and on the sides.

It looked as if Uncle Chester hadn't had enough to do.

It was hot in there and the dust we'd stirred hung about in the dead air and around our heads like a veil. It choked me.

We went out of there and back into the living room, started out the front door to get some air, and that's when we noticed that besides the lock the key worked, there were no fewer than five locks or barricades on the door frame, you wanted to use them. There were two chain locks, a dead bolt, and a metal bar that fit into slots on either side of the door, and at the bottom and top of the door were swivel catches.

"He wasn't fucking around on security," I said.

"The assholes next door, I reckon," Leonard said.

We stood on the porch and the air was still not moving and it was still hot, but it was a hell of a lot more comfortable than the decaying air inside the house. Another couple of hours, the temperature would be down to ninety and the wind might be stirring, and inside the house, you had all the windows open and a fan going, you might be able to breathe without a respirator.

I looked over at the crack house. No one was visible. I said, "You did all right for a fella on a cane."

"Motherfuckers are lucky I can't get around good as usual. Another week, I'll be taking a dance class."

"That post with the bottles. What the hell is it? Ornamentation?"

"It's mojo shit. Protects you from evil spirits. Spirits supposed to go into the bottles and get trapped. Or maybe they go in and are tossed out and transformed into something safe. Don't know for sure. I remember seeing them now and then as a kid. Hearing about them. But Uncle Chester, he never believed in that shit. He was always practical as a hangman."

"There's things about people you never know, Leonard. Even people close as you and me. Hell, I might listen to polka records, all you know."

"Reckon so. Listen here, Hap. I got to see that lawyer tomorrow. Think I could get you to stay with me here tonight?"

"If I don't want to?"

"Long walk home."

"What I figured."

Though we hadn't planned on staying, we had brought a change of clothes with us, in anticipation of stopping somewhere to shed our suits so we could maybe get a bite to eat and go to a movie.

We put on the clothes and set about tidying the place up some. I drove into town proper and bought some plastic trash bags and some cleaning stuff, and when I got back, Leonard had started washing dishes in the sink.

While he did that, I pulled back all the curtains and opened all the windows and picked up the trash and bagged it and took it out to the side of the house.

Time I got that done, Leonard had finished the dishes and was doing general cleaning. Sweeping, mopping, beating down cobwebs with a broom, polishing the window bars, spraying Lysol about.

"There's roaches in here big enough to own property," Leonard said.

"I know. One just helped me carry the trash out."

Time we finished what we were willing to do, we were sweaty and dusty, and we took turns in the bathroom, washing up best we could. There wasn't any hot water.

We turned on the porch light and closed the windows and locked up the joint and stuffed the trunk and backseat with garbage bags and drove off. We put the garbage in a university dumpster when no one was looking, and went to a Burger King and ate. We went to a movie after that and came back to the house solid dark, watching to see if any of our friends next door were waiting to surprise us.

Guess they were still mulling over the ass kicking earlier that day. We could see a knot full of them out on the dark front porch over there, looking at us. We picked up the newspapers in the driveway and waved at our crack house buddies and went on in the house.

Leonard gave me the bedroom and took the couch in the living room. We laid about and read newspapers for a while, then sacked out. I left the bedroom door open to keep air circulating and I raised the window and turned on the overhead fan.

From where I lay, I could turn and look out the doorway and see Leonard lying in there on his back on the couch, his arm thrown over his eyes.

"I'm sorry about your uncle," I said.

"Yeah."

"Everybody has to go."

"Yeah. I wish things had worked out better between us."

"He loved you, Leonard. Otherwise he wouldn't have left you the house."

"I'd have liked for him to have told me he loved me. Sometimes, when I'm stupid, I feel guilty for being homosexual. Like I had some choice in how my hormones got put together. Uncle Chester found out, he treated me like I was a pervert. Like being gay means you molest children or take advantage of weaker men for sex."

"He wasn't any different than a lot of folks, Leonard."

"I've never forced anything on anyone else, and mostly I don't bother with sex at all. I got the problem of being attracted mostly to straight men and that doesn't work. Lot of gay guys act gay and that bothers me."

"That's odd, Leonard."

"No, that's pretty standard with a lot of gays. I think somewhat like a woman, I guess. I want to have a relationship with a man, but somehow, gay guys don't normally do much for me. I guess I've been taught they're odd, and I'm one of them. Go figure. I tell you, nature played a fucking joke on me."

"Ha. Ha."

"Hap, you ever feel funny being my friend, knowing I'm gay?"

"I don't normally think about it. I mean, you're not exactly a gay prototype."

"No one is."

"I mean, I'm not aware of it much, and when I am, I guess it strikes me odd. I accept it, but don't understand it. I don't see gays as perverts. Some are, some aren't, same as heterosexuals. But I am an East Texas boy and my background is Baptist—"

"I'm East Texas and Baptist background too."

"I know. I'm just saying. Sometimes, I am aware of it. It doesn't bother me exactly, but I'm aware of it and I feel a little confused."

"Think *you're* confused. Life would be easier, I was straight."

"Yep, but you ain't."

"Damn. Wish I'd thought of that."

"You ever watch *Leave It to Beaver?*"

"Yeah."

"End of that show, way I remember it anyway, the two brothers, Wally and the Beaver, they used to share a room and

23

have a talk before they turned out the light and went to bed. In that talk they summed up the episode you just watched, and the problems they'd gone through, and everything was capped off and solved in those last few minutes and they moved onto new stuff next week with no baggage. You know what?"

"What?"

"Life ain't like that."

"No, it ain't. Good night, Wally."

"Good night, Beave."

5.

Next morning Leonard called and made an appointment with Florida Grange and we drove over there.

Uptown or not, her building was in the cheap section, right next to a burned-out apartment complex on a red clay hill that had a highway cut through it. The apartment complex had burned down three years back and had yet to be rebuilt, and the clay on which it lay had started to shift toward the highway.

We entered her building and rode the elevator upstairs and saw a middle-aged woman exit a door holding her jaw. We passed the office she had come out of. It was the office of a dentist named Mallory. Florida Grange, Attorney at Law, was between it and a bail bond office.

We went in. No secretary. No lobby. The room was about the size of the men's restroom at the YMCA and it was mostly taken up with desk and chairs and file cabinets and a word processor. On the wall were framed degrees and certificates that vouched for Florida Grange's professional abilities.

Florida Grange was sitting behind her desk. She smiled when we came in and stood up and extended her hand, first to Leonard, then to me. When I shook it, the two large silver bracelets on her wrist rattled together.

She was wearing a short snow-white dress that made her chocolate skin and long kinky black hair radiant. I figured her for thirty years old, maybe thirty-five at the outside. Sweet chocolate in a smooth white wrapper.

I felt a bit self-conscious being there with her, wearing the clothes I'd slept in. I had brushed my teeth with some of Uncle Chester's toothpaste and my forefinger.

We took seats and Florida Grange sat back behind the desk and picked up a folder and said, "This is simple and won't take long. But it is a private matter, Mr. Pine."

She smiled at me when she said that, just to make sure I didn't break out crying.

"Me and Hap ain't that private. Nothing you got to say he can't hear. You already said I get the house and some money. There anything else?"

"It's a matter of how much . . . You're right, Mr. Pine. I'm being melodramatic."

"Leonard. I don't like to be called Mr. Pine. Call him Hap."

"Very well, Leonard. It's not a complicated will, so I'm going to forgo all the formality, if you don't mind?"

"I don't know," Leonard said. "I live for formality. I don't get some of it, I might get depressed."

She smiled at him. I wished she'd smile at me that way. "He left you the house and some money. One hundred thousand dollars."

Maybe that's why she didn't smile at me the same way. I didn't have one hundred thousand dollars.

"Where in hell did he get money like that?" Leonard said. "He was a security guard when he was working."

She shrugged. "If he'd been saving a while, that's not that unusual. Perhaps he had some bonds come due. Whatever, you inherited that much money. I'll arrange for you to receive it. One last thing, he left you this envelope and its contents."

She opened her desk drawer and removed a thick manila envelope. She handed it to Leonard. He opened it and peeked inside. He gave it to me. I peeked inside. There were a lot of newspaper clippings in there. I saw that one was a coupon for a dollar off a pizza. Good. We liked pizza.

I shook the envelope. Something heavy moved inside. I held the envelope so that whatever it was slid out through the clippings and into my palm.

It was a key. I gave it to Leonard.

"Looks like a safety-deposit box," he said.

"My thoughts exactly," I said.

"Goddamn, Doc!" came a clear voice through the wall.

Florida Grange, Attorney at Law, looked embarrassed, said, "I don't think he's a very good dentist. People yell a lot."

"That's all right," Leonard said. "We don't plan to use him."

"I keep planning to move," she said.

Leonard said, "Which was Uncle Chester's bank, you know?"

"Certainly. LaBorde, Main and North."

Leonard nodded, put the key back in the envelope. "You said you didn't know him, but you're his lawyer. You talked to him. You must have got some kind of impression."

"I met him about a month ago," she said. "He came to me and wanted me to handle his affairs."

"Did he seem sick?" Leonard asked.

"He seemed stressed. Like he was having some troubles. He thought he had Alzheimer's. He said that much."

"And did he?"

"I don't know. But he thought he did. He wanted to square things up in case his mind was going or his time was up. That's the way he expressed it."

"What I'm really asking is, did he say anything about me, other than what I inherited?"

"No. I'm sorry."

"That's all right," Leonard said, but I could tell it wasn't all right.

"I guess you know this, he shot a number of people a few months back. Or so the story goes."

"What?"

"I don't mean he killed anyone. I heard about it through the grapevine. I'm originally from that part of town. Where your uncle lived. My mama still lives there. Seems your uncle had some trouble with the people next door. Supposed to be a crack house."

"It is," Leonard said.

"Someone over there was playing around, shot some bottles off a post in his yard. I suppose they were talking about a bottle tree."

"They were," Leonard said.

"Your uncle was on his porch when it happened and a shot almost hit him he said, so he got his shotgun and went over there and shot some men on the porch. He had rat shot in the gun. Way it worked out, the police showed up and he got hauled in and the men went to the hospital to get the shot picked out. Your uncle was let go, and far as I know, it wasn't even in the papers."

"Happened in nigger town is why," Leonard said. "Bunch of niggers popping one another isn't news to the pecker-woods. They expect it."

"I suppose," Florida Grange said. "Anyway, that's something I can tell you about him, but that's about all."

I could tell Leonard was secretly pleased. It fit his memory of his Uncle Chester. Strong and upright, didn't take shit from anyone.

Grange had him fill out some papers and gave him some to take with him. By the time they were finished, the dentist drill had begun to whine.

"I'm sorry," Florida Grange said. "Let's go out in the hall."

We went. Leonard said, "I guess I don't really have anything else to ask, Miss Grange. Sorry I pulled you out here."

"I'm tired of the drill anyway," she said. "And if you're going by Leonard, call me Florida."

"OK, Florida. Thanks."

"You have any other questions, give me a call," she said.

"Is it OK I ask a question?" I said.

"Yes," she said.

"Are you married?"

"No."

"Anyone significant in your life right now?"

"Not really."

"Any possibility of me taking you to dinner?"

"I don't think so, Mr. Collins."

"I clean up pretty good."

"I'm sure you do, but I think not. Thanks for asking."

On the way down in the elevator, Leonard said, "Hap Collins, Lady Killer."

6.

In the car, while Leonard drove, I looked through the contents of the envelope.

"Anything there mean anything?" Leonard asked.

"Got a bunch of pizza coupons. Some for Burger King. And you get real hungry, we can buy one dinner, get one free at Lupe's Mexican Restaurant."

"That's it? Coupons?"

"Yep."

"Christ, he must have been losing it."

"I don't know. Coupons save lots of money. I use them. I

figured up once I'd saved enough on what I'd normally have spent on stuff to buy a used television set."

"Color?"

"Black and white. But I bought some Diet Pepsi and pork skins instead."

"Coupons seem a strange thing for Uncle Chester to give to a lawyer to hold for me. He could have left that stuff on the kitchen table."

"Maybe he wasn't thinking correctly. Coupons could have taken on valuable import. And the key was with them."

"Goes to a bank safety-deposit box, I figure."

"You said that, Sherlock."

"We'll check it out right now."

"Leonard?"

"Yeah."

"These coupons, I just noticed, they're a couple years expired."

Inside the LaBorde Main-and-North First National Bank, I took a chair and Leonard spoke to a clerk. The clerk sent him to a gray-haired lady at a desk. Leonard leaned on his cane and showed her the key and some of the papers Florida Grange had given him. The lady nodded, gave him back the key, got up, and walked him to a barred doorway. A guard inside the bars was signaled. He opened the door and Leonard went inside and the guard locked it behind him. A few moments later, Leonard was let out carrying a large manila envelope and a larger parcel wrapped in brown paper and twine.

"You'll love this," he said, and held up the envelope. "Inside's a paperback copy of *Dracula* and a fistful of newspaper clippings, and guess what? Another key. There's not a clue what it goes to. Uncle Chester's brain must have got so he didn't know his nuts from a couple acorns."

"What about that?" I said, indicating the larger parcel.

"I opened it already."

"I can tell that by the way the twine is rewrapped. What is it?"

Leonard was hesitant. "Well . . ." He took it over to one of the tables and untied the twine and unwrapped the package. It was a painting. A good painting. It was shadowy and showed a weathered two-story gothic-style house surrounded by trees; fact was, the trees grew so thick they seemed to imprison the house.

"Your uncle do this?"

"I did. When I was sixteen."

"No joke?"

"No joke. I used to want to paint. I did this for Uncle Chester's birthday. Maybe he's giving it back to me now, letting me know things aren't really forgiven."

"He's certainly giving you other things. Money. The house."

"Coupons and a copy of *Dracula*."

"That's right. Is that all there was? Nothing else?"

"Nothing, besides the fact you're right. There's the house and I'm gonna get one hundred thousand dollars and you aren't."

So, I thought Leonard was gonna be richer, and that would be all right, and we'd go back to normal, except for him not working in the rose fields, and me, I'd be heading on back to the house and back to the fields, provided I could get my old job again, or another just like it, and Leonard, he'd be putting his uncle's place up for sale and living off that and his inheritance, maybe put the dough into some kind of business.

I was sad for Leonard in one way, losing a loved one, but in another, that Uncle Chester was a sonofabitch far as I was concerned, way he treated Leonard, and I was glad Leonard had gotten some money and a house to sell, and a secret part of me was glad the old sonofabitch was dead and buried and out of sight.

So, that afternoon after seeing the pretty lawyer who wouldn't go out with me, Leonard drove me home and dropped me off and went away. I figured he was at his place, his feet propped up, listening to Dwight Yoakam or Hank Williams or Patsy Cline, smoking his pipe full of cherry-tinted tobacco, perhaps reading his uncle's copy of *Dracula* or contemplating his loss and gain, wondering what he'd end up doing with his money.

In the long run, except for the fact he was gonna wither and die like everybody else ever born, I figured things for him were going to be fine as things can get fine.

But I hadn't counted on the black cloud of fate.

7.

The black cloud of fate came with rain, of course.

Two days later, early afternoon, I was sitting on my front porch taking in the cool wind and the view. One moment there was just the same red, empty road that runs by Leonard's place, and beyond it, great pines and oaks and twists of vines, and above it all, clouds as white and smooth as God's own whiskers, and the next moment, the wind abruptly changed direction, blew harder from the north, turned damp and sticky, and the clouds began to roll and churn and go gray at the edges. Out of the north rolled darker clouds yet, and they filled the sky and gave up their rain and the pines became purple with shadow and the road turned from red to blood-clot brown, then darker. The rain slammed down hard, and the wind thrashed it onto the porch in steel-colored needles that stung my face and filled my nostrils with the aroma of wet earth.

I got out of my old wooden rocking chair and went into the house, feeling blue and broke and missing Leonard.

I hadn't heard from him since he'd dropped me off, and I'd called his place a couple times and only got rings. I wondered if he'd finally gotten his money. I wondered if he were spending it. It wasn't like me and him to go more than a couple of days without touching base with one another, just in case we needed to argue about something.

I thought I'd call him again, maybe drive over there after the rain, see if his phone might not be working, but about then the phone rang and I answered it.

It was my former boss, Lacy, the Old Bastard. He sounded friendly. A warning flag went up. I figured whoever had taken my place in the fields had gotten a better job bouncing drunks or shoveling shit, or maybe died of stroke or snakebite, or taken up preaching, which was a pretty good career, you had the guts not to be ashamed of it.

"How's it hanging, Hap?"

"To the left."

"Hey, that's my good side. Nut over there's bigger. You ready to come back to work?"

"Don't tell me you're calling from the field?"

He forced a laugh. "Nah, we had a down day."

That meant either no one showed up, or certain supplies couldn't be coordinated, or they'd expected the rain.

"That little thing the other day," he said. "Let's let it go. I won't even dock you. Tomorrow we got to have a good day, losing this one. So, hell, Hap. I can use you."

"Man or woman's got hands and isn't in a wheelchair, you can use them."

"Hey, I'm offering you a job. I didn't call up for insults."

"Maybe we can jump that shit pay a little. Another fifty cents an hour you'd almost be in line with minimum wage."

"Don't start, Hap. You know the pay. I pay cash, too. You save on income tax that way."

"You save on income tax, Lacy. Wages like that, I don't save dick. I'd rather make enough so I had to pay some taxes."

"Yeah, well . . ." And he went on to tell me about his old mother in a Kansas nursing home. How he had to send her money every month. I figured he probably shot his mother years ago, buried her under a rosebush to save on fertilizer.

"Couldn't your old mother whore a little?" I said. "You know, she's set up. Got a room and a bed and all. If she can spread her legs, she can pay her way."

"Hap, you bastard. Don't start fucking with me, or you can forget the job."

"My heart just missed a beat."

"Listen here, let's quit while you're ahead. You come on in and I'll get you working. Tell the nigger to come on in when he's ready."

"Shall I tell Leonard you called him a nigger?"

"Slipped on that. Force of habit."

"Bad habit."

"You won't tell him I said it, all right? You know how he is."

"How is he?"

"You know. Like that time in the field, when him and that other nig—colored fella with the knife got into it."

"That guy ever get out of the hospital?"

"Think he's in some kind of home now. I'm surprised Leonard didn't do some time for that. You won't tell him about the 'nigger' business, will you?"

"I did tell him, there's one good thing about it."

"Yeah?"

"You already got the roses for your funeral."

He rang off and I had the fifty-cent raise for me and Leonard both, just like I thought Leonard might actually go back to it.

Frankly, I had a hard time seeing me going back to it, but a look at the contents of my refrigerator and a peek at the dough in the cookie jar made me realize I had to.

My mood moved from blue to black, and I was concentrating on the failures of my life, finding there were quite a few, wondering what would happen ten years from now when I was in my midfifties.

What did I do then?

Rose-field work still?

What else did I know?

What was I qualified for?

I wasn't able to tally up a lot of options, though I spent considerable time with the effort.

I was considering a career in maybe aluminum siding or, the devil help me, insurance, when the phone rang.

It was Leonard.

"Goddamn, man," I said. "I been wondering about you. I called your place and no answer. I was beginning to think you'd had an accident. Refrigerator was lying on top of you or something."

"I didn't go back home," Leonard said. "Not to stay anyway. I packed some of my stuff and came back here to Uncle Chester's."

"You calling from there?"

"His phone got pulled from lack of payment. Months ago. I'm calling from a pay phone. You want to know what I'm wearing?"

"Not unless you think it'll really get me excited."

"I'm afraid clothes have to have women in them for you to get excited."

"Maybe you could talk in a high voice."

"Cut through the shit, Hap. I'm gonna live at Uncle Chester's awhile. I been going through his stuff. I feel like I want to do that, get in touch with who he was. And more importantly, find out what this fucking key goes to."

"His main coupon collection."

"Could be. I've looked everywhere. I got other reasons too. I want to fix the house up some. Maybe sell it for more than I can get now."

"Sounds smart, Leonard. Things are swinging here too. I got my old job in the rose fields back."

"Lose it again."

"Easy for you to say."

"Hey, you toted me some, move over here a bit, least till I do what I got to do, and I'll keep you fed and in toilet paper."

"I don't know. That's more charity than I like. I don't even have a bum leg."

"Me neither. Hardly. I've been moving around some without the cane. Mostly without it. I don't plan to pick it up again, I can do without it. Look, Hap. It ain't charity. You can help me fix the place up."

"What I can't fix, which is nothing, I shit on. You know that."

"You can tote a hammer, hand me nails. And there's something else. These fucks next door. I got no problems with them yet, but I feel one brewing, way they watch me. They're biding their time. I'd like to have you at my back, and there's always the chance they'll get you first, instead of me. I like the idea of a buffer."

"Well, I can see that."

"Good. Can I count on you?"

I considered working for Lacy again. I thought of the rose fields, the heat, the sticks, the dynamic pay.

"What the hell do you think?" I said.

8.

The real repairs and cleaning began in earnest.

I went to live with him in Uncle Chester's house the next day, and he got the bed from then on and I got the couch. During the days we did repairs, or rather Leonard did. I walked around with a hammer and nails and fetched things, hummed and sang to myself. I do some pretty good spirituals. Leonard said that's the way it ought be, a black man with a honkie servant could sing a little gospel.

We spent a lot of time on the roof, taking off the old tin and putting down some real roofing. I trimmed the big oak that was scratching the roof all by my ownself, managed to saw off the offending limbs without sawing through a finger or busting my ass on the ground.

It was hot as hell up there and the glare was bad enough you had to wear sunglasses while you worked. I began to tan and lose weight, and I liked the feeling so much I gave up beer and excessive numbers of tacos.

When I wasn't holding down roofing for Leonard to hammer, wasn't fetching something, I'd look off at the crack house and wonder who was inside. People came and went there pretty brisk come late afternoon, and right on through until morning. Come full day, things got quiet. Selling crack wore you out, you had to get some rest before the next tide came in.

Whole thing depressed me, seeing kids and adults, and even babies on the hips of female druggies a couple years into having their period, lining up over there like it was a cafeteria.

I saw a couple of cop cars during that time, and there was even a bust and some folks were hauled in. In fact, it was Leonard made the call, but the next day, same guys that left the house were back. One of them was Mohawk, the other was Parade Float. Great strides in my understanding of our judicial system were made without leaving the house and yard.

Way it worked was simple. I'd had it all wrong. You broke the law you didn't have to really suffer. See, a guy sold drugs to kids or anyone else, they could come get you, they could lock you up, but come morning, you knew somebody, had some money, a good lawyer, a relationship with the bail bondsman, you could go home, get a free ride back to your house. Have some rest, a Dr. Pepper and a couple of Twinkies to lift your spirit, and you were in business again, if come nightfall you had the supplies.

It was depressing, and the folks next door must have known we felt that way, 'cause they liked to hang out on their front porch come dark and stare at us. We could see them over there beneath their little yellow porch light, congregating like the bugs that swarmed the bulb above them.

And their light and our porch light, when we used it, was about all the light there was for Comanche Street, because the street lights had long been shot out and no one had come to replace them. If they had, the crack house people would have shot them out again. The only beacon they wanted on the street was their beacon, one that called people to their place to buy something to make them spin and float, help them coast through another few hours.

There were a couple houses across from us, but they kept their porch lights off, and what lights they burned were filmy behind curtains, looked like lights seen from a distance and underwater. Decent folks on Comanche Street didn't come out of their houses at night, lest they encounter the dealers or the druggies themselves, the latter looking for a quick few dollars to purchase a hunk of rock.

For that matter, during the day you didn't see folks much. The working people came and went, but didn't linger. The kid we had seen on Leonard's front porch that day, we began to see more often. He wore a beeper on his hip. Acquired a cool walk. Had some nice clothes. He looked as if his soul was melting.

The bars and locks on Uncle Chester's door began to make sense. You didn't nail something down in this neighborhood, it'd show up at the pawnshop, and the money received for it would finance some druggie to do some business.

Got so we left the house, we had the impression we might come back to the front door off the hinges, rammed in, and all the little goods that Uncle Chester had left would be gone, except the coupons. Or maybe the shits next door would start to think they ought to get even with me and Leonard, and we'd come back to worse: smoke and charred wood.

Considering all that, way we did, was something had to be bought, one of us nearly always stayed while the other went to get it.

Got so Leonard stayed pissed all the time. Kept his brow furrowed and his uncle's shotgun oiled and loaded, and not with rat shot. He made jokes about how many niggers next door it would take to roof the house, he sliced them real thin.

We cleaned inside the house, too. Uncle Chester and his odors finally departed. The flies went in search of deader pastures.

Nights, after a hard day's work, was when we did our cleaning and searching for what the key went to. No safe or locked box or locked floor or wall panels were found. Some of the coupons from the deposit box were good, though. We used them for eat-outs, one of us running into town to pick up pizza or burgers.

At night, we worked to the sounds of Leonard's country music; hillbilly voices fighting it out with the rap and rock sounds next door, stuff I sometimes preferred to lost loves and drinking in the barroom, but Leonard, he used the decibel knob to drown them out. 'Least they were drowned out in Uncle Chester's house. I don't know they noticed next door. Nobody called the law on either of us. In that neighborhood, somebody wasn't getting hurt or robbed, a little loud music didn't mean much. For all the good the law did down there, they might as well have just drove near the neighborhood and honked, tossed out a few Don't Do Drug leaflets.

Last room we tackled was the one with the newspapers. It was hot in there, and the little fan managed to stir the dust and make you choke. The roof had leaked, gotten on the papers and mildewed them, and in some places the water had soaked through and joined the wood beneath them and rotted out sections of the floor. We could hear it squeak, feel it sag when we walked.

We decided best thing to do was remove the papers, glance through them quickly as possible, see if there was anything there really meant anything.

After a couple pickup loads to the recycling center, we quit looking through the rest, quit thinking they meant anything. Only thing we noticed were gaps in pages, where Uncle Chester had liberated coupons with scissors.

All doubts were cast aside. It was pretty clear by then. Uncle Chester had been off his nut. The key had probably gone to something no longer owned, long lost to time, but significant somehow in the watery cells that made up Uncle Chester's brain.

Leonard put the key away and forgot about it and read *Dracula*. He said he liked it pretty good and thought it would have scared him more had it not been for the crack house next door. Look out there and see that happening, it's hard for some guy with fangs to scare you much. Guys next door were bigger vampires: clutch of assholes made you want drugs way a vampire wanted blood. Made it so you'd do anything to have it. Rob and lie, murder your lovers, take up astrology and reading cozy mysteries.

After we'd been there about a week, Leonard quit using his cane and replaced the broken bottles on the bottle tree. I think he was taunting the folks next door to shoot them out, looking for some excuse to exchange their heads, mix up their internal organs.

One night he woke me up calling out "You sonsabitches" in his sleep. He was making me nervous. He kept the shotgun a little too close. I felt things were coming down on Leonard that were bigger than he was. Somewhere in all this, he had determined the assholes next door were the cause for Uncle Chester's death. And maybe they were. Old Uncle Chester had been everything Leonard knew about manhood.

Leonard had been raised by his grandmother, but it was his uncle he came to see summers, and it was his uncle who taught him what it was to be masculine. Taught him about the woods and guns and carpentry and the appreciation of books. Encouraged him to make something of his life, gave him backbone. Then, when Leonard was a young man and realized he was gay and told his uncle, it had all fallen apart.

But be that as it may, his uncle had formed him, had taken him like dough and shaped him and baked him and made him who he was, and no matter how I felt about Uncle Chester's disowning Leonard, I had to admit, he had done a good job. Or a job that had held up till now—up until Uncle Chester came back into Leonard's life, came back after he was dead like some kind of ghost. And not a happy one.

One Saturday afternoon, hot as the blazes, I was up on the roof with my shirt off, cooking up a skin cancer, considering breaking my ban on ice-cold beer, and Florida Grange showed up. She was driving a little gray Toyota, and when she got out of the car I saw she was outfitted in a simple sky-blue dress that showed lots of leg and happily threatened to show a little more.

She stood in the drive and put a hand over her eyes like an Indian scout and called up to me. "Leonard here?"

"He's in town. Went to get some supplies."

"Oh. Well, I came to visit my mama, thought I'd drop by and see how things are coming along. And I got another paper for Leonard to sign. I missed it at the office."

"One minute."

I got my shirt off a sawed oak limb and pulled it on. It was a cotton jean shirt with the sleeves bobbed short and it felt good and soft against my warm, sweaty skin. I sucked in my gut while I buttoned it, just in case Florida was watching. I climbed down by method of the oak.

I dropped out of the tree, wiped my hands on my pants, smiled, and went over to see her. I stuck out a hand and we shook. She had the same soft hand and the same rattling bracelets. Her hair was dark and wild, like a storm cloud. The wind picked up the smell of her perfume and gave it to me. I needed that like a punch in the teeth.

I caught my reflection in her car windshield. I looked like shit, but my teeth were clean. I'd brushed with my own toothbrush not long ago, and I'd even used mouthwash. Progress was being made.

"Would you like something to drink, Miss Grange?"

"Florida?"

"Yeah. That's right. Florida."

"Yes. I would like something to drink."

"I'll get it. It'd be best to sit out here on the porch. We don't have air-conditioning."

"That'll be fine."

"We've got Coke. Diet Coke. Ice tea. Beer. We've got some nonalcoholic beer too. Sharp's. It's pretty good."

"I'll have ice tea. No sugar."

I went in the house and poured her tea and got myself a Sharp's. I had discovered I actually preferred the nonalcoholic beer to the real thing. It was the taste I liked, not the results.

I carried the tea and Sharp's onto the porch. Florida was seated in the glider Leonard and I had installed. I had fastened the bolts to the porch roof. I hoped I had done a good job. I'd have hated for Florida Grange to bust her shapely ass.

I gave her the tea and sat down on the other side of the glider and mentally groped for small talk. I almost said something about the weather but restrained myself. I tried not to look at her legs, which were bare and smooth looking. I wondered if they were as soft as her hand.

"You living here?" she asked.

"For now. I'm helping Leonard get the place in shape to sell."

"I see."

We sat in silence and sipped our drinks. An old black Chevy chugged along the street and an elderly black face looked out of it at us, looked away, and looked back. The driver was trying to determine if any miscegenation was going on.

It wasn't, though I was hopeful, in a fantasy sort of way. Actually, seemed to me, from here on out, I'd have to be content to look at Florida Grange's legs and sneak a look at her panties when she got in or out of her car, way I used to do with girls when I was in high school.

Thought of that made me feel sort of ill. Guys, they're some piece of work. Next thing I knew I'd be putting quarters in filling station restroom rubber machines, trying to get those special gift items you bought when you really didn't need a rubber. The Instant Pussy, a French Tickler that looked like a plastic squid, and the little book of sex jokes.

Here was an intelligent professional woman, and all I could think about was how much I'd like to dork her. I had to think about something else. Thing to do was to talk to her the way you'd talk to any interesting professional in the law business, male or female.

"You get many whiplash cases?"

"What?"

"You know—"

"Oh. Now and then. I mean, a couple. I mainly do wills, stuff like that."

That was good, Hap. Real good. Why don't you just call her an ambulance chaser?

"Nice day, huh?"

"Yeah. Well . . . "

"I mean, it's hot, but it's OK. It's not as humid as usual. I mean, it's usually more humid."

Florida Grange looked at her watch. "When do you think Leonard will be back?"

"Soon. Hell, Florida. I'm acting like a fool. I get around a beautiful woman lately, I act like a jackass. I don't mean to."

"That's all right."

"No. No, it isn't. If you prefer, I'll just be real quiet and sit here. . . . You interested in Leonard?"

She smiled at me. "Leonard's gay."

"You knew that? I was hoping to break the news to you, and you'd be so disappointed, I'd have to do in a pinch. I'm not gay, by the way."

"Gee. I'd never have guessed. Most everyone around here knows Leonard's gay. He spent time here in the summers. My mother knew his uncle and knew Leonard all the while he was growing up. She told me about him."

"Ah."

"Listen, Mr. Collins . . . Hap. I owe you an apology."

"You owe me one? Way I've been ogling you? You got to forgive me, Florida. I been out in the country too long. No female companionship. I'm almost completely fueled by adolescent hormones."

"The other day, when you asked me out, I told you no—"

"Hey, no problem, that's your right—"

"Will you shut up a minute?"

"Sure."

"I got a confession. I didn't go out with you because you're white. That's it."

"You don't like white guys?"

"It's not that. It's that I'm as much a product of racism as anyone else. I don't really think about it much, don't think I'm doing it. But, you see, I feel all that stuff about the white man's world. How, as a black woman, I have to battle uphill for everything I get. How it always seems when I get to a point where I'm ready to advance, there's some kind of white hurdle."

"I guess there is."

"Sometimes there is. Sometimes there isn't, but I've got a chip on my shoulder just the same, so when a white man asks me out, I get to thinking he's thinking, 'This black bitch will be glad to go out with me. I'm white. And because I'm white, I can get me some of her nigger ass,' then Massuh can go on about his business and hook up with someone white, someone respectable."

"Well, to be honest, I was thinking about the 'get me some ass' part."

"I know. I can tell. You sort of ooze musk. But it's the other part. The racist part. I didn't really think you were thinking that. Not then, not now. But conditioning dies hard. I've thought about it a lot since then, and I've regretted it, me thinking that, and you see, I knew you were here, 'cause my mother said she's seen you here, and she knew you from the funeral, and well, I wanted you to know, I'm sorry I was racist. Damn, I'm sort of running things together."

"That's all right. I get your drift. It's very honest of you. It makes me feel like shit, but it's honest."

"Yes, it is. And I still don't want to go out with you."

"I see."

"Know why?"

"I'm ugly?"

"No. Actually I find you attractive, in a gnarly, old-fashioned male sort of way."

Gnarly?

"But the problem is I like to dance and white boys have no rhythm. And you know what else they say about you white boys?"

I watched a beautiful smile spread across her face.

"What do they say?" I asked.

"You've got itty-bitty dicks."

9.

When Leonard came back, Florida gave him the paper and he signed it and she took it back. We talked her into returning that night for supper. Leonard promised to cook spaghetti and sauce, and I promised to make a salad. Leonard eyed me when I said that, and I said, "Really."

I tried not to watch too pointedly as Florida climbed into her car. When she was driving off, Leonard said, "Man, you need to jack off or something. You're starting to look at that woman like she's a chocolate eclair."

"Yeah, and I'm embarrassed by it too. I can't help myself. I been alone too long. I made progress, though. While you were gone we had a polite and intelligent conversation about the size of white guys' dicks."

"Those little things?"

I climbed back on the roof and Leonard came up with me and looked over what I had done, and was pleased to see he wouldn't have to redo it.

"You know, you gonna get where you can flush a toilet without instructions," Leonard said.

"Yassuh," I said. "I's catchin' on. Ya wants me to sang one them spirituals now, Massuh Leonard?"

"I want you to shut up."

We knocked off at five to clean up. Leonard had paid for a tank of butane, so now there was hot water. When I finished showering with the hot water, I turned the faucet to pure cold and rinsed in that. By the time I got out of the shower and dried and was stepping into clean underwear, I was already sweating and the old boards and wallpaper in the bathroom, damp from moisture and heat, had taken on the aroma of the ass end of a camel.

I pulled on my jeans and T-shirt and slid my sockless feet into my deck shoes and went into the kitchen. It smelled good in there, which was a nice change. Leonard was hustling about, chopping mushrooms and stirring meat and garlic in a frying pan. There was a big pot of water on to boil.

"Can I help?"

"Yeah," Leonard said. "Stay the fuck out of the way."

"I could do the salad."

"You could, but it's too early. Made it now, time we ate, the lettuce would be wilted and the tomatoes would taste like wet golf balls."

"Maybe I'll just read."

I got one of the books I'd brought along, Neal Barrett, Jr.'s, *The Hereafter Gang,* went out on the back porch and sat in a creaky old rocking chair. The left side of the porch was blocked with plywood, most likely so Uncle Chester wouldn't have to look at the drug dealers next door. The rest of the porch was screened in. The screen door had the bottom part of its screen knocked loose, and it curled up as if suffering from heat stroke.

Out behind the house there was a pile of burned garbage, some of it black, twisted plastic, some of it blackened cans and dark wisps of paper.

On out a ways was a butane tank, and beyond that, a trickle of woods and brambles that gradually became more than a trickle. It turned into full-fledged woods. I wondered how far it went. Had it been in a white section of town, where property values were up, it would have long been cut down and concrete would have been spread over it.

Here, it was a strange oasis of green in the midst of a disintegrating neighborhood that was a slice of human pie neither completely rural nor urban, a world unto itself.

I read from *The Hereafter Gang* until Leonard came out the back door and called to me, "Why don't you go down and rent us a VCR and a movie. And don't get none of those damn socially redeeming films or anything you got to read at the bottom what they're saying. And let's don't see *It's a Wonderful Life* anymore."

"Three Stooges OK?"

I drove into town and rented a VCR and checked out a couple of movies. *Jaws*, which I'd never seen, and *Gunga Din*, which I saw when I was head high to a cocker spaniel's nuts.

By the time I got back to the house I was hot and sweaty and nervous. I was wondering if I should put the move on Florida, or just watch the movies like a good little boy. Frankly, I didn't know how to put the move on anybody anymore. I was too long out of practice. I began to wonder if she'd show up. Maybe she'd bring a date. That would be cozy. Perhaps I could loan him some condoms.

While Leonard hooked up the VCR, I made the salad. I can break lettuce and slice a tomato with the best of them. I didn't even screw up when I put on the bacon bits and the croutons.

About fifteen minutes after I finished, there was a knock on the door and Leonard let Florida in. She was carrying a bottle of wine and a long loaf of French bread. She had a little black pocket book on a strap draped over her shoulder. She was wearing canary yellow this time. It was like all her other dresses, plain in design, but tight and short and flattering to what it covered. She didn't have a date.

"Who're the sweeties next door?" she asked, giving Leonard the bread and the wine.

"Just the local crack house," Leonard said. "They're a real fun-loving bunch."

"They certainly are. They just gave me a verbal anatomical lesson."

"Sorry," I said.

She smiled. "That's all right. I hear worse in court. From my own clients sometimes."

We seated ourselves at the table and started on the salad. She ate some of it, but nothing was said about its excellence. Personally, I thought the croutons and bacon bits were very fresh. She bragged on the spaghetti, meatballs, and sauce. Leonard, a regular reader of *Bon Appetit*, bragged on her choice of wine. To me, all wine tastes pretty much the same. Bad. But I said I thought it was pretty good, too.

After dinner, we watched the movies. *Jaws* first. The TV was a little-screen affair Leonard had bought at a pawn shop, but the movie, cropped at the corners, scared the shit out of me anyway. I've never liked water, and I like sharks even less. Florida sat in the middle of the couch, and during the scary parts she didn't leap into my lap for protection or grab my hand. I thought it would be most unbecoming of me to leap into hers, though I found myself pulling my feet up onto the couch, in case any floor sharks drifted by.

Between the movies we took a coffee break, and Florida took off her shoes, then we watched *Gunga Din*. I loved it again. About midnight the movies were over and we talked about them for a while, then Leonard went out on the porch to smoke his pipe.

I stood up from the couch and found I didn't know what to do with my hands. I didn't know what to do with my mouth either. Should I say "Good night?" How about "What about them Mets?"

Florida didn't help. She kept her seat and smiled up at me. She said, "I'm sleepy."

"Yeah, well, it is late. You need me to drive you home? You can get your car tomorrow."

"I'm not that sleepy. I would like to stay here, though."

"'Cause you're tired?"

She smiled at me again. This was the sort of smile you reserve for the feeble-minded. "You want it spelled out?"

"That would help," I said. "I think I know what you're saying, but if I'm wrong, boy, am I going to be embarrassed."

"You're not wrong. Let's go to bed. Together."

"One minute."

"One minute?"

I went out on the porch. Leonard was sitting on the glider. The smell of his cherry tobacco drifted back to me.

He said, "Well, what's the score?"

"Can I use the bed tonight?"

"Yeah, but you do the laundry tomorrow. I don't want the wet spot."

"Right."

Back inside I tried not to look too much like I was waiting for dessert. "Well, you ready?"

She laughed at me. It was a nice sound. Like bells tinkling. "Where's the bathroom?"

I showed it to her. Before she went inside, she said, "Go out and look in my car and bring my overnight bag, will you? Keys are in my purse."

I got the keys out of her purse, went out and got the bag. She knew she was going to stay all along. I began to feel a little taller. When I walked past Leonard, he said, "I hope you still remember what to do."

"It'll come to me," I said, and went inside.

The overhead fan moved moon shadows and stirred the hot air. The shadows fluttered over me and the sweat on my chest dried slowly and comfortably.

I was lying on my back, naked. Florida lay beside me, on her stomach, sleeping. I had my hand resting on one of her smooth, dark buttocks. I couldn't resist playing my fingers over her flesh. I replayed what we had done time and again in my head. It was a good picture show no matter how many times I rewound it. I liked it better than *Jaws* or *Gunga Din*.

The bedroom window was up, and from where I lay, my head propped on a pillow, I could see out clearly. Across the way there was some laughter and some lights and shadows moved between the windows and the laughter moved with them.

I rolled on my side and put my arm across Florida's back and kissed her ear. She smelled of sweat and sex and perfume. She moved and made a noise I liked. I ran my hand down the small of her back, over her buttocks, down one of her legs, letting my hand hydroplane over the beads of sweat. She spread her legs and I ran my hand between them. She was soft there and moist, and she moved like she thought she might do some business, but then she went still again and started snoring like a lumberjack.

That was all right. After all we'd done, my ambition might be bigger and better than the tool I needed for the job. And I was thirsty.

I rolled away from her, eased out of bed, and untangled the sheet from my ankles. I stretched, got the sheet off the floor, shook it out silently and tossed it over Florida, taking a good look at her before I did.

I found her panties on the floor, along with the little nightie she had worn so briefly. I folded them and put them at the foot of the bed, went to the window and took hold of the bars and looked out. Still busy over there.

The sound of the wind in the bottle tree came to me, like the faraway hooting of ghostly owls. I listened to the bottles and thought about going to get a drink, then, behind the sound of the bottle tree, I heard a scraping noise. It was coming from the next room.

I found my jockey shorts and slipped them on, then my jeans. I had brought a little .38 revolver from my house, and I got it out of the dresser drawer from under my socks and eased over to the bedroom door and listened.

No sound.

I opened the door carefully and looked into the living room. I didn't see Leonard on the couch. I heard the scraping noise again.

I slipped into the living room and saw there was a light coming from the open door of the newspaper room. I held the gun down by my leg and went over there and looked inside. Sitting on the floor, damp newspapers pushed in a heap behind him, was Leonard. He was pulling at the rotten boards in the flooring, prying them loose with a crowbar, stacking them by the papers. The little fan was pointed in his direction and was set not to rotate. It hummed pleasantly, like a bee at flower.

I went inside.

"I was going to shoot you," I said.

He looked up at me.

"Who the hell did you think it'd be?"

"Guess I've got the jumps a little, those guys next door."

57

"Did it come back to you? The sex stuff, I mean?"

"Yes, but we did some things I don't remember doing before. I guess it's OK, though. Neither of us got hurt."

"What do you think of her?"

"Well, we haven't sent out wedding invitations, but I like her. She's smart. Witty. Fun to be with."

"And she's fucking you."

"There's that."

"Come here and give me a hand. I've found something interesting."

I put the gun on the table next to the little fan, went over and got down on my knees and grabbed hold of the board he was holding and helped him pull it up. There was a screech of nails as it came loose.

"I couldn't sleep," he said. "I came in here and started looking around, moved some papers and found this spot. You'll notice, not all these boards are rotten."

"Meaning?"

"Meaning what happened was the floor was repaired here with untreated wood to replace old wood, and some of that has rotted because of the roof leak. I think Uncle Chester took advantage of replacing the floor to make a hiding place."

He pointed. "For this," he said.

In the gap in the floor I could see something large lying in the dark against the ground. There must have been about four feet between the floor and the dirt.

"When I moved the papers, I spotted it through the hole and got busy pulling the rest of the lumber out," Leonard said. "I didn't wake up Florida, did I?"

"From what I can tell, she doesn't sleep. She hibernates."

"Help me get this out of here, would you?"

I leaned down and got hold of the heavy metal trunk, for that's what it was, and we pulled it out of there and set it on the floor beside us. It was army green and there was a padlock on it. It had CHESTER PINE stenciled in white letters on the lid. It smelled of damp earth.

Leonard got the crowbar and put it inside the loop of the padlock and started to give it a flex, but I grabbed his arm.

"Before you do that," I said,."I was thinking there might be another way."

He looked at me, and slowly it dawned on him.

10.

Leonard went to get the key while visions of outdated coupons danced in my head.

When he returned, he tried the key and the lock sprang open. Leonard removed the lock and lifted the lid. There was a puff of dust and a smell came out of there I couldn't quite identify. Musty, a little sharp. Leonard leaned over and looked inside, and stared. I looked too.

It wasn't coupons.

There was a small, yellowed skeleton, blackened in spots. The skull was turned toward me. Some of its teeth were milk teeth. Probably a male, though I was no expert on that. Eight, nine years old. From the forehead to a spot square between the eyes, the skull was cracked like the Liberty Bell. The legs had been sawed off at the knees so that it would fit in the trunk, and the arms were pulled free at the shoulders, twisted from their sockets like chicken wings. Beneath and around the bones were moldering magazines, and I realized that much of the smell was from rotting paper, but that certainly wasn't the whole of it. The bones were old, however, and most of death's stench had long left them, and perhaps what I did smell on the bones was not death at all, but mold.

We held our positions for a while, soaking it in. Leonard got one of the newspapers and crunched it over his hand and made a makeshift glove out of it. He got down on his knees and reached inside and picked up one of the arm bones. When he lifted it, it pivoted at the elbow and some of it powdered and fell back in the box. The bones that made up the hand broke loose from the wrist and rattled back into the box, fragmenting pages from one of the old magazines; the fragments wisped and fluttered like a shotgunned bird.

Leonard held the arm bone and looked at it for a while, then carefully put it back. He used the newspaper to get one of the magazines out of there. He dropped it on the floor. Pages came apart and powdered the way part of the bone had powdered.

The magazines had been mostly photographs. A lot of the photographs were still visible. I didn't like them. They were of children, male and female, in sexual positions with adults and each other. Leonard got out a couple other magazines and put them on the floor. More of the same. They were even some with children and animals.

I looked at them longer than I wanted to, to make sure I was seeing what I was seeing, then I squatted back on my haunches and took a deep breath. The breath was full of rotting paper and that other smell.

Leonard picked up the magazines and returned them to the trunk. He dropped the newspaper he was using as a glove inside and closed the lid of the trunk and put the padlock on it and locked it.

He stood up and wiped his hands on his pants and walked around in a small circle, then went to the desk chair and sat down and turned the little fan on his face. He was breathing as if he had just finished a hard workout.

"Uncle Chester," he said. "Jesus Christ."

I don't know how long we stayed like that, me on my haunches, Leonard in the chair, the fan blowing on his face. Finally, I said, "It may not be like it looks."

"How can it not be like it looks? This is the key he left me. It goes to the trunk and it's got what it's got inside. That skeleton is a kid's skeleton."

"I know."

"And those magazines. That filth . . . Jesus, was he getting even with me for being gay? Was he telling me he was a sicko, because he thought I was? Or did he get so far gone in the head he thought he had him a real treasure here? That I'd be one happy sonofabitch to have it. What did he do? Get this out now and then, look at the skeleton, the magazines? Jack off?"

"You're jumping pretty far."

"I'm jumping where there is to jump. The sick fuck had the gall to criticize me, and he was . . . Jesus, Hap. You think there are others?"

"I don't know what to think. But you'll need to tell the cops."

"Yeah, they're so fucking efficient. Jesus, Hap."

I stood up slowly. "You could just put the trunk back in the hole, you know. He's done what he's done, and now he's beyond punishment and can't hurt anyone else. You could just go on with things."

"You don't mean that?"

"No. . . . Just a small, sad part of me means it."

"This child needs to be identified. There might be others. Jesus. How long could this have been going on? There might be a whole slew of bodies under the house here. They could have been down there when I came for summers. He's up here teaching me to tie a fishing fly, reading me a story, tucking me in bed, and underneath our feet, children are rotting."

"He was sick in the head, Leonard. You know that. It could have just happened recently."

"That only makes it a little better. Shit, it don't make it any better. . . . Don't tell Florida. Not yet."

"I wouldn't."

"Christ."

"Tell you what, Leonard. Let's put the trunk up for now. Nothing can be changed tonight. Absorb all this best you can. Tomorrow, after Florida leaves, we'll do what you want to do. Of course, once the police know, it isn't a secret any longer."

"Yeah. Help me with the trunk, Hap."

We put the trunk back. Leonard put a few boards over the hole and we stacked some of the newspapers over that. When we were finished, Leonard said, "Thanks, man."

"Not at all."

We washed up and I got that drink of water I'd been wanting. I went back to the bedroom.

Florida had kicked off the sheet again. She lay on her back. Her face was smooth and beautiful, and her lips fluttered slightly. Her breasts and pubic hair caught my attention, but somehow, having seen what I had just seen, I couldn't hold any sexual interest.

I took off my clothes and eased back in bed and lay on my back and watched the fan go around and around. I listened to the wind in the bottle tree and hoped the souls of the drug dealers were being sucked inside. I wondered if Uncle Chester's soul had gone in there, the soul of his victim . . . or victims.

I thought about the trunk and the magazines and I thought about Leonard. The world had certainly come down on him. I thought about the child's skeleton and what the child had been like when he was alive. Had he been happy before it happened? Thinking of Christmas? Had he been sad? Had he suffered much? Had he known what was happening?

Across the way, in the crack house, I heard someone laugh, then someone said something loud and there was another laugh, then silence.

The shadows changed, broadened. A slice of peach-colored light came through the bars and fell across the bed and made Florida's skin glow as if it had been dipped in honey. I watched her skin instead of the fan, watched it become bright with light. I rolled over and put my arm around her. Her skin was warm, but I felt cold. I got up and got the sheet and spread it over her and crawled under it and held her again. She rolled against my chest and I kissed her on the forehead.

"Is it morning yet?" she said.

"If you're a rooster," I said.

"Umm. I'm not a rooster."

"I noticed."

"Your breath stinks."

"Not yours. It's sweet as a rose. . . . Of course, it's growing by the septic tank."

"You know, you're my first peckerwood."

"And how was it?"

"Except for the itty-bitty dick part, great."

"Nice."

"I'll show you nice. In a moment."

She got out of bed and pulled the sheet off and wrapped it around herself. "I'm going to brush my teeth. Right back. Then you're going to brush your teeth."

"Are we going to check for cavities?"

"There's one cavity I'd like you to look at," she said, and left the room. I actually began to get the trunk and the body and the magazines off my mind. At least off the front burner.

When she came back, she said, "Leonard's up. He always get up early?"

"Sometimes."

"You think we woke him up last night? You know, we were kind of loud."

"It's OK. Why don't you take off the sheet?"

"Teeth."

I went and brushed then. I heard Leonard in the newspaper room. He seemed to be pacing. The old floorboards squeaked.

When I came back to the bedroom, Florida had taken off the sheet and was lying in bed with an unwrapped rubber on her abdomen, a folded pillow under her ass and her legs spread.

"Hint, hint," she said.

11.

It was noon and hot and no breeze was blowing. Florida was long gone to visit her mother. The curb was bordered with cop cars and unmarked cop cars. Leonard had called the police about an hour back.

Next door, the crack house was up early, surprised it wasn't them being paid a visit. They sat and stood on their porch and watched. Mohawk called to one of the plainclothes cops in the yard—a fat guy with a bad toupee—by name. The fat cop waved back.

An old black woman on a walker came out of the house across the street and stood on the porch and looked at us. It was the first time I'd seen her. She reminded me of an ancient, oversized cricket. Above her, on a high line, a crow cawed as if it needed a throat lozenge.

Leonard and I were on his front porch, sitting in the glider. Leonard looked to have shrunk during the night. His complexion had grayed.

A big black detective, fiftyish and hard looking, wearing a loose blue suit coat, was hunkered down by the glider asking us questions, while a white detective in a green Kmart suit like I had wanted to buy took notes and did battle with a fly that kept trying to light on his sweaty, balding head.

"Goddamn fly," he said.

"They go straight for shit," the black cop said.

"Yeah," said the white cop. "Guess they're gonna be all over you."

The big black cop didn't look at the white cop. You got the idea they did that kind of dull banter all the time, just to keep themselves awake. The black cop got a turd-colored cigar out of the inside of his coat and put it in his mouth and chewed it. He didn't light it. He said, "That's about it for now. The both of you will have to talk again. Maybe come down to the station."

Inside, we could hear boards being ripped up. A couple of guys in jeans and T-shirts went by us, carrying shovels into the house.

"My name's Lt. Marvin Hanson," said the black cop. "I guess I should have already told you that. My manners are short. You two might want to hang somewhere else for a while. They're gonna be digging and looking for a time. . . . You fellas want to go with me and have lunch? I'll make the city pay."

"Thanks," Leonard said. "We'll do that. OK, Hap? I wouldn't mind getting out of here."

"Yeah. Sure."

"What about me?" said the white cop.

"Blow it out your ass, Charlie," Hanson said.

Charlie chuckled and slipped his notepad inside his coat. Hanson stood up and I heard his knees pop.

"Be a minute," he said.

He went in the house and we stayed put. Charlie didn't say anything. He didn't look at us. He just leaned on the porch post and did battle with his fly.

Over at the crack house, a pizza delivery truck pulled up at the curb and a nervous black kid wearing a cockeyed paper cap got out and carried half a dozen large pizza boxes up to the porch.

Some jive talk and some dollars were passed around. The kid got off the porch without his paper hat. I noticed Mohawk was wearing it. It was too small and made him look like a black Zippy the Pinhead. Charlie looked over and saw him. He yelled, "Give it back, asshole."

"Ah, man," Mohawk said.

"Give it back."

"That's all right," the pizza kid said, one foot in the truck, one foot out. "They got another one they can give me."

"Naw," Charlie said. "You look good in that one."

"Whatch y'all got over there?" Mohawk said. "Dead people?"

"Butane leak. Give him the cap back."

"Yeah, sure," Mohawk said. "Come get it, kid."

"Naw," said Charlie. "You take it down to him. And be polite. Or we might have to look your place over. See if you got any illegal substances behind the commode."

"You got to have some cause," Mohawk said.

"A stolen paper pizza hat."

"I didn't steal it. I borrowed it." Mohawk looked around at his porch buddies and smiled, and they all smiled with him. Parade Float came out of the house and let the screen door slam like he meant some kind of business.

68

"That's right, ain't it, kid?" Parade Float yelled to the kid. "My man just borrowed that hat, didn't he?"

"That's all right with me," the kid said. "Damn. You know I don't deliver this other pizza quick, I'm gonna have to pay for it. I better rush."

The kid got in the truck and started to close the door.

"Naw. That's all right kid," said Charlie. "Keep your spot. I got money. And you, Melton. Let me give you some cause to give that hat back. You don't, I'll shove a pipe up your ass. One shoots bullets out the end of it."

Mohawk—or rather, Melton—smiled. "Well, since you're talking sexy, Sergeant. I'll give it back."

Mohawk went down the steps and toward the kid. He walked slow and cool, like he was styling his duds. He threw the hat at the kid and the kid grabbed at it and missed it, picked it off the ground, put it on his head, got in his truck, and cranked it up. He rolled away from there bent over the wheel.

Mohawk gave us a hard stare, like any minute he might move over and whip all of us. Leonard got up and stood at the end of the porch and looked at him, said, "Why don't you come over for coffee, later. I'd like to visit . . . Melton."

Mohawk smiled loosely and went back to the porch. Some talk floated around over there and the word *motherfucker* came up. Mohawk went inside and slammed the screen door. The little crowd on the porch shuffled positions like dogs looking for the right place to shit, and finally settled down.

"One day, that place over there might have a fire," Leonard said.

"Yeah, I'd hate that," said the white cop. "Me being friends with Melton like I am."

"I could tell he liked you too," I said.

"We can't get enough of each other," Charlie said. "We see each other time to time at the station. Melton Danner's who he is, but he goes by Strip to them guys. I went to high school

69

with him. I was a couple years up on him. He was OK then, I guess."

I said, "What I can't figure is why you can't just take those fucks off the street for good."

"We're figurin' on that one ourselves," Charlie said. "We've asked Uncle Sam about it, but he don't have any answers, and I guess we're not smart enough to come up with any on our own. Shitasses like that, they got rights, you know? And they got expensive lawyers 'cause they got lots of dope money. Kind of makes us feel inefficient, running them in at night so they can get out in the morning after a hot meal and a shower."

Hanson came out of the house. He took his chewed cigar out of his mouth and flicked it gently and put it back inside his jacket. He walked to the edge of the porch and spat out a little hunk of tobacco. He looked at Charlie and he looked at us. "What?" he said.

"We were just talking to Melton," Charlie said.

"Sweet boy, that Melton," Hanson said. "And already got his door fixed from last time we knocked it off the hinges."

"He's a beaver, all right," Charlie said.

Leonard said, "Find anything else?"

"Not yet," Hanson said. "Come on. Let's go. Don't fuck things up, Charlie."

"Hokeydoke," Charlie said, and we followed Hanson out to his car.

12.

A burger joint was Hanson's idea of fine dining. I got coffee, a cheeseburger, and fries. The coffee tasted as if a large animal had crapped in it, but the burger and fries had just the right amount of grease; you wrung out their paper wrappers, there was enough oil to satisfy a squeaky hinge.

Hanson said to Leonard, "You doing OK?"

"Not really," Leonard said, "but another hundred years, things will get better. You didn't just invite us to eat so you could cheer me up, did you? You got something on your mind?"

Hanson experimented with his coffee. His was good too—

I could tell the way his upper lip quivered. He put the cup down and got out his cigar and put it in his mouth, talked around it. "I knew your uncle. He'd been down to the station."

"For shooting my neighbors in the ass," Leonard said.

"And he reported them a half-dozen times. We take them in, they get out, they start over. It's like fighting back the Philistines with the jawbone of a hamster."

"A game," Leonard said.

"Yep," Hanson said. "And there's a nasty, persistent rumor that some of the cops take bribes."

"Naw," Leonard said. "Say it ain't so."

"All I got to say on the matter is I'm not one of them, and you damn well better believe it. As for your uncle, he fancied himself something of a policeman. You know about that?"

"I know he was a security guard. That he wanted to work in law enforcement. Wanted to be a detective. I remember he read a lot of true-crime magazines and books, read mysteries. Anything associated with crime. I know he tried to get a job on the police force, but by the time he tried he was too old, and before that, they weren't gonna have no black man on the LaBorde cops."

"Trust me," Hanson said, "it ain't no bed of roses now. We still got the legacy of Chief Calhoun."

"As I remember," I said, "in the late sixties the first Chief Calhoun gave his cops six feet of looped barbed wire with a wooden handle and told them to use it on some civil rights folks, a peaceful assembly downtown. He had his cops hit the protestors with the wire. Women and children. The town council was so broken up about it, they issued all the cops new batons and brought some martial arts guy in to show them how to use it. The batons left more legitimate marks."

"That Calhoun was before my time," Hanson said. "But his heritage lives on. Fact is, except for the rhetoric, chief we've got now, his son, makes the original Calhoun look like a liberal. I'm the only black on the police force, and it's not because they want me. Calhoun sees me, his stomach hurts and his dick shrinks up. A nigger with a gun makes him nervous, makes him dream of white sheets and burning crosses. Worse, I'm a former city nigger, a concrete and neon jigaboo. Add insult to injury, I been here nearly ten years and I'm still an outsider, and last but not least, I'm a good cop."

"And modest," I said.

"That's my most pronounced trait," Hanson said.

"You didn't invite us to lunch for this either," Leonard said, "to tell us you knew my uncle and the department thinks you're a nigger. You damn sure didn't bring us here to tell us what a good cop you are."

"I'm not sure I brought you here for any reason makes sense. I wanted to ask some more questions, kind'a."

"The sphinx would make more sense than you do," Leonard said. "You haven't asked a question one."

Hanson sipped the bad coffee without removing his cigar, said, "I don't have any reason to doubt your uncle committed this murder."

"Hey," Leonard said, "thanks for the news flash. But I'm gonna tell you something. My first impression was same as everyone else's. But I've thought on things some, and my uncle could be an asshole, but he didn't kill any kid. I knew him better than that. There's something else to all of this, I don't care how it looks."

Hanson shrugged and spread his hands. "Chester came to the station talking about child killings not so long ago. You know that?"

"No," Leonard said. "What do you mean he talked about child killings?"

"What I'm saying, is there may be more murders, more bodies than this."

"Didn't think you were ripping up my flooring looking for nickels had fallen through the cracks," Leonard said, "but you still haven't answered my question."

"And if he was murdering children," I said, "why would he tell you?"

"Frankly, everyone thought he was nuts," Hanson said. "I think he was too, toward the end there. As to why would he tell us? Throw us off. A cheap thrill. Or he was trying to prove what a good cop he could be. Uncover the murders, but not turn up the killer."

"Which you think was him," Leonard said.

Hanson shrugged again.

"A friend of ours thinks Chester may have had Alzheimer's," I said.

"Could be," Hanson said. "But Chester said there were child murders, and now there are. One, at least."

"Didn't you guys check into what he said?" I said. "You do that sort of thing, don't you?"

"When we're not at the doughnut shop. . . . All Chester said was there were child murders going on in the black neighborhood, and that no one outside of the neighborhood gave a damn."

"Was he right?" I asked.

"There were reports over the years of missing children."

"How many years," I said.

"Ten at least. And according to the files all those cases had been looked into, but nothing had been solved. According to written remarks made by a couple of officers no longer on the force, they felt the parents had done the children in because they were too much trouble to care for, but they couldn't prove it, and they didn't give a damn. In fact, written at the bottom of one report was 'One less nigger won't hurt anything.' That was just ten years ago. Civil rights is sinking in slow here. At least in the area of law enforcement."

"There's always a difference when a crime is a black crime," Leonard said, "especially if it's against another black and done in the black section. Black man killed a white, cops'd be on the case like hogs on corn. Listen here, Lieutenant, this lunch is scrumpdillyicious and all, but you're trying to be too clever. You're talking, but you're not saying anything. You're trying to see if I've got any strings you can play, aren't you? Think maybe I'm holding something back, something could help your case?"

"Could be you've forgotten something," Hanson said. "Could be you know something about him from the past might have something to do with now, the murders."

"Knew anything, I'd tell you. Him being my uncle or not. Maybe 'cause he is my uncle. You don't have to burger-and-coffee me to find things out. I told you about the keys, the coupons, the paperback of *Dracula*. Turned the skeleton in, didn't I?"

"That's what you're doing?" I said to Hanson. "Trying to see if Leonard knows more than he's told?"

"He ain't hip," Leonard said to Hanson. "He can't see the signs they're on his face."

"Yeah, hip's a problem," Hanson said. "But you may not be so hip yourself, Leonard. I'm merely being polite here. Getting you away from that place, feeding your face and your partner's too. I mean, I got a few questions, but they're all routine."

Leonard smiled at Hanson.

Hanson smiled back.

A couple of sharks trying to outflank one another.

Leonard said, "Why don't you run your program by me one more time, and you can leave out the cryptic stuff that's supposed to scare me, stuff where I'm supposed to think you know more than you know, so if I know more than I'm letting on, I'll get scared and go all to pieces and spill the beans."

Hanson said, "All right then. The bare bones. Your uncle said there were child murders. There was no evidence of that. Just evidence that over the years children had come up missing. It wasn't a case I was familiar with. I gave the file notes on missing kids in the black section a once-over. It didn't look good, but there wasn't anything there to go on. What your uncle wanted was for us to give him a team, some men to work with, and he was going to solve the case."

"He said that?" Leonard said.

"Said he and his associate would prove to us something was happening and who did it."

"Who was his associate?" I asked.

"He wouldn't name him. Said it was best he kept his man on the outside. Said he wasn't willing to turn it completely over to the department because it would be swept under the rug. Said he needed our facilities. Maybe he didn't even have an associate. Maybe he did."

"You mean maybe it was me," Leonard said.

"I didn't say that," Hanson said.

"Needless to say," I said, "you didn't give Chester his own team."

"No," Hanson said. "He was pretty erratic, so he was hard to take seriously. He didn't really present any evidence, just talked. And sometimes kind of randomly. Like he'd forgotten what he'd come around for. Everytime he showed up, he was a little less with it. Not that we'd have given him his own team if he hadn't been nuts. No insult intended there, Leonard."

"None taken," Leonard said. "But I still don't know any more than I've told you."

Hanson removed his cigar and put it inside his coat pocket. "OK then," he said, "I'm through being clever. For now. You fellas want more coffee?"

"I'll have a Coke," Leonard said. "Long as you're buying."

13.

Three days later and the morning was very bright and the light that came through the windows was splotched with eyeshade-green patches from the sun shining through oak leaves and there were intervals of jet-black shadows made by the bars over the windows.

We had spent the time since the discovery of the body out at our places outside of town, but now we were back. The cops were through and no more kid skeletons had been found, though Leonard had profited fifty-five cents found on the ground beneath the flooring, turned in by Hanson, who may have done it to prove to us he was an honest cop. Hell, it might have even come out of his pocket.

The law had been nice enough to haul off the newspapers and the rotten lumber, just in case a clue was lurking in a knothole or behind the sports sections, and Leonard bought some one-by-eight pine boards and a sack of nails and we went to putting in new subflooring. That's what we were doing the morning I'm talking about. The boards were fresh cut and the weather so hot you could smell the resin on them and feel a powdering of sawdust on your hands. It was a little odd, putting that flooring down and living in a house where just a few days ago Leonard had made a bony discovery, but with the newspapers hauled off, the smell of new lumber, and the hot sunshine sticking through the windows, the house seemed different somehow, as if it had never held the remains of a long-dead child.

When we had a good chunk of flooring replaced with Lap 'n' Gap decking, Leonard said, "Let's break it."

We poured some lukewarm coffee into our cups and went out on the porch and sat in the swing. It was not so humid this day, so maybe that was better, though it's always been my contention that at the bottom of it all, the distinction is bullshit. Bake or fry, hot is hot. Least when it's humid, I know I'm hot, when it isn't, I get the feeling I'm being cooked up secretively.

We sipped the coffee for a while and looked at the street and watched a few cars go by. Over at the crack house, it was quiet.

Leonard went back into the house and came out with a bag of his favorite cookies, vanilla creme. Well, actually his favorite is vanilla anything. He kept the bag on his side of the swing and didn't volunteer me any cookies. He made me ask for one.

"You haven't been the most talkative about all this," I said.

"A board's a board," Leonard said. "You do what I say, you won't fuck up."

"Your uncle, Leonard. You haven't talked about your uncle."

"I'm still putting it together. Not just the stuff with the skeleton, but my life."

"Is this going to be one of those insightful moments?"

"I think so. You see, all I ever wanted was to be loved and comfortable and fulfilled in my work. Way it stands, the family I cared about is dead, and has been dead for years, except one, and he just died, and without ever saying he was sorry or just taking me as I am. I guess I'm more comfortable now financially than I was a short time ago because he's dead, but the house I inherited and loved turns out to have a dead kid under the floorboards, and my uncle is supposed to have put him there, and if that ain't shitty enough, I've got no work to go to or feel good about. Think I sound sorry enough for myself?"

"You could maybe throw in a favorite dog got hit by a truck or something. And you didn't mention Mama or a train, like in the country-and-western songs."

"Yeah, I guess you're right. And I do have my cookies. What about Florida? What's she think about all this?"

"She came out to my house day before yesterday. She was sorry about the whole thing. Shocked. What you'd expect. She said to give you her best."

"I notice she hasn't been back over here."

"Yeah, well, we just got back. What'd you think, she'd be waiting on the porch?"

"I guess I'm getting sensitive in my old age."

"She'll be back. Or I think she will. I hope she will."

"How's the relationship?"

"I'm not sure. We like each other. We have sex and we can joke with each other, and I want there to be more to it than there is at the moment, but I get the feeling she doesn't want to be seen with me in public."

"I have the same problem."

"Seriously. I think it's because I'm white. She said as much once, but I thought she got past it."

"She may know better than feeling that way, but that doesn't mean she can get completely past it. Not in that short time anyway. Hey, look at it this way, she's made great strides. She's fucking you, and you're white."

"That's what I like about you, Leonard. You're such a romantic."

"Hap, you think my uncle killed that kid?"

"I don't know. It looks that way. Main thing is you don't think so."

"I did at first, and you told me not to jump to conclusions. Remember?"

"I'll be honest. I thought he did it the moment you found the body. I said what I said to be nice to you. There's things point to him having done it, besides the obvious, the skeleton under the floorboards. Stuff like him being a cop freak. That by itself doesn't mean anything, but lots of times, people who are into wanting to be cops and can't, people obsessed with it, have some kind of control fixation. Child abuse, the abuse of anyone weaker than you, is a form of control. Like rape. Wife-beating. Maybe your uncle was an abused child and it affected him. It all goes together."

"I know my uncle."

"You knew your uncle."

"He didn't change that much. I never got any indication from him he was an abused child. And if he was, it didn't make him a child abuser. Lots of abused children aren't child molesters. He was the one taught me how to live, how to think. He didn't just turn around one day and start wanting to kill children."

"It could have been going on for a time."

Leonard shook his head. "Nope. And I don't think he had a power fixation. I think the man wanted a job with respect, and law enforcement was it. He just never got it because of who he was and where he was. He may have begun to lose his head some at the end, but that doesn't mean he lost his ethics. I want to know what happened, Hap, no matter what the results, and I want you to help me."

"What makes you think you have to ask?"

14.

We finished our coffee and were about to go back to work, when across the street we saw the old, black lady on the walker come onto her front porch. It was a slow and dutiful process, her coming outside, and watching her made me nervous. The screen door slammed her in the hip because she couldn't move away from it fast enough, and she wobbled and the porch groaned loud enough for us to hear across the street. I bet she didn't weigh ninety pounds, but I could see boards sagging as she went.

She looked across the street at us and we waved. She

waved back, careful to do it so her arm didn't come off at the shoulder.

She stood in the frame of her walker and watched us awhile, then slowly lifted her hand and flicked a come-over signal with her fingers.

We went over and stood at the bottom step of her porch and looked up at her. The hot sunlight lay on her like a slice of thin cheese and showed her to no advantage. She looked as if she had been boiled down and wrung out and left to dry. The wrinkles in her face were very deep and rivered with sweat. Her prune-colored eyes were runny and the whites were no longer white; they were a Hiroshima of exploded blood vessels: pink, red, and blue. Her false teeth hung too low in her mouth at the top and were set too high at the bottom, giving the impression of living things trying to climb out of a hole. Her head was mostly bald and her hair was spaced in gray tufts and looked like dirty cotton that had been blown by the wind to collect on a damp, black rock. Her breasts sagged and wobbled against her ribs inside her simple blue shift. She wore fuzzy pink house shoes on her feet and one black toe, like a water-logged pecan, poked through a hole in the right one.

I tried to imagine her younger, middle-aged even, but it was impossible to envision that she might ever have looked any different.

I said, "We help you with something, ma'am?"

She took a deep breath, collecting enough wind to speak, ignored me, and turned to Leonard. "You," she said, "the colored boy," just in case Leonard might be confused on his ancestry. "I heard about your uncle. I don't believe it for a minute. I don't care if they found babies in his toilet, he didn't murder and saw up no chil'ren. I've known that boy all his life."

"Word sure gets around," Leonard said.

"Ain't no secrets in nigger town," she said.

"No, ma'am, guess not," Leonard said.

"And if the policemens catch anybody it'll be an accident. They done decided it was Chester, and that will be the end of it."

"What I'm afraid of too, ma'am," Leonard said.

"Them boys next door," she said. "Y'all don't have nothing to do with them niggers. They're on drugs."

"Yes, ma'am," Leonard said. "We was kinda thinkin' they were."

"You can tell way they walk," she said.

"Yes, ma'am," Leonard said.

"And they sell'm too," she said. "Every little chile you see go in over there and come out, they done sold them some drugs. They kill'n their own, and I betcha some fat-cat peckerwood somewheres is on the gettin' end of the money."

"Yes, ma'am," Leonard said.

She looked at me, as if examining my fat-cat white peckerwood tendencies. I guess none showed. Her wrinkles shifted. She said, "Listen here, I got some apple and pear pies baking. You boys come on in and help me get 'em out of the oven a'foe they burn up. I wore myself out bakin' 'em."

We mounted the porch and it screamed at us. I looked down and saw a split in the boards and the ground looking up at me. That old lady fell through those boards, she'd break a leg or kill herself.

The smell of baking pies from inside was rich and fine and made me hungry. I opened the screen door and held it. Leonard stood beside her while she used the walker, and after she made a few short steps she said to me, "Close the screen door, son. You're lettin' in flies. I'm gonna be coming for a bit."

I closed the screen until she got closer, which, true to her words, took awhile, and when she was close enough, I held the screen open and she and Leonard went past to the tune of straining boards.

I followed inside and closed the screen and left the front door open because it was hot in there with all the heat from the oven and there being only a little rotating fan on the kitchen table to cool the place. I felt mildly dizzy, as if I had been riding too fast on a merry-go-round. When I looked back at the screen door, it had begun to bead and buzz with house flies hoping for a chance to wipe their shitty legs on some pies.

The kitchen was very clean, and beneath the smell of the pies I caught a hint of Pine Sol. I wondered if she cleaned the place herself, and couldn't figure the how of it if she did. Being frail as she was, a bathroom trip would be like an expedition through the South American jungles.

One wall was quite amazing. It was papered with snapshots taped to it, some in color, some black and white, some very old and very faded. Where the wall gave them up was a doorway, and through the doorway I could see another room, and the part of the wall I could see in there was also covered in photographs.

Over the stove hung an ancient dime-store painting of a serene Jesus dressed in red robe and sandals, a worshipful beggar at his feet. The painting was in a frame behind clean glass, but the frame was too big and the glass wasn't pressing the picture and the picture had started to fade and heat-curl at one corner, giving the impression that Jesus's robe was rolling up and would soon expose private matters to the beggar.

The rest of the kitchen was cabinets and pot-holder hooks with pot holders and transparent, time-yellowed curtains over a slanting window.

"Turn the oven off and get the pies out," she said, and leaned forward on her walker as if getting lower would help her breathe better.

Leonard turned off the oven and got a gloved pot holder off a hook and opened the oven and took out three thick and beautifully crusted pies and sat them on top of the stove. The smell of pies filled my head thick as an allergy.

The old lady said, "You don't remember me, do you, Lenny?"

Leonard closed up the oven and looked at her for a long moment, then shook his head. "No, ma'am. Guess I don't. Haven't been back here in a time. I came to visit my uncle, it was the Browns lived here. Mr. Brown, he worked for the railroad or somethin'."

"Browns are all dead and buried," she said. "They call me MeMaw."

"MeMaw?" Leonard said. "MeMaw Carter. You used to live over on Sheraton. I used to go over to the park there. My uncle brung me. Y'all visited while I played."

"That was just for a couple of years," she said. "So I ain't surprised you don't remember me. You was practically a baby. I don't never forget nothing, though. You know there ain't no park there now? None you can use, anyway."

"No, ma'am."

"Drug niggers took it over. Kids with them beepers and needles and pistols in their pants. Ain't no place to do nothing 'round here anymore but get killed. My youngest son, Clarence, moved me here ten year ago. Thought it was a better place than Sheraton Street. Was, then. Old house was falling apart and all them drug niggers around. Now I got them 'cross the street and this old house ain't much."

"You used to tell me stories about Br'er Rabbit and such," Leonard said.

"And you ate my cookin' when you come with your uncle. You liked pies and vanilla cookies. Any kind of vanilla cookie."

"Yes, ma'am, that's me. I oughta remembered you right off."

She showed Leonard an acre of dentures and some of her wrinkles straightened out. "I've changed a little, Lenny. You know how old I am?"

"No, ma'am. I'm no good guessing ages."

"Don't guess no woman's age," she said. "That'll just cause you trouble. 'Course, you get old as me, it don't matter no more. One day to the next couldn't make me look no older. 'Foe long I'll be bakin' pies for Jesus. . . . I'm ninety-five years old."

"You don't look it," Leonard said.

She made a noise in her throat that sounded like crisp crackers being crumbled. "You don't start lyin' to MeMaw now. I look a hundred and ninety-five. You boys, help me sit down."

We got hold of her arms, which felt like sweaty sticks covered in foam rubber, and helped her away from the walker and onto a hard-backed chair at the kitchen table.

She sighed and said, "Thank you. That sittin' part and gettin' up by myself tuckers me. Turn the fan on me."

I twisted the fan around so that the rotation stayed mostly in her direction. I said, "You like a drink of water?"

"No," she said, "I'm OK, but I'd like you boys to help me eat some of that pie."

Leonard sliced us pie and poured us milk and we ate. The pie was good. It made me nostalgic for home and my mother, but my mother was long gone and so was the home where I had been raised.

I turned and looked at the photographs. They were of all manner of folks. People black and white and brown. The clothes and hairstyles and backgrounds revealed just how long ago this whole photographic display had begun, though a lot of the photos appeared to have been taken in recent years on MeMaw's front porch, or in her yard, or right here in the kitchen. A healthy number of them showed people eating at her table.

"Quite a collection of photographs you have there, MeMaw," I said.

She turned her head toward the wall and looked at them. "Got a whole nuther room of 'em. I always take pictures of folks. Cheers me, all them I've met. I look at them walls, I got memories."

"Who are they all?" Leonard asked.

"Some family," MeMaw said. "Most ain't, though. There's people come by to check the gas meter or the water or bring the mail, and they're nice enough, I'll take their picture and put it up there, try and remember what we talked about that day. This here," she waved her finger at a row of photos, "is all my family."

Some of the photos she was pointing to were old and some were new, and some had been taken by someone other than MeMaw, because she was in a number of the photos with her children. In the earlier ones she didn't look a lot different than she did now until you got to the oldest black and whites, and even then she looked elderly, but with darker hair and more of it, less wrinkles maybe, and a few of her own teeth.

She pointed out and named her children, and there were eight of them, five girls and three boys. The first seven close together, the last, a boy, born when she was forty-five, way past the time she thought she'd have another child.

"Ain't one more loved than the other," MeMaw said, "but Hiram, he's the baby. A surprise. Lives in Tyler, but travels a lot. He's a salesman."

I looked at her baby. In the most recent picture she had of Hiram he looked my age and size, but with thicker shoulders. He had a personable face.

The latest photograph of her eldest child, Pleasant, showed a woman who looked seventy-five if she was a day. MeMaw said she was retired and had a little check, but was in business for herself, selling leather-stitched white Bibles.

We got a look at all the grandkids and great-grandkids, and she told us their names and stories about each one.

"How come you started doing this, MeMaw?" Leonard asked. "Taking all these pictures? Puttin' 'em on the wall?"

"All my family done gone 'cept one boy, Cletus. Moved off tryin' to get somethin' decent for themselves. I wanted somethin' to do, and after my husband, Mr. Carter, died, I took to takin' even more pictures. Anyone I liked, I took their picture and taped it to the wall. Bet I've gone through half-dozen of them Polaroids. Every time I wear one out, my children buy me another. There's pictures of your Uncle Chester in the other room, and an old one of you. I took it when you was just a child."

"No joke?" Leonard said. "Be all right I see them?"

"Have to look for them," she said. "I ain't aimin' to get up right now. They'll be in the other room."

I went in there with Leonard, and it was stuffy and hot and all the walls were full of photographs, some relatively fresh, some wrinkling from age and heat and turning green. It made me feel a little lonely somehow.

On one wall near the floorboard Leonard found a black-and-white picture of his uncle and himself sitting on a merry-go-round in a park, most likely the park Leonard talked about over on Sheraton Street. Leonard was probably about ten years old and his uncle was our age.

The photograph wasn't too good, and Leonard's features faded into his black skin. His teeth showed white in his face and he looked happy. His uncle had caught a ray of sunlight and was more defined. He looked a lot like Leonard looked now. I took a minute to make fun of Leonard, just so he knew I loved him, and he showed me his middle finger to show he cared about me too.

We checked around for a long, hot time and found more photos of his uncle at different ages, and finally, on the way out, we came across one near the door. The Uncle Chester there looked a lot like the Uncle Chester I had seen in his coffin, only a little less puffy and a lot less dead. He was standing next to a tall angular black man about his age, and he had his arm around him. They weren't exactly smiling. They looked self-conscious, as if preparing for a hemorrhoid operation but bound to make the best of it.

"Who's that with him?" I asked.

"I don't know," Leonard said.

MeMaw heard us. "I'm pretty sure that's Illium," she said. "Take it off the wall and let me see it."

Leonard freed the photo and took it into the kitchen and gave it to MeMaw. She said, "That's who it is. Illium Moon."

"Who is he?" Leonard asked.

"He and your uncle was near growed together at the hip," she said. "You seen one, you near saw the other. Illium moved here from San Antonio. He'd been a policemans or somethin' like that. He and your uncle met at the domino shack up by the highway."

"Illium still around?" Leonard asked.

She studied on that for a moment. "I ain't seen him for a bit. Couple weeks, I reckon. Hadn't really thought about it.

Your uncle not around, I ain't expected to see him. Got so you couldn't think of one without the other."

"You know where he lives?" Leonard asked. "Being a friend of Uncle Chester's, I thought I might like to talk to him."

"No, I don't," MeMaw said, "but he works over to the colored Baptist church sometimes. I know that much. He used to drive the bookmobile too."

"For the library?" I asked.

"It wasn't the real library, the one downtown," she said. "Illium, he was like your uncle. He wanted to do good by folks, so he got this bus . . . or what do they call them now?"

"Van?" I asked.

"That's it," she said. "He had him a van fixed up with his own books, and he went around and loaned books here in the East Side, like a library. I never did take none of 'em, ten year ago I quit reading anything 'sides the good book since I couldn't get around good enough to go to church. I figured God would let mé slide on that, I kept knowledge of His word. But I thought Illium was a good man. Sometimes your uncle helped him out, rode around with him."

"Can you tell us where this church is where Illium works?" Leonard asked.

"I can," MeMaw said. "But first, Lenny, you go over there and open that cabinet."

Leonard went over to the cabinet she was indicating with a cadaverous finger and opened it. There was a snapshot camera inside.

"Bring me that camera," she said.

Leonard did.

MeMaw looked at me, said, "What's your name now, son?"

"Hap Collins," I said.

"Hap, you and Lenny sit together at the table."

We sat and pulled our chairs close and leaned our heads together.

"Ya'll'd make good salt and pepper shakers," she said, raised the camera to her face, grinned, said, "Now, boys, say cheese."

15.

"Do you remember seeing Illium at the funeral?" I asked.

"No," Leonard said, "but I wasn't looking for him. He could have been there."

"I don't think so, and if he and your uncle were as close as MeMaw claims, he oughta been, don't you think?"

I shifted gears on my old Dodge pickup and we climbed a hill full of potholes and crumbling slabs of weather-heaved blacktop. The sun was near midsky, and it shone on the faded gray hood of my truck and made me squint, and the hot wind blowing through the open windows made me sweat as if I were in a sauna. I reminded myself that in another couple of hours it would really be hot.

I had brought my truck back with me when we returned to Uncle Chester's house from our three days in the country, and I was glad to have it, old and uncomfortable as it was. When I first moved in with Leonard, he had picked me up and brought me here and left my truck back home because it was giving me trouble. Turned out the trouble was burned-out rings and cheap gas and no money to fix it.

But on our return to Uncle Chester's, Leonard needed a way to haul lumber, so he paid for me to get a ring job and real gas. Now, I was no longer polluting half of East Texas, and felt better about that, and without my telltale cloud of black smoke following me I was less embarrassed to be seen driving it.

We were following MeMaw's directions, looking for the First Primitive Baptist Church, and along the way I got a good look at the East Section, saw parts of it I had never seen before, realized just how truly isolated I was from the way of life here. Along with decent houses, there were houses next to them without electric wires, houses broke down and sagging, their sides actually held up with posts, and out back were outdoor toilets and rusted-out appliances in which garbage had been burned and not collected because the garbage trucks didn't always come down here.

Black children with blacker eyes wearing dirty clothes sat in yards of sun-bleached sand and struggling grass burrs and looked at us without enthusiasm as we drove past.

It was near midday and grown men of working ages were wandering the streets like dogs looking for bones, and some congregated at storefronts and looked lonesome and hopeless and watched with the same lack of enthusiasm as the children as we drove past.

"Man, I hate seeing that,'" Leonard said. "You'd think some of these sonofabitches would want to work."

"You got to have jobs to work," I said.

"You got to want jobs too," Leonard said.

"You saying they don't?"

"I'm saying too many of them don't. Whitey still has them on his farm, only they ain't doing nothing there and they're getting tidbits tossed to them like dogs, and they take it and keep on keeping on and wanting Whitey to do more."

"Maybe Whitey owes them."

"Maybe he does, but you can be a cur or you get up off your ass and start seeing yourself as a person instead of an under-dog that's got to take those scraps. I've always worked, Hap. Be it in the rose fields or as a handyman laborer or raising hunting dogs, and you ain't never known me to take handout checks because I'm black, and my uncle didn't either."

"Most of the people taking handout checks are white, Leonard."

"That's true, and I ain't got nothing for those sonofabitches either. Unless you can't walk or you're in temporary straits, there ain't no excuse for it."

"One minute it's things are bad here because it's the black section of town, and next time you open your mouth you're saying it's the blacks' fault. You can't have it both ways."

"Yes, you can. Ain't nothing one way, Hap. Everything's got two sides and sometimes the same problem's got two dif-ferent answers. It's the ambition and pride these folks are missing. They don't want nothing but to exist. They think God owes 'em a living."

"And some of them just haven't got jobs, Leonard, and it's as simple as that."

"Some of them," Leonard said. "Some gonna tell you too they got to sell drugs to survive 'cause things are bad, and I say you can rationalize anything. 'I got to sell drugs, I got to sell myself, I got to eat shit with flies on it.' You don't got to do nothin' like that. You grew up poor, Hap. You ever want to sell drugs or hire out to get your dick sucked or maybe lay back and take a check?"

"Government could mail me a check, they wanted to. But I'd want someone to go out to the mailbox and bring it to me. Maybe getting my dick sucked wouldn't be so bad either, especially someone wanted to pay me for it."

"Bullshit. I know you. You got pride."

"Not everyone has had the chance to have pride, Captain Know-It-All. You don't come with it built in. Like new cars, there are some options got to be installed."

"Yeah, but there's them that go out and get the options, use their own tools to put them in. Like your dad and my uncle. From what you've told me, your dad didn't have it so easy."

He hadn't. His mother had died when he was eight, and his father had put him to work in the cottonfields, and when Dad didn't pick the same cotton as a grown man, his father had put the horsewhip to him. I remember as a child seeing my father without his shirt, lying on the floor in front of the TV after a hard day's work at his garage, and there were thin white lines across his back, scars from the whip. My father could neither read nor write. He never missed a day's work. He never complained. He died with mechanic's grease on his face and hands. I'm glad I never met my grandfather. I'm glad he was dead before I was born.

"I had advantages still, Leonard. I'm white. Even the worst of the whites, the white trash, have had it better than minorities."

"Minorities are one thing. Choice is another. Check and see how many Orientals are on the welfare rolls. You ain't gonna find many."

"Check and see how many of those Orientals have ancestors were owned by white folks and sold on slave blocks. Frankly, Leonard, I think a Bible quotation is in order here. 'Judge not least ye be judged.' That's close, anyway."

"Yeah, well, I got one too. 'Decide to be a fuckup, you're gonna be a fuckup.'"

"What bible's that in?"

"Leonard's Bible."

I shut my mouth and brooded. There was some truth in what Leonard said, but ultimately, in my mind, there's no one more obnoxious and self-righteous than the self-made man. And no one more admirable.

Leonard told me to take a right and I did and we rolled off the ravaged blacktop and onto a smooth cement street with beautiful sweet gum trees and broad-limbed pecans skirting it on either side. The sunlight made bruise-blue shadows out of the trees and laid them on the street and behind the trees on either side were nice, inexpensive houses with clean sidewalks leading up to them.

Leonard looked at the house and said, "See, ain't everybody down here got to live in the garbage and walk the streets."

"They got jobs, Leonard."

"My point exactly."

"Remind me to kill you in your sleep," I said.

Soon the street gave up its trees, and there was just the blistering sunlight and on the right a couple acres of land and on it a parking lot and a whitewash church with a plain black-and-white sign out front that read FIRST PRIMITIVE BAPTIST CHURCH. REVEREND HAMIL FITZGERALD OFFICIATING.

Behind the church was a simple blue frame house with a well-tended lawn with a sprinkler spitting on it and onto a number of circular, brick-enclosed flower beds. In the driveway was a recently washed last year's blue Chevy and parked nearby was a small blue-and-white bus with FIRST PRIMITIVE BAPTIST CHURCH painted on the side. The bus looked fairly old, and a few of the back windows had been replaced with plyboard. I figured if you scratched the blue-and-white paint deep enough, you'd find a yellow school bus underneath—

one of those they used to call the short bus, the one the retarded kids rode to school.

I pulled up in the lot and parked.

Leonard said, "I see a church and I get to thinking how black folks are mostly taught how to accept their misery through God. It pisses me off."

I didn't say anything. We got out of the truck and Leonard looked at the church sign, said, "Never can figure that 'Primitive' part out. What's that mean? Everybody carries spears?"

"Leonard," I said. "You got a bad attitude. We find the Reverend, maybe I ought to do the talking."

"A white guy?" Leonard said. "I don't think so. Trust me, I know how to warm a guy like the Reverend up. I grew up here, remember. I can play the game, I have to."

We walked alongside the church and on toward the house out back. Back of the church was green grass and a playground that broke into the side yard of the house. The air smelled like mowed grass and floral perfume.

We could hear a sound coming from the back of the church, a thumping sound, so we stopped to listen to it and to the sound of the sprinkler sputtering, and within seconds we both knew what the thumping sound was because we had both made that sound before.

It was the sound of fists striking a speed bag, quick and rhythmic, sweet and sure.

16.

The sound came from an elongated, low-roofed addition to the back of the church, and from where we now stood, we could see the church was much larger than it appeared from the street. We walked toward the sound.

The back door was propped open, and we went in and down the hall, following our ears. We came to a closed door on the right, and the sound came from behind it. I opened the door and looked inside and felt the air-conditioning and liked it.

It was a small but nice gymnasium. The floor was smooth and shiny and there was a basketball goal at one end, and

JOE R. LANSDALE

against one wall some pull-out bleachers. In a corner of the
gym was a speed-bag prop, and striking the bag was a bare-
to-the-waist black man wearing blue jogging pants and black
boxing shoes. He was fortyish, about five-ten with thick
shoulders and sweaty skin and close-cropped graying hair. He
looked strong, if a bit thick in the middle, but the middle was
solid as a truck tire, and the muscles in his arms and chest
coiled and released as he hit. He moved quickly and expertly
and the bag sang to him as he did.

We stood there for a moment, watching him work, admir-
ing it, then he paused for a moment, caught the bag with one
hand, blew out some air, turned his head and saw us.

"I do something for you gentlemen?" he asked, and started
slipping off the bag gloves.

We walked over to him and he tossed the gloves aside and
we shook hands and introduced ourselves. He turned out to be
the Reverend Fitzgerald, his own sweet self.

"You look pretty good," I said.

"Golden Gloves when I was a kid," he said, but not to me.
He was studying Leonard. "I teach some of the neighborhood
boys. I know you?" he asked Leonard.

"I don't think so," Leonard said.

"Mr. Fitzgerald," I said. "We're looking for a man we've
been told works here. Illium Moon."

"Illium?" he said. He used his hands to wipe sweat from his
chest, then wiped his hands on his pants. "Haven't seen him
in days. Does a bit of handy work around here now and then.
He's retired, so he doesn't want anything steady. Sort of
chooses his own hours. I pay him a little. He helps run some
of the children's programs from time to time. Assistant-
coaches volleyball and baseball."

"Drives a bookmobile too," I said.

"That's right," he said. "But not for the church. That's his
own project. He's got all manner of projects."

"When did you see him last?" Leonard asked.

"I don't know," Fitzgerald said. "Week or two ago. You men don't look like cops."

"Aren't," I said. "We just need to find him on a personal matter."

"Serious?" Fitzgerald asked.

"He was a friend of Leonard's uncle. We'd just like to talk to him. Know where he lives?"

"Out in the country. Somewhere off Calachase Road. To be honest, I'm not entirely certain. Here, let's step into my office."

We followed Fitzgerald out of the gym and down the hallway and into a small paneled room with a desk and the expected religious paintings: Jesus on the cross. Jesus being baptized by John the Baptist. Some guy wrestling with an angel. On his desk Fitzgerald had one of those old clay ashtrays like get made at camp. It was gray-green and cracked and I had an idea about it and thought I'd warm him up. "Your kid make that?" I said.

"I'm not married," he said. "Actually, I made that when I was a kid. For my father. Sit down."

So much for warming him up. There were a couple of leather chairs in front of the desk, and a similar one behind it. Fitzgerald took his position behind the desk, and me and Leonard manned the remaining chairs. Mine had something wrong with the swivel and wouldn't move, but Leonard's worked just fine. He was turning slowly left to right. He always got the best stuff.

We sat for a moment listening to the air-conditioning hum. Fitzgerald clasped his hands together. He had a friendly face. The kind of face you'd tell your troubles to. He said, "Just as part of the job, may I ask you boys a question?"

"Sure," Leonard said, "but would it be OK not to call us boys? It's not that I'm overly sensitive, but I'm getting a little long in the tooth to visualize myself in short pants."

Fitzgerald smiled. "All right. It's a habit. We preachers get so we can't help calling every one boy, or son, or daughter. But the question was, are you fellas Christians?"

"Well, you've put us on the spot," Leonard said. "And the answer is no. For both of us."

Fitzgerald looked at me for agreement. I nodded, said, "Yeah. And no offense, Reverend, but we didn't come here to discuss religion. We just need to find Illium Moon."

"I've told you all I know about where he lives," Fitzgerald said. "I've never been to his place. I just know generally where it is."

I didn't believe that. I felt he didn't trust our motives, and that he wasn't about to give out Illium's address to a couple guys he didn't know, and infidels to boot. I respected that, but I still wanted to know where Illium Moon lived. I was considering an approach when suddenly Fitzgerald waved a finger at Leonard. "Wait a minute," he said. "I didn't think I knew the face, but something was bothering me. It's the name. Pine? You the nephew of Chester Pine?"

Leonard assured him he was.

"I've heard about you," he said.

"Word gets around," Leonard said. "And so do newspapers."

"Yours is a family with problems," Fitzgerald said.

"You might say that," Leonard said. "But not of our own choosing. Actually, far as family goes, taking or leaving—let's make that leaving—a few not-too-close and boring cousins, I'm all the family I care about.'Cept Hap here."

"He appears to be a very distant relation," Fitzgerald said, and smiled when he said it.

"We couldn't keep him out of the bleach," Leonard said.

Fitzgerald looked at me and I grinned, way you do when you're trying to let a third party know you know the guy with you sees himself as a real card, but you merely tolerate him.

Fitzgerald turned back to Leonard. He said, "Your uncle had a quick mouth too. Like you. I didn't like him."

"That's honest."

"He came around with Illium from time to time. I had a few unpleasant conversations with him."

"About what?" Leonard asked.

"About God and religion," Fitzgerald said. "He had a kind of cavalier attitude about the subjects."

"That was Uncle Chester, all right," Leonard said.

"I assure you I wish no one ill," Fitzgerald said, "but the Lord seems to have made his statement with your uncle."

"That didn't have quite the Christian ring I'd have expected," Leonard said. "You sound a little too goddamned happy."

"I prefer you not use the Lord's name in vain," Fitzgerald said. "Especially in His house."

"And I'd prefer you not malign my uncle," Leonard said.

"Sincerely," Fitzgerald said, "I didn't mean to put it that bluntly. I apologize."

Leonard didn't respond. He just studied the Reverend's face. I said, "Reverend. We didn't come here for a fight, and I don't see how we've gotten into one. We got a couple questions to ask. That's it, and we'll be out of your hair."

"You're not in a fight," the Reverend said. "I'm suggesting, respectfully, that you don't use that kind of language here, and I'm apologizing for what I said. I'm overly zealous sometimes. You see the things I see, hear the stories I hear, you get so you want to crusade, do something about the badness out there. Open the world up to God."

"All right," Leonard said. "Apology accepted. And I apologize for my language. Not because I think it matters, but because it is your church."

"However you prefer to see it," the Reverend said. "Listen, about your uncle. Let me say a little more. I'm not happy about what happened to him. I merely meant to point out that

103

we all face judgment in the eyes of the Lord. Not just your uncle, you and me as well. I'm suggesting only that we should all strive to stand in the Lord's light without blinking. I didn't mean it the way it sounded. Or perhaps there *was* some bitterness there. Your uncle was a witty man, and quick with a quip. He seemed to have a special hatred for religion."

"Hypocrisy is what bothered him," Leonard said. "Not religion."

Reverend Fitzgerald refused to be baited. He was very pleasant when he said, "It's unusual that your uncle and Illium Moon were such good friends. Mr. Moon is quite religious. Very involved in church activities. Especially those dealing with youth. And considering what I've read in the papers . . ."

"Don't believe everything you read in the papers," Leonard said.

"Very well," Fitzgerald said. "I'll keep that in mind. You know, I've been sitting here trying to recall what I've heard about you, Mr. Pine, and now it comes back to me."

"I hope it's flattering," Leonard said.

"You're a homosexual and you flaunt it," Fitzgerald said.

"I don't wear Easter hats and high heels and study floral arrangements, that's what you mean," Leonard said, "but I don't hide out in the kitchen under a chair either."

"You take pride in it," Fitzgerald said.

"You're no one I have to answer to," Leonard said.

"No," Fitzgerald said. "You don't have to answer to me. The Lord is who you answer to. I've nothing against you. I'm merely saying, your way is not the way of the Lord. Are you acquainted with your Bible, Mr. Pine?"

"Me and Hap here were just quoting Bible verses on the way over."

"Are you familiar with the story of Sodom and Gomorrah?"

"Yep," Leonard said. "It's a favorite Baptist queer allegory. I just get cold chills all over when I hear it. Which is pretty

104

often. I especially like where Lot's wife gets turned into a pillar of salt."

"You know the story, then learn from it, sir. Lot met the angels of the Lord at the gates of Sodom and took them to his house for a feast, and the house was soon surrounded by homosexuals who wanted to know them."

" 'Know them' means 'fuck them,' right?" Leonard said.

Fitzgerald batted his eyes a couple of times but pretended not to hear and plowed ahead. "And the homosexuals gathered around Lot's house and demanded that he bring the angels out and give them to the crowd, and the angels struck the crowd blind. Does that sound like tolerance for homosexuals, Mr. Pine?"

"All right," Leonard said, "you didn't get to the pillar-of-salt part, but you left out some good stuff. Like how Lot, wanting to protect these angels who needed no protection, offered his daughters to the crowd. Now there's the exemplary father I'd like to have. 'Hey, girls, we got these guests the queers want to screw, but, well, hell, they're angels and they haven't finished their chicken-fried steaks, so I'm gonna give them you instead. Shuck your panties and hit the porch.' "

"You have an unfortunate turn of phrase, Mr. Pine," Fitzgerald said. "The problem you have is not dissimilar to that your uncle had. And for that matter, I've had. Yeah, even preachers can have a crisis of faith. But in time it came clear to me. What you're doing is what I was doing. You're looking for God to operate on human levels. Forget that. God lays down the law, and the law is there, and it's not for us to question. It makes no difference if it seems just in our eyes or not. It is the law, and that is the long and the short of it."

"Religion's not the question here," I said, "and we didn't mean to get off on it."

"It's always the question," Fitzgerald said. "Mr. Pine, be proud now, for when you leave this world of the flesh and meet your Maker and you are cast down into the fiery lava pits of hell, your pride will fail you. Rationale will fail you. The law is the law."

"Now I know why you call this church primitive," Leonard said.

I thought: *That's warming him up, Leonard. That's playing the game.* Only way we could have made a worse impression was if we'd come in with our pants off swinging our dicks.

"Sin is a primitive act," Fitzgerald said. "Our beliefs here are as basic as I've stated. They're not to be debated, because they are the law and the law is made by a Judge wiser and more powerful than we. In time, in the hereafter, we'll understand His judgments. And if not, that is not ours to consider. It is our job to obey the law of God. It's that simple. And if there was ever a time we needed the laws of God, it's now. Look what this world is coming to. Forget the world. Look right here. We have a tremendous drug problem right here in LaBorde, Texas. Especially right here in the black sector. Kids sticking poison in their veins. Children prostituting themselves for money and dope. Did you know that many of the mothers here in our black community are unmarried? Their children are illegitimate?"

"I've heard that rumor, yes," Leonard said.

"They don't see that as sin, Mr. Pine. The world says that's OK. Fornicating is acceptable. These girls, children really, as young as thirteen and fourteen, have produced baby boys conceived by lust and born of the bile of sin. And who is to take care of these children? The children who bore them? What sort of future will they have? The children of children."

"What you need here is something practical," Leonard said. "Not more religion. Lessons in birth control and disease prevention are the ticket."

"That doesn't stop the sin," Fitzgerald said. "The act itself. Sex out of wedlock. Abstinence is what's needed."

"That's all right too," Leonard said. "But for those who don't plan to abstain, they need rubbers."

Fitzgerald took a deep breath, but when he spoke, he was as patient as ever. "That's exactly the problem, Mr. Pine. Tolerance. Too much tolerance. There will be punishment for those who sin against God. That includes you. Homosexuals will not enter into the House of the Lord. Ask God to forgive you for the perverse things you've done with other men. Turn your life over to Him."

"I ain't gettin' down on my knees for nobody," Leonard said.

Fitzgerald turned his attention to me. "What about you, Mr. Collins?"

"Hey, I didn't do anything," I said.

"You have to believe to be saved," Fitzgerald said.

"I'll think it over," I said. "Who knows? I might be back."

Fitzgerald smiled politely. "Well, it doesn't seem I can be of much aid to you gentlemen, in the areas of the spiritual, or with directions. I've told you all I know about Mr. Moon's address. Somewhere off Calachase Road." Fitzgerald put his hands on his desk as if to rise. "I'd really like to get back to my workout, now."

Outside, where the church lawn met the lawn of the little blue house, a huge man stood in the yard. He was over six feet, wearing gray cotton work clothes and his skin was black as sin and everything about him was big and tight and round, as if he were made up of boulders carefully stacked. In fact, there may have been enough of him there for a mining claim.

He was moving the sprinkler and hose, and when he did, little boulders ran up his arms and crunched and ran back down again. His mouth was open and he was studying us. From a distance, he seemed to have very small teeth. He wasn't concerned that the water from the sprinkler was spraying all over him. He watched us as we went, and may have watched us after our backs were turned.

Out in the parking lot, I said, "That went well, don't you think? Seldom have I seen two people warm to each other so quickly."

"Yeah," Leonard said. "Bet me and Fitzgerald ride together to the next Baptist convention."

17.

East Texas weather, being the way it is, by the time we got back from the church to the house, ready for lunch, it changed. Before we could get mustard plastered on our ham sandwiches, the hot, blinding sunlight was sacked by hard-blowing clouds out of the west. They swept down black and vicious and brought with them Zorro slashes of lightning and lug bolts of rain.

The rain fell cool and solid for two days, hammered the house, churned pea gravel out of the driveway, broke loose the packed red clay beneath, and ran it in bloody swirls beneath the porch and on either side of the house to collect in the sun-burned grass like gore in a crew cut.

The rain was so constant the birds quit hiding. You could hear them singing and chirping between flashes of lightning and rolls of thunder. Not a good sign. It meant the rain would continue, and most likely for some time. Outside, except when lightning zippered open the sky, it was black as the high stroke of midnight on a moonless night.

On the second day of the rain, late afternoon, I glanced up from reading *The Hereafter Gang* by lamplight and looked at Leonard's hard profile framed before the living-room window. He had pulled a hard-backed chair there and assumed the position of *The Thinker*, elbow on knee, fist under chin. He was observing the rain, and I watched as a snake tongue of blue-white lightning licked the outside air above and beyond the bars and strobed his skin momentarily blue. Inside the house, the air became laced with sulfurous-smelling ozone, and I could feel my hide and hair crackle like hot cellophane.

Leonard looked at me. "You told Florida to stay home?"

"Sure, but she listens way you listen. Not at all."

"Then she ought to be here pretty soon?"

"If she didn't run off in a ditch."

Earlier, bored out of my mind and tired of working on the flooring with Leonard, I'd braved the storm with a flimsy umbrella and gone over to MeMaw's and used her phone and called Florida at her office.

Turned out Florida was doing almost as much business as a nun in a whorehouse. She wanted to come by and eat supper with us. I tried to talk her out of it, the weather being like it was, but she told me she was coming anyway and she'd bring a big Pepsi. I wondered if that was some kind of bribe.

I left MeMaw's after being happily force-fed a slice of fresh cornbread slathered in butter, and waded back to the house through ankle-deep water that flooded down the street and tried to trip me.

Back inside and dried off, I looked at my watch and calculated when I had talked to Florida and told her not to come and she'd told me she was coming. I computed the normal rate of travel from her office to Uncle Chester's, doubled it because of the rain.

"She doesn't show in a few minutes, I'm going to look for her," I said.

"Then I'll have to go look for you," Leonard said. "You drive for shit in bad weather."

"You're brooding, Leonard, my friend. What's the problem?"

"I blew it with Fitzgerald."

"I don't think you're giving yourself enough credit. It was more like a nuclear disaster."

"Just can't stand shits like that guy, hiding behind the Bible and a church, judging everyone's got a view doesn't fit tight with his."

"All you had to do was hold your tongue for five minutes and we'd have known where Illium's house is. I think he knew exactly where he lived, but he didn't entirely trust us. After we got what we wanted, you didn't like the Reverend, we could have soaped his windows or shit on the lawn. Actually, I thought the old boy was pretty polite. He's at least trying to deal with his community's problems, and I guess religion is a better way than nothing. Truth is, you were itching for a fight."

"Have me shot, will you?"

"Not the first thing you've fucked up. I can think of all kinds of stuff."

"Thanks, Hap."

"Seriously, pal. Reverend's not the only one knows where Illium lives. It's not like he's hiding. We'll find him when the rain stops."

About ten minutes later, I heard a car sluicing through the rain. I went to the front door and opened it. The rain was like a steel-beaded curtain hanging off and all around the porch. It slammed the ground with a sound like ball bearings. The wind was the coolest it had been since last fall.

I could see car lights in the drive, and they were all I could see. They went out, I heard a door slam, a black umbrella and a yellow, hooded rain slicker split the curtain of water, and Florida was on the porch, her beautiful face staring out of the slit in the slicker hood. She grinned and held the umbrella down and shook it and collapsed it and leaned it against the wall next to the door.

"Hi," she said.

"You should have stayed home," I said.

"Good to see you too."

We went inside.

"Hello, Leonard," Florida said.

"Florida," Leonard said. "I was hoping you wouldn't get out in this. We been worried."

Florida slipped off her raincoat, and I hung it on a wood-frame chair by the door. She had on laced workboots, blue jeans, and a loose-fitting plaid shirt with the sleeves rolled up to the elbows. Under the coat she had been carrying a cloth bag. She sat it on the seat of the chair and spread the mouth of it and pulled out a three-liter Pepsi and a bag of those vanilla cookies Leonard likes.

"Hap told me you were nuts for these," she said to Leonard.

Leonard got up and took a look. "He's right. Thanks." He hugged her.

"You know I'm sorry how things are," she said.

"Yeah," Leonard said. "Thanks."

"First time I haven't seen you in a dress, Florida," I said.

"I was doing office cleaning," Florida said. "I felt like grubbies. Make us some cocoa or something, Hap. I don't think I'm ready for Pepsi."

"It's coffee or tea or slightly curdled milk warmed on the stove," I said. "Take your pick."

"That curdled milk sounds good," Florida said, "but guess I'll go for the tea."

I made us a pot of tea, and we were sitting at the kitchen table drinking and eating cookies instead of having supper, when I heard another car come up in the drive.

"Would you get it?" Leonard said. "I'm kind of comfortable next to the cookies."

"Yassuh, Massuh Leonard, I's on it."

I went to the door and opened it and a big shape in a black slicker mounted the porch. He looked a little like the Spirit of Christmas Future. He pushed back the hood of the slicker and smiled at me. It was Lieutenant Hanson.

"Come in," I said.

Hanson slipped off the slicker, and I took it and led him inside. I hung the slicker over a chair and let the water from it puddle on the floor. I said, "Hey, gang, look who's here."

"Damn," Leonard said, looking through the dividing space between kitchen and living room, "if it ain't Sherlock Holmes, and come all the way in the rain just to visit. Can I hold your gun, sir?"

"No," Hanson said, "but you can wear my badge a little while, you promise not to lose it."

Hanson and I went into the kitchen, and Hanson smiled broadly and said, "Hi, Florida."

"Hi, Marvin." Florida had a pretty big smile herself.

"You two know each other?" I said.

"We've met a time or two," Hanson said. "I've arrested a couple of her clients." Hanson nodded toward the cup Florida was sipping from. "That coffee?"

"Tea," Florida said. She smiled. Rather nicely, I thought.

I offered Hanson my chair and poured him a cup of tea and took my cup and went over and leaned against the kitchen counter and watched him watch Florida out of the corner of his eye. Watched Florida watch him for that matter. I didn't blame him, she was beautiful. And I didn't blame her, Hanson was powerful and charismatic and likable, if big and ugly and old enough to be her father.

Hanson looked at his tea and said, "You got any milk for this? I like milk in mine."

"They just have curdled milk," Florida said.

"I don't like it that bad," Hanson said. "What about sugar?"

"Would you like a rose in a vase to go with it?" I said.

"No," he said, "but I'll have some of those cookies."

Leonard pushed the cookie sack at Hanson, a little reluctantly, I thought. In fact, I didn't think he'd been sharing them all that well with Florida and myself.

Hanson crunched a few cookies and sipped some tea.

"You got questions for us, Lieutenant?" Leonard asked.

"No," Hanson said.

"Then you have something to report?" Leonard said.

"I do," Hanson said. "I thought you might like to know the preliminary forensic findings."

"That's awful chummy of you," Leonard said.

Hanson shrugged. "I'm divorced. I'm lonely. And I got nothing better to do."

"Why don't I think that's why you're here?" Leonard said.

"You're one suspicious sonofabitch," Hanson said. "Your uncle's house is involved. Possibly your uncle. You found the body. I thought it would be only fair I kept you informed."

"Don't pay any attention to Leonard," I said. "He was raised in a barn."

Hanson took a sip of his tea and frowned. He put the cup down, said, "We had a forensics guy come in from Houston. He's taken the bones back with him, but he looked them over here, gave us a preliminary report. He could revise his opinion somewhat, he gets a good look, but the forensics guy says the skeleton in the box belongs to a nine- or ten-year-old boy, and he probably died of severe trauma to the head. After that, the body was cut up to fit into something small."

"The trunk," Leonard said.

"No," Hanson said. "Originally, the body was in a cardboard box. On the bones were paper fibers and remnants of a kind of glue found in cardboard. Could I have some more tea?"

His cup was half-full, but I poured him some more.

"You're saying the body was put in a cardboard box, then the box was put in the trunk?" Leonard said.

Hanson shook his head. "Nope. There's not enough remains of the cardboard in the trunk for it to have ever been put in there whole. What about that sugar?"

I got Hanson the sugar bowl and a spoon.

"You got a longer spoon? You can't stir good with these short ones."

"No wonder you're divorced," I said. "And no, no teaspoon."

Hanson stirred sugar into his teacup. He said, "The body was put in the cardboard box originally, but by the time the bones were put in the trunk, the cardboard had, for the most part, disintegrated. Some of the cardboard fibers stayed with the bones. Another thing. The clay on the bones doesn't go with your uncle's dirt beneath the house. The dirt found on the bottom of the trunk."

"Then the body was moved from somewhere and put in the trunk?" Leonard said. "And before it was moved, it had been in the ground for some time."

"Looks that way," Hanson said. "But that doesn't let your uncle off the hook. Sometimes a murderer kills in one spot, moves the body, buries it, then moves it again. If your Uncle was sick, he might have thought about the body enough he wanted to be near the corpse, went and dug it up. Put it here."

"Uncle Chester wasn't sick," Leonard said. "That kind of thing isn't sick anyway, it's sickening."

"I'm not saying anything concrete about him," Hanson said. "I'm just speculating. We don't even know this was a sex crime. It could have been murder, flat and simple."

"Does it matter?" I said.

"Yes," Hanson said, "it does. It's a sex crime, it may not have ended with one victim. It was a murder, maybe a blow struck in anger, whatever, this could be the whole of it."

"Can the forensics guy tell from the skeleton if the child was sexually molested?" I asked.

"No," Hanson said. "Least not preliminarily, and I doubt later. Just not enough left to work with. He did determine the child was killed some eight or nine years ago."

"The magazines in the trunk indicate a sex crime, though, don't they?" Leonard said.

"They point that direction," Hanson said.

"Any take on the magazines?" I asked. "Were they buried as long as the body? Seems to me, had they been, they'd have gone the way of the cardboard box."

"Smart question," Hanson said. "They were added to the trunk in bad condition, but not bad enough to have been re-covered with the skeleton when it was moved from its grave to the trunk. They weren't in the ground as long as the corpse."

"So you haven't any proof this skeleton is tied in with the child disappearances?" I said.

"Nope. Other than circumstantial. Leonard's uncle talking about child murders, a skeleton being found here. Children missing in the community over the years. That's it, really."

"What do you think, Marvin?" Florida asked.

"I don't know," Hanson said. "It do be a puzzle, and I hate them. Agatha Christie shit. Never can figure that stuff out."

"Any chance I might see those files about the missing children?" Leonard said.

"I don't think so," Hanson said. "What good would that do?"

"Seeing them, knowing my uncle like I did, maybe I might see something that'll shed some light."

"I doubt it," Hanson said.

"Very conscientious," Leonard said. "But sounds to me you could use all the help you could get. I think maybe you might even be asking for help."

"Well," Hanson said, "the subconscious is a tricky sonofabitch, but my conscious mind knows better than to bring a civilian in on this. To be honest, after all this time, someone figures out exactly what happened here, even who the child is, it'll be an accident. That's how most of this gets solved, by accident. If it gets solved."

Hanson tipped his teacup up and got up from the table. "Gentlemen. Lovely lady, who I apologize to again for my past rudeness, and stupidity. I have to go. I have work to do."

"Tonight?" Florida said.

"Every night," he said. "It's either that or watch TV, so I take files home and work."

"Considering most of it gets solved through accident," I said, "any of what you do matter?"

"Very little," Hanson said, "very goddamn little."

18.

That night, with the rain heavy on the house, a sweat-cooled sheet drawn over us, I held Florida in my arms and had the sad, dreamy sensation that no matter how tight I held her, she would soon slip away.

I kissed her on the nose, and she opened her eyes and blinked and closed them again, said softly, "Can't sleep?"

"No," I said.

"Horny?"

"Not really."

She opened her eyes again and looked at me. "It's the rain."

"I guess so."

"What's the matter?"

"How are we, Florida?"

"What?"

"How are we? You and me?"

"We're OK."

"I mean, really?"

She eased out of my arms and raised up on one elbow. I couldn't see her features clearly in the dark. "We're how we've always been."

"And how is that?"

"You're not going to get complicated."

"Maybe."

"We haven't been together that long."

"Long enough for me."

"The cliché is women are the ones who always want to get married."

"I didn't say anything about getting married."

"But if we get serious, that's what you mean?"

"I guess so."

"Every guy I've dated has been ready to put a ring on my finger, Hap. A few dates, especially if they get a piece of ass, they want to tie the knot."

"I don't want to hear about that part . . . dating. Is that what we're doing?"

"Yes, we're dating. We're fucking too, but that's sometimes part of dating."

"I thought we made love."

"Oh, Hap. Don't get technical."

"Fucking's technical. Making love is the same as the flow of a river. A cloud in the sky."

"Where in hell did you get that shit?"

"I think the big-cheese monk on *Kung Fu* said it to Grasshopper. Ever watch that? David Carradine didn't know kung fu from shit."

"Before my time. I'm twenty-nine."

"No shit?"

"You think I look older?"

"No. I just thought you were older. Lawyer and all."

"See, Hap, way it works, some of us go to high school, get out, go to college, and in my case, law school, then go right into gainful employment. Some of us."

"Is there a hidden slight in that?"

"Some. Hap, I like you. I like you a lot. You're funny. You're a decent guy. You're not bad looking, and you make love beautifully. But you don't strike me as a secure bet."

"You're boiling it down to financial prospects. What happened to love?"

"I'm not in love—hear me, completely. But I could be. In love, I mean. But..."

"But what?"

"My mother married for love. My father married to be mothered. After I was born, he decided he'd work when he wanted to. He had a college education, Hap. He was smart. He was a sweet man. But my mother ended up working and supporting him and me both, and every now and then, the time of year was right, he'd work at a pecan orchard over by Winona. He liked to make just enough for a six-pack or two before he came home. I love my father. But my mother was miserable. Is love worth that?"

"Who says I'm going to lay around with my feet propped up watching TV reruns while drinking six-packs of beer?"

"What's your profession, Hap?"

"I do field work most of the time."

"That's not a profession. That's a temporary job. Or should be. You're in your forties, correct? And right now you're living off Leonard—"

"He lived off me for a while. Hey, listen. I pay my bills. I tote my load. I'm not your father."

"Maybe you aren't. But I like ambition. I like someone who gets up in the morning and has a purpose. A real purpose. I have one. I want whoever I love to have one."

"I always look forward to breakfast."

"You dodge behind jokes too much too."

"And you don't listen to your heart enough."

"My heart isn't as smart as my head, Hap. And who says I can't find someone I love who has ambition and purpose? For that matter, maybe my heart isn't telling me what you want it to hear."

"I'm not without ambition. I've just been temporarily derailed, that's all. Something will come along—"

"That's exactly what I mean, Hap. You're waiting for luck. Waiting to win the lottery. Waiting for something wonderful to show up on the doorstep. You're not out there trying to make anything happen."

"I've got enough money for now."

"For now. And it's not money, I tell you. It's purpose. Ambition. You'd rather coast."

"And maybe it looks bad for a beautiful black lawyer to have a rose field worker for a husband too. And I'm white. Let's throw that turd out and dissect it. Not once since we've been...dating, as you call it, have we gone out together. Really out. You come here or out to my place, and we eat here and go to bed and make love, and then in the morning you leave. You don't want to go to a movie with me, out to dinner, because someone might see you with a white man."

She rolled over on her back and looked at the ceiling. She pulled the sheet up tight under her chin. "I never said anything other than I had problems with it."

"So it boils down to I'm white, I'm lazy, I don't have money, and I could have a better job."

"That makes it all sound so harsh. I don't mean it that way. Not exactly. If those things really bothered me, I wouldn't be here." Florida rolled over and put her arm around me. "Are you really in love with me, Hap, or are you in love with being in love?"

I thought that over. I said, "You're right. I'm pushing things. Maybe I just been lonely too long, like the *Young Rascals* song."

"Who?"

"Before your time. Like *Kung Fu*."

"Do you want me to go?" she asked.

"In this rain?"

"Do you want me to go in the morning and not come back?"

"Of course not."

We lay quietly for a while. Then she said: "Hap, even though I'm a racist castrating bitch that wants you to be better than you are, wants you to do something with your life besides be a knockabout, do you think you could find it in your heart, in your itty-bitty white man's dick, to get a hard-on for me? In other words, want to fuck?"

I rolled up against her, kissed her forehead, her nose, and finally her lips. She reached down and touched me.

"Is that your answer?" she said.

"Sure," I said. "I have no shame."

19.

In the gray morning I awoke to the smell of Florida's perfume and the dent her head had made in her pillow. I had not heard her leave. It was still raining.

After breakfast, Leonard and I went to work on the sub-flooring, our hammering not much louder than the pounding of the rain on the roof.

We worked off and on until about suppertime. Then the rain quit and so did we. We locked up and took Leonard's car and went out to a Mexican restaurant to eat, then decided to try and drive out to Calachase Road and see if we could find Illium Moon's place. That didn't work, we'd do what you're supposed to do. We'd scout around till we found someone who knew where Illium lived.

It was still light, the summer days being long here in East Texas, but the sun was oozing down over the edge of the earth, and the sky in the west looked like a burst blood vessel. The air was a little cool and it smelled sweetly of damp dirt.

Calachase Road is a long road of clay and intermediate stretches of blacktop and gravel. It winds down between the East Texas pines and oaks, and in the summer the air is thick with their smell, and the late sunlight filtering through them turns the shadows on the road dark emerald.

We drove around for a while, saw some houses and trailers, but no mailboxes that said Illium Moon. We finally pulled up to a nasty shack that looked as if a brisk fart might knock it over. It was gray and weathered with a roof that almost had a dozen shingles on it. The rest of the roof was tar paper, decking, and silver tacks. The tiles that belonged up there were in ragged torn heaps beside the house, and leaning against the house was a crowbar and a hammer. A couple window screens were swung free of the windows, dangling by single nails. The front porch and front door were flame-licked black. There was a healthy stack of beer cans by the porch that weren't even damp, and it had been raining solid for nearly three days. Budweiser was a major label.

Beside the house was a man. He was black and bald and bony and wore a T-shirt that was stained to a color that wouldn't be found on any paint charts. He had on khaki pants with red-clay knees. His once-black loafers were colored with red clay and gray something-or-other. He had a shovel and he was digging, and he was somehow managing to hang onto a beer can while he did. He looked up when we pulled into the yard.

We got out of the car and walked over to him. The gray something-or-other on his shoes was immediately made identifiable by smell. Sewage.

Up close, we could see he had quite a trench going.

"Hello," Leonard said.

The man looked at us. His face was boiling in sweat. He opened his mouth to speak and revealed all his front teeth were missing. When he spoke, his missing teeth made him sound a little like he was talking with a sock in his mouth. "Shit, man. I thought y'all's comin' tomorrow." He stood up and pushed his chest out. "I know y'all seen them beer cans, but we ain't no algogolic's here."

Algogolics? What was that? An alligator with alcohol problems?

"You've got us confused with someone else," I said. "We've just come to ask directions."

"Y'all ain't from Community Action?" he said.

"Nope," I said.

"Damn, that's good," he said. "I'm hoping to get them cans up."

"What's Community Action?" I asked.

"They come and see I deserve to have my house weatherproofed or not. It's for the underprivileged. Figure I tear a few more shingles off the roof, they got to fix the whole thing instead of just spots, which is what they did last time."

"I don't know," Leonard said. "I doubt that dozen or so up here is worth bothering with. I'd go with what I got. But I'd move the shingles in the yard outta sight."

"I'm gonna tell 'em the wind done it," the man said. "There was some bad wind with that rain. 'Course, I took 'em off fore the rain."

"That crowbar and hammer look suspicious," I said.

125

"I'll throw 'em up under the house," he said. "Say, you fellas was Community Action, seen my roof like that, would you fix it?"

"I'd be all over that sonofabitch," Leonard said.

"That's what I figured," the man said. "Wish I hadn't started taking them shingles off 'fore it rained. Leaks between them tacks. Top of the TV's all fucked up. Run into the VCR and fucked it too, but I got it at Wal-Mart. They take anything back and give you another. One time I wore some shoes a year and took 'em back. You got to keep your sales slip, though."

"Digging a new sewer line?" I asked.

"Naw," the man said, swigging from the beer can and tossing it on the ground. "I'm digging in the old one. I lost my teeth."

"Ah," Leonard said.

"Got so drunk last night I was puking in the toilet, and I pulled out my bridge and flushed it. It's here in the line somewhere, it didn't go into the septic tank. It's in the tank, reckon I'm fucked."

"Sorry about the teeth," I said.

"They ain't gone yet," he said. "We ain't flushed the commode since, so I'm kinda thinkin' them teeth's here somewhere in the line. It runs slow."

I looked at the line. It was a ditch seething with broken red sewer tile and gray sludge. Flies pocked it like jewels.

"I don't want to buy no new teeth," the man said, "and I need to get 'em now so I can flush the crapper. Damn wife shit in there a couple of times knowing it ain't supposed to be flushed. Can't go in the house it stinks so much."

I looked at the house and thought a little shit stink might actually give it some charm.

"We wanted to know about someone might be a neighbor of yours," I said.

"Shit," the man said, "these neighbors 'round here are all motherfuckers. Our house caught on fire and these motherfuckers didn't even bake us a casserole or a cake."

"That's cold," Leonard said. "Listen, this guy may not be a main neighbor of yours. He lives on this road."

"This a long road, man."

"Illium Moon's the name," I said. "Drives a bookmobile."

"That motherfucker," the man said. "Shit, he tried to come by here see we wanted to read some books. I told him I got the *TV Guide*, and my wife can read it, so what I need a book for?"

"*TV Guide* does hit the highlights," Leonard said.

"That motherfucker's crazy," the man said. "He come by here 'nuther time and wanted to know I wanted to fix my place up with some scrap lumber he's got. Said me and him could do the work. Shit on that. Community Action, they use new lumber and do the work too."

"You know where this guy lives?" I said.

He pointed. "Down the road a piece there."

"We been down the road a piece," I said, "and we don't know what we're looking for."

"He has that van, one with the books, parked out 'side the house," the man said. "It's white. And there's piles of that old sorry-ass lumber and things under tarps there. You didn't see that, you just didn't go down a good enough piece."

"Thanks," I said. "Good luck with Community Action, and I hope you find your teeth."

"You do," Leonard said, "what you gonna do with them?"

"Rench 'em off and use 'em," the man said.

"That's what I figured," Leonard said.

"I'd do more than rinse them," I said. "You ought to use a little Clorox to kill germs, then rinse 'em in alcohol and then water."

"I don't go in for that nonsense," the man said. "I ain't never seen a germ, and I ain't never been sick a day in my life."

"Okeydoke," I said.

We left him there, poking his shovel around in the sewage. In the car, Leonard said, "I know it's an ugly thing to say, him being ignorant as a post and all, but maybe, luck's with the world, that shiftless sonofabitch will die in his sleep tonight. He ain't doing nothing but makin' turds."

"Yeah," I said, "and his teeth are in them."

20.

Red fingers of sunlight were all that remained of the day, and they clawed at the trees on the horizon. By the time we found the place described to us by the man with no front teeth, the sunset was still bleeding, but in the east the full moon was out and clearly visible and the color of fresh coconut.

The man with no front teeth was right. We had not gone far enough. Illium Moon's place was a small cottage-style house set off the road. We recognized it by the tarp-covered stacks we presumed to be lumber and by a mailbox across from it with MOON painted on it in black letters.

To get to the house you had to go through an open gap in a

barbed-wire fence and over a cattle guard and down a muddy-white sand drive. The house was white with a blue roof and shutters, and beside it was a little open carport that sheltered a very clean-looking '65 white Ford. The yard was impeccable. Out to the far side of the house were several neat stacks of something with huge gray-green tarps pulled over them. No bookmobile was visible.

We parked by one of the stacks and got out. I took hold of the edge of the tarp closest to me and pulled it back. Underneath was lumber on treated pine pallets. The lumber on the pallets was used lumber, as the man with no teeth had said, but it was good lumber and free of nails.

We knocked on the front door and waited, and no one answered. We walked around the house and didn't see anyone. Out back we walked a ways into a large, recently mowed pasture. The pasture smelled sweet, like a fruit drink. Off to the far left was a small, weathered-gray barn. From where we stood we could see a little brown-water pond with a big oak growing by it, and behind it, a long dark line of pine trees. The leaking sunlight visible above the trees was like a fading flare.

As we walked out to the barn, grasshoppers leaped ahead of us. The barn door was partially open and we went inside and called Illium's name, but no one answered. Inside it was stuffy hot, and there was a tractor and some equipment and a few bales of low-quality hay. I was uncertain how much land Illium Moon owned, but I didn't get the impression he ran livestock. Most likely he had a little cash crop of hay, and that was it.

Behind the tractor were two small piles under tarps. I looked under one. Stacks of newspapers on pallets. Under the others were neatly stacked cardboard boxes, and in the boxes were aluminum cans and plastic bottles. A few things clicked around inside my head like Morse code, but they didn't click long, and I couldn't decipher it.

We walked back to the house and stood on the front porch.

"No bookmobile," I said, "and no Illium."

"Let's leave a note," Leonard said. "Tell him I'm Chester's nephew, see if he'll get in touch."

Leonard went out to his car and got a pad and a pencil. He came back and leaned the pad against the front door and started to write. The front door swung open under the pressure.

"Open sesame," Leonard said.

I peeked inside. It was a very neat house. The living room furniture wasn't new, but it was well cared for. The white walls looked to have been painted a short time ago. There was no carpet, but there were some colorful throw rugs. The blue-and-brown couch had plastic protection sleeves over the arms. There was a cardboard box on the couch.

I called out, "Illium."

No answer.

"He ought to lock up," I said.

"Maybe he couldn't lock up," Leonard said.

I let that lay, and Leonard went in the house, and I went with him.

"We could get our ass in a crack for this," I said, but we kept right on looking.

We went through the house. Illium's kitchen was even neater than MeMaw's place and smelled of some sort of minty disinfectant. The bedroom was very tidy and the bed was made. The bathroom was neat except for the tub. It had a sandy ring around it and there were little hunks of damp hay. We went back to the living room.

I looked in the box on the couch. There were magazines in the box. I saw immediately by the cover of the magazine on top that it was the same sort of magazine we had found in Uncle Chester's trunk. I picked it up. There were more magazines of the same ilk underneath. Unlike the magazines in Uncle Chester's trunk, these magazines weren't as aged. They looked as if they might have been damp once, but they were in pretty good condition. I said, "Uh-oh."

Leonard was looking at them too. He said, "Yeah, uh-oh."

Under the magazines was a pile of clothes. Pants. Shirts. Underwear. All little boys' clothes.

"A bigger uh-oh," I said.

"I don't know," Leonard said. "We come by and Illium ain't here and he's left the door unlocked and he's got him a box of kiddie porn sitting right here on the couch with kids' clothes. Seems awful damn convenient."

"Nothing says he couldn't be stupid."

We put the stuff back like it was and went out and closed the door. I used my shirttail to wipe the door knob and wondered what all I'd touched in the house besides the magazines.

"Let's look in the carport," Leonard said.

We looked in the old Ford first. Nothing there.

"Must be doing the bookmobile route," I said. I turned then, and in the corner of the carport, on shelves, were a number of large jars, and in the jars there were little cuts of paper, and even though I wasn't close to them, I guessed what they were right away.

Leonard saw what I saw. He went over and got one of the jars and twisted the lid off and pulled some of the pieces from the jar and held a handful out for me to look at.

I'd guessed right. Coupons.

Leonard replaced the coupons and screwed the lid on the jar. "While we're snooping," he said, "why don't we look under those tarps?"

We checked under all the tarps. Under some was lumber, and under others were mechanical parts of all kinds, everything from plumbing to automotive. Illium seemed to be a neat pack rat. Maybe he used the stuff to fix up his house and car, tried to be neighborly to folks like No Front Teeth down the road by sharing his goods.

And in his spare time he cut hay and sold it and worked at
the church and free-lance drove the bookmobile, and in the
evenings, after a hard day of public service, he read child
pornography with a young boy's underwear stretched over his
head. It could happen.

We walked back to Leonard's car and leaned on the front of
it and we crossed our arms and watched the sky grow darker
and the moon grow brighter. Stars were popping out. In the
distance, the pond sucked up the moonlight and turned the
water the color of creamed coffee.

"What the hell is it with the coupons?" Leonard said.
"First, I thought Uncle Chester had gotten to be a nut shy a
pecan pie, but now I'm wondering. This guy's got the same
thing going."

"Hate to bring it up," I said, "but another stretch of coinci-
dence is kiddie porn showing up here as well as your uncle's.
And there's the fact they knew each other, and were good
friends. Lots of circumstantial evidence. It's beginning to
look bad for a certain good friend's relative, and I say that
with all due respect."

Leonard was quiet for a time. He said, "Doesn't matter. I
believe in Uncle Chester. He didn't kill anyone, not a kid anyway. Someone fucked with him, he might have killed them,
but a kid, no way. And he wasn't reading kiddie fuck lit.
There's an answer to all this, I don't care how it looks."

I hoped so, for Leonard's sake. I glanced down at the
ground and watched the moonlight silver the rainwater collected in a set of deep tire ruts in front of us, ruts from the
bookmobile, I figured.

Where was the bookmobile? Where was Illium? Did moss
really only grow on the north side of trees, and why did the
Houston Oilers keep losing football games?

I took a careful look at the ruts. They ran on out across the
grass and hay field. The grass and hay was pushed down, but
starting to straighten slowly. That meant the grass had not

been pushed down too long ago, but with the rain beating for a couple of days, it probably hadn't had the chance to pop back up. It would have taken this warm day and this much time for it to come back to its former position. Those tracks had been made three days, four days before.

I said, "Look here."

Leonard and I squatted down and looked more closely. The night was bright and we could see well. We also knew what we were seeing. Put us in a city and we couldn't hail a taxi, but we'd both grown up in the woods and had learned to hunt and track when we were head high to a squirrel dog's balls, so we could read sign. Animal sign, or human sign. A paw print or a tire track, it was all the same to us.

We got up and went across the grass and the mowed hay field. Another couple days and the hay stubs and the grass would spring back up completely, and there wouldn't be any trail to see. Not unless you knew to look for it.

It didn't take an expert in nanotechnology to figure where the ruts were leading. They played out at the lip of the pond, and there were deeper tracks in the bank where the vehicle had gone over. There were a couple of hardback books in the mud by the water, and the moon rode on the pond's brown surface like a bright saucer. I could smell the pond, and it smelled of mud and fish and recent rain. A night bird called from a tree in the distance and something splashed in the water and rippled it, turned the floating moon wavy.

Leonard eased down the bank and got hold of one of the books and came back up with it.

"Don't tell me," I said. *"The Old Man and the Sea."*

"No. *How to Repair Your Fireplace.*"

"Bound to have been a big run on that one," I said.

I looked at the pond, then looked at Leonard. He said, "I'd go in, but I got a problem with my leg."

"I thought it was well."

"Sometimes it gives me trouble."

"Like now?"

"Right."

"That figures. Look, we know it's there."

"For all we know, he run an old tractor off in there, or some drunk came through the cattle guard and run out here in the pond thinking it was a parking lot."

"Sure," I said.

I unbuttoned my shirt and tossed it to Leonard, stood on one foot and took off a shoe and sock, switched feet, and repeated the process. I pulled off my pants and underwear. I folded the underwear and pants together and tossed them to Leonard and put the socks in the shoes.

"Aren't you embarrassed undressing in front of a queer?" Leonard said. "All you know, I might be sizing up your butthole."

"Just call me a tease."

I slipped down the bank and started to go in the water.

Leonard said: "Hap, be careful, man. We haven't finished that flooring yet."

The water was warm on top, but three feet below it was cold. The bank sloped out and was slick. I went in feet first and slid down and under. The water flowed over me, and I looked up and could see the moonlight shining through the murk.

Going down the bank like that I had stupidly stirred up the mud, and a cloud of it, like ink from a squid, caught up with me, surged over me and frightened me. For a moment I was in complete darkness, then the mud thinned and I went down deeper, feeling for the van I knew was there.

The water, though less muddy down deep, was darker. I wondered what ever had possessed me to do this. We should have called the cops, let them look. I should never have promised Leonard I'd help him out in this matter. I should have finished college and gotten a real job. I wondered how long Florida would remember me if I drowned.

The pond was not deep, and soon I could reach down and touch bottom with my hands and feet. I crawled along like that a little ways, stirring mud, raised up and swam forward, felt myself starting to need air.

I rose up swiftly in the blackness and hit my head sharply on something solid and nearly let go of what breath I still had; it was as if the water above me had turned to stone. I swam left and hit a wall and something from the wall leapt out and touched me and I kicked out with my feet and pushed backward into another wall, and things jumped off it and touched me too. I clutched at them and they came apart in my hands.

My lungs were starting to burn, and I couldn't go up, and I couldn't go left or right. I pivoted and swam forward and hit a low barrier and reached above it and touched something soft. I grabbed at it, held with one hand, and my other hand touched something else.

Suddenly I realized where I was and what I was touching.

The back doors of the bookmobile must have been loose and popped open when the van went over. That would explain the books on the bank; they had bounced out when the vehicle went into the water, and due to the way the bank was sloped, the van had landed at a slant with its rear end up, and I had accidentally swum inside. The walls I had hit were the sides of the bookmobile, and the things that had jumped off the walls were books.

What my right hand was touching now was a steering wheel. That's what had cued me. Tactile memory reaction. Common sense, something I seemed short on these days, told me what my left hand was most likely touching. A water-ballooned corpse. I made myself reach around and feel along what I thought to be the face. I couldn't tell much about features, nose, jawbone, the like. The flesh was too swollen.

After a few seconds, I'd had enough. I jerked my hand away from the corpse but held to the steering wheel with the other.

I was beginning to pass out from need of air. Black spots swirled inside my head. It was hard to remember not to try and breathe.

I pulled myself over the seat and reached between the corpse and the steering wheel to where the driver's window ought to be. It was open. I yanked myself through and shot up, surfacing like a dolphin at a marine show. The moonlight jumped on me. The air was sharp, and I took in deep breaths that seared my lungs.

I swam to the bank where Leonard stood watching. He leaned out and gave me a hand and pulled me up. I coughed and shivered, said, "Next time, you go in."

"The van down there?"

"Yeah," I said. "And I believe Illium Moon is too."

21.

"I think we should go to the police," I said. "Talk to Hanson."

"Not yet," Leonard said. "Let me think on it."

My shirt was still damp from dressing while wet, but it felt comfortable in the close heat. I smelled faintly of pond water. We were back over on the East Side, at a little, smoky black juke joint called the Congo Bongo Club, having a beer. Well, Leonard was having a beer. I was having a nonalcoholic beer. The place served them, but they seemed embarrassed about it. The bartender, who was also the waiter, kinda slunk over and put it on the table like a patient giving a pretty nurse a urine specimen.

The lights in the joint were not too good. Most of what light there was came from red-and-blue neon beer signs at the bar and the blue-white glow from the jukebox. In fact, it was so dark in the back of the place you could have pulled your dick out and put on a rubber and no one would have known it. It wasn't the kind of place had a no-smoking section either. The cigarette and cigar smoke was thick enough to set a beer glass on.

The joint smacked of fire hazard. If there was a rear exit, you probably had to go through a back office to get to it. A fire started here, the office was locked, and the front door got blocked, you could kiss your charred ass good-bye. The music on the juke was great, however. John Lee Hooker.

We were trying to figure our next move. Or Leonard was figuring our next move. I was wondering what the cops did to you if they found out you had discovered a body in a pond and went away and didn't tell them. I was certain dire consequences hovered above the question. I had already spent some time in prison, and I didn't want another stretch. I wasn't even crazy about a small fine.

"There's things here don't jive right," Leonard said, "but I can't put my finger on the problem."

In the glow of the jukebox, I saw a big black man eyeballing us from a table across the way, throwing back beer like water. Actually, he was eyeballing me, as carefully as a birdwatcher might a rare yellow-throated two-peckered brush warbler. I suddenly realized just how white my skin was. Maybe we'd have done better to have picked up a six-pack at a convenience store.

I didn't say anything to Leonard, as the faintest hint of intimidation made his dick hard, but I kept my eye on the guy.

We shouldn't have gone in the Congo Bongo anyway. In my old age it seemed I was becoming less wise and cautious.

It was supposed to be the other way around. Maybe, after forty, a kind of self-destruct button kicks in.

"I don't know for a fact there was a body in the van," I said, blinking away tobacco smoke. "It just seems likely, because it damn sure didn't feel like a bundle of books I was touching. Question is, if it is a body, and it is Illium, why is he in the pond?"

"Bad driving?"

"That's not high on my list. Seriously, Leonard."

"Suicide?"

"Actually, I thought of that one. Don't get pissed, but let me throw out a theory, OK?"

"Toss it."

"Say your uncle and Illium met and took to one another like flies to shit, discovered they had something in common. They liked little kids, and not to pet on the head."

"I see this coming."

"Say your uncle did kill the child under his flooring. Killed him somewhere else and brought him back to the house."

"To play with?"

"I'm trying to be delicate here."

"That don't mean you ain't thinking it."

"Illium and Uncle Chester find they both like this kind of thing, and Uncle Chester likes to show Illium what he's got in the trunk under the floorboards, and they share a few magazines, and let's say when your uncle dies, Illium begins to feel guilty. . . . No, let's say lonely. I mean, this isn't a club. You can't go to Child Molesters United and find a bunch of guys like you."

"Way I understand it, it ain't as hard as you think."

"So Illium misses your uncle. Gets tired of looking at the kid fuck magazines by himself, just sitting around in the house, waxing his well rope—"

"So he gets all dewy eyed, puts his box of pornography on the couch, and his kid's clothes, possibly acquired from murders he's committed, or my uncle's murders if Illium was just a fantasizer, and he says, 'Good-bye, cruel world' to his box of toys, jumps in the bookmobile, runs off in the pond and drowns himself."

"It's a theory."

"It sucks, Hap. It sucks the big ole donkey dick. I don't buy any of it. And what's with the coupons? And you know that book I picked up on the bank? It had a mark in it that's in the copy of *Dracula* Uncle Chester gave me. A black circle with a red heart on the inside."

"It's my turn to say that's nothing. They were friends. Makes sense Illium marked the books he loaned that way, and your uncle got one."

"Yeah, and my uncle left me a safety-deposit box containing a book with that inside, and some coupons, so maybe it means more than it seems like it ought to. The coupons seemed nuts until we found those coupons at Illium's, now I'm beginning to think Uncle Chester was trying to tell me something."

"And he left you a painting," I said.

"Yeah, and there's that," Leonard said. "And if he was trying to tell me something, why didn't he just write it down and explain it? Or get in touch with me and tell me? Why the code business? What's it all mean?"

"I'm afraid Hanson's right," I said. "This is starting to sound like Agatha Christie shit, and I don't know from puzzles. They make my head hurt."

"Reckon we need Miss Marple?"

"Could be she's coming over right now," I said.

The big black guy who'd been watching strolled over to our table. Well, not exactly strolled. He listed a little. He'd had just the right amount of beer. I sized him up, looking for striking zones just in case it wasn't his intention to discuss politics or summer fashion.

He stopped at our table, said to Leonard, "What the fuck you doin' in here with this honkie, brother? You trying to get a job promotion? This ain't no honkie place."

Leonard leaned over the table, said, "He's talking about you."

"Yeah?" I said.

"Yeah," Leonard said. "You see, *honkie* is a very derogatory black term for whites," Leonard said to me. "You see, stuff like *peckerwood, ofay,* and *honkie*, it's very insulting. It's like whites calling us *nigger* or *coon* or *jungle bunny*."

"No shit?" I said.

The big black guy glared at me, said, "You ain't never heard *honkie* before, motherfucker?"

"He's sheltered," Leonard said. Then to me: "*Motherfucker*, Hap, is a common term meaning you fuck your mother. Even if you don't fuck your mother, folks say it anyway if they're mad at you or want to make you mad. It's designed to be derogatory."

"I see," I said.

"You cocksuckers best quit fuckin' with me!" the big black guy said.

"*Cocksucker*," Leonard said to me, "is a common term—"

"Cut it out, you motherfuckers!"

A lot of folks were looking at us now, wondering how much blood would be involved. The jukebox wrapped up its tune and the air went silent with the threat of murder.

The bartender said over the bar, softly, "Clemmon, ease off, these fellas just come in for a drink."

"I ease off I want to ease off," said the big black guy.

I glanced out of the corner of my eye at the front door. About twenty steps. Five, if you were leaping.

"Hey, buddy," I said, showing more confidence than I felt, "I'm not bothering you."

"You come down here and slum with the niggers, is what bothers me," said the big black man. "You white pieces of shit always lookin' down your noses at us. Come in here, smart-mouth me. It's gonna get you hurt. I bet you think I'm on food stamps."

"I hadn't thought about it," I said.

"Well, I ain't. I own my own business."

"Congratulations," I said, "but I'm warning you, go on about your business. 'Cause you fuck with me, tomorrow your relatives will be splitting up your belongings."

"What's that mean?" the big man said. "What the fuck you talkin' about?"

"He's threatening to kick your ass plumb to death," said someone at a nearby table.

"Appreciate that translation," I said.

"You're welcome," said the man at the table.

It finally registered with the big black guy that he was being insulted, and the game was over. He reached for me.

I batted his hand to the inside with my palm and raised out of my seat and hooked my other arm behind his head and dropped down quick with all my weight, brought his head into the edge of the table, sharply. The bottles on the table jumped and fell over. I slammed the guy behind the neck with my forearm and he came down and met my knee and rolled over on the floor and made a sound like he might get up, but didn't. He lay there in a ball and tried to look comfortable. I was glad he was drunk.

Leonard stood up. A lot of folks were standing up. I heard the click of a knife opening nearby. I picked a fallen bottle off the table and held it by the neck. Some of its contents ran out and splashed on my shoe. I reached in my pocket with my free hand and got some money and put it on the table. I wished I was wearing a wide-brimmed black hat and a serape. A damp shirt and pants would have to do, though.

The bartender said very softly, "Go 'head on and leave, boys."

I turned and looked at him. He was a little jet-black man wearing a white shirt with black bow tie. The neon throbbed colors on his shirt. He was holding a sawed-off pump shotgun, gauge of twelve. He wasn't holding it tensely, just showing it off. If he'd thought it through, he'd probably loaded it with slugs. You let down on it, you cleaned out fewer innocent customers that way.

"We were just leaving," I said.

"I thought you was," he said. "Don't forget the tip."

22.

When we got back to Leonard's place, Florida's car was parked in the drive and she was on the porch sitting in the glider. It was a bright-enough night I could see she was wearing some kind of cartoon character T-shirt, blue jean short-shorts and big wooden shoes that reminded me of miniature pontoons. She looked cute as a new puppy.

Next door there was the usual activity of drug selling, and I could hear Mohawk's, alias Strip's, alias Melton's, voice above everyone else's. When Melton got excited, his vocal cords achieved a kind of shrill quality, like something oily was trying to crawl up his ass and he was liking it.

"Not a real good place for a lady to hang out this time of night," I said to Florida.

"They think I'm inside, I bet."

The way the glider was positioned, the shadows, that was possible, but I still didn't think it was a good idea. Guys like the ones next door knew we were gone, saw her car over here, they might decide to investigate.

"You'll promise me you won't do this again, though, won't you?" I said.

"I promise," she said.

"Want to come in?" Leonard asked her.

"No," she said, "I'm going to steal Hap from you. I'm taking him on a picnic."

"Picnic?" I said. "This time of night?"

"I been waiting since dark," she said. "I'm hungry. And I don't care if you just ate dinner, we're picnicking, and you will eat. I made the stuff myself."

"Yes ma'am."

"I don't mean to be rude," Florida said to Leonard, "stealing Hap off and not inviting you, but—"

"That's all right," Leonard said, hanging his head and pretending to be sad. "I have a TV dinner, meatloaf, I think, and they're having a *Three's Company* rerun marathon on channel nine. I wouldn't want to miss that. And right before it, there's an hour of *The Brady Bunch*."

Florida giggled sweetly and Leonard raised his head and smiled.

I said to Leonard, "We'll talk later."

"I want to sleep on a few things anyway," Leonard said.

"Pretty mysterious, you two," Florida said.

"That's us," Leonard said, "The Mysterious Duo."

I got in the car with Florida and she drove us out Highway 7 East. I reached in the back for the picnic basket, an official wicker one with handle, and she said, "Uh-uh."

"I just wanted to know what we were having on this picnic," I said.

"It's a surprise. You find out as you eat it. But I bet you can guess what dessert is."

"Is it chocolate colored and sweet and shaped like a taco and you keep it in a warm place?"

"My God," she said, "The Amazing Kreskin. Come over here and ride bitch, big boy."

I slid over next to her and she smelled sweet and delectable. She said, "What's that cologne, Hap? Frog and Pond?"

I slid away from her. "Do I smell that bad?"

"Get back over here," she said. "Always did like a man smelled faintly of frog. Maybe you'll tell me how you came by that aroma?"

"Maybe," I said, and slid back and kissed her softly on the neck.

We continued until we came to a turnoff that announced a Scenic Overlook. The idea of an overlook in East Texas, especially if you've ever been to Colorado, someplace with mountains, is pretty funny. What it means here is a high hill, and not all that high.

We drove up there, and at the top were a couple of concrete picnic tables, a chained-down metal trash receptacle, and a whitewashed chain that ran between thick white posts that designated the area.

We got out of the car, and I carried the basket over to a table. Florida put her arm around me, and we walked to the chain barrier and looked down. You fell, you'd go almost six feet before you were in a pasture. Not exactly scary or breathtaking. But the deal was this: Here, on this hill, you looked straight out, there was a big V in the usual line of trees, and you could see a long ways, and the trees in the distance, especially now at night, looked like blue and purple mountains, and above those trees, the stars were like glitter being poured into a funnel. Directly overhead, it was so clear the stars seemed close enough to snag with a butterfly net. The air was invigorating.

The depression I was feeling after the rush of adrenaline from discovering the body in the van and the brief bar fight was subsiding.

"This is nice," I said.

"Yes, it is," she said, and hugged me tighter. "You can see forever itself from here."

"You come here a lot?"

"Now and then. An old boyfriend in high school showed it to me."

"Never mind. I'd rather not hear it."

"He was an astronomer-to-be," she said. "He was interested in the stars."

"Right," I said.

"Well, he did have a theory or two on black holes."

"Ha. Ha."

She laughed. "I've never been here when someone else was. Not yet. I've always had it to myself."

"Good," I said.

A shooting star flamed across the sky and snuffed out. We oohed and aahed it.

Damn, what a day. A nude swim. A dead body. A bar fight, and now a picnic with a beautiful woman, and a shooting star. What next? A UFO encounter?

The picnic basket contained barbecued chicken, egg salad and ham and cheese sandwiches on wheat bread, and sweet pickles and hot peppers and chips and potato salad.

"That's a lot of food," I said.

"Figured an old guy like you might need to recharge himself later."

"Honey, I look at you, I don't need any jumper cables."

We put the food on paper plates and ate and drank sweet tea out of a large thermos. There was another thermos with coffee; when we finished eating, I reached for it, but Florida stopped me. She said, "After dessert."

She stood up and took off her shorts and she wasn't wearing panties. She put the shorts on the picnic table. She slipped off her shirt and she wasn't wearing a bra.

"You saving on laundry?" I said.

She put the shirt with the shorts. She moved up close to where I sat on the stone picnic bench, and I kissed her belly button. She pushed away from me and smiled and gathered her clothes and walked back to the car. She looked funny and sexy wearing nothing but those big shoes. She opened the back door and sat on the seat with her legs outside and unfastened her shoes and put them on the floorboard. She crossed her legs and looked at me. "Do I have to write you a letter?" she said.

"Don't even need to send a telegram," I said, and I got up and went over there.

Later, we dressed and had coffee while we lay on the hood of the car, our backs against the windshield. We must have seen a half-dozen shooting stars.

"This was a nice surprise," I said. "I especially liked the part where you shucked your shorts."

"Glad you liked it, but could I say—without intent to hurt your fragile male ego, because I enjoyed myself very much—you seem a little distracted?"

"I've had a big day."

"Hap, I've been thinking, and I got to tell you, what I said the other night—"

"That's all right. I was pushing."

"What I mean is, I really don't have the right to judge you. You are who you are, and that's a pretty good thing. I shouldn't try and make you something else."

"You made some good points. I am coasting."

"I suppose another thing is we haven't had time to know each other that well. One day I see you and you're this grungy guy, and the next day I see you you're on top of the house sucking in your stomach—"

"You noticed that?"

"Sure. And then we're in the sack, and I like you. I like you a lot, and I don't really know who you are."

"What do you want to know?"

"You don't know me either. Not really. Let me tell you something about myself. Something to clear the air a little. I'm laying on you how ambitious I am, right? Telling you what a ball of fire I am, and what a wet ball of twine you are. So let me be honest. I'm not living up to my ambitions either."

"Maybe no one does."

"It was my plan to be a serious criminal lawyer. I wanted to try murder cases. I wanted to specialize in cases dealing with blacks, helping them get fair trials in a white world. The whole nine yards. But I've settled for divorce work and a little ambulance chasing. I've been in that shitty office of mine for three years, and half the time my clients don't pay me, or if I get a percentage of something, it's not a percentage of much, and I haven't made one bit of real difference in the world, and I thought I'd make oodles."

"Everyone starts somewhere, Florida. Hell, you're young. You'll build into a bigger career."

"I've got to be willing to do that, though. You see, I found out most of the people I was dealing with, defending, white or black, were guilty. If they weren't guilty of the crime they were up for, they were guilty of two others they got off from. Most of them were guilty as hell."

"That could have just been your experience so far. There're bound to be innocent people who need you."

"Yes, but I was trying to get guilty people off. Trying to find loopholes. And I'm disillusioned with people. Not just the crooks I've dealt with, people in general. Not long ago there was a murder near here, over in Mud Creek. A husband lost it and shot his wife and two kids and even the dog."

"I remember."

"People talked about the crime for a month or so. A lawyer friend of mine was assigned to the case. She proved the murderer was insane. She told me people asked her about the case all the time, and you know what she said their most common question was about what happened?"

"I don't know."

"What kind of dog was it? Yeah. What kind of dog? Like the people didn't matter. But if it was a cute dog, then we're talking tragedy. How could someone think that way?"

"You're running idealism up against reality, Florida. It happens to everyone eventually. But don't think the two aren't compatible. I've been through that myself."

"Point is, I've lost a lot of my ambition this last year or so, and just that stupid thing about the dog had a lot to do with it. What I'm saying, Hap, is who am I to cast the first stone? And another thing. You're right. I am nervous about being seen with you because you're white—"

"You never denied that."

"But that's not an excuse. I'm going to change."

"Hot damn, you're gonna take me to a movie."

"Yeah, but you have to wear gloves and a bag over your head."

"It's a start."

"I don't think of myself as prejudiced, but when I was a little girl we lived briefly up North. My mother had gone up there to stay with relatives. She left my father for a time, and she thought, up there, out of the South, she had a chance to do something without skin color mattering. That was in New Jersey. Well, there wasn't much more in the way of jobs there, and the relatives we were staying with were living in a white section of town and had been for a couple of months, and one morning we woke up with snow on the ground and a cross burning in the yard. Burned into the yard with gasoline was the word *nigger*. We moved back here, and the relatives moved out of that neighborhood and into a black one, and the whole idea of sanctuary, that there was somewhere you could go where there wasn't any prejudice, any racial hatred, was gone.

"It made an impression, Hap. I don't blame all whites for the stupidity of those people who put up that cross and burned those words into my relatives' lawn, but it left something here," she touched her heart, "that has to do with me and white skin. I'm smart enough to know it's a knee-jerk response at times, and I fight against it, but it's there, and what really makes me mad is, late at night, sometimes I wake up bitter. Memories like that don't go away easy."

"So now you don't trust whites, and you don't care to be seen with them—romantically, anyway?"

"It makes me feel dirty. I even feel a little inferior a lot of the time. Like I should be grateful I'm doing what I'm doing, and that I'm doing good for a little colored girl from East Texas. I know better intellectually, but emotionally, I feel maybe I am a nigger. That I'm second-best. I fight against it all the time."

"Do you feel dirty right now?"

"No. You don't make me feel that way. In this setting. But we went out in public, the old feelings would come back. I'm not saying I'm not willing to fight them. I'm being honest. But they'll come back. And maybe that's OK, as long as I confront them. All right. I've showed you my dirty laundry. Told you stuff I've never told anybody. Now, tell me something about yourself. Help me learn who you are."

"I'm a guy who hopes he can show you there's more to white guys than someone who just wants in your pants. More to this white guy, anyway. I don't deny that getting in your pants is on my mind. I look at you and biology takes over, and

I'm enjoying the sexual aspect of our relationship, but I want more. I'm not going to push you on the matter, but I want you to know that.

"OK. Enough on that. Let's see. What else? I'm a college dropout. I was a draft resister during the Vietnam War, and I'm proud of it. I stood up for something and didn't wimp out. Didn't run off to Canada. Didn't get religion. 'Course, there was a down side. I went to prison for refusing to step forward at the induction ceremony. I did eighteen months. Let's see. What else? I was married. The woman made a fool out of me, even after we were divorced. She was like catnip to me. She waved her butt and I followed. She nearly got me and Leonard killed once."

"What?"

"I'm only going to talk so much about this right now. Later, maybe I'll have more to say. But the gist of it, without being too specific, is I let her pull us into something I should have known better about. A way to make quick money, easy. Only it wasn't easy. Leonard knew it was a dumb idea and he told me so, but I was headstrong, and he went along with it anyway, because of me. Ended up my ex-wife, Trudy, got killed and I got injured, and Leonard got his leg hurt bad. He was lucky it healed up the way it did. They thought for a while he'd lose it."

"My God, Hap. . . . That explains those scars you've got?"

"Some of 'em. So, I'm an ex-con and I nearly caused my friend to lose his leg because I couldn't keep my dick in my pants."

"I don't believe that."

"You're right. I'm giving myself too much credit. It wasn't my dick leading me around. It was some foolish vision of true love. I used to believe in that. Sometimes I still do. Maybe that's what sapped my ambition, there not being any true love. Though to be honest, before Leonard got hurt, I wasn't exactly a ball of fire either.

153

"Trudy and prison could be blamed, but I guess finally, you always got to blame yourself. I let my idealism get stepped on, and I began to think it was a sham, that there never was anything to it, because nothing ever changed. But I've come out on the other side, now. I'm not ambitious, but I'm not lost either. I've got my faith back in humanity, and it's people like you that do it.

"There's bad stuff out there, but you look around, there's good too. I'm not saying I'm ready to wear flowers in my hair and tell everyone to just love one another, but I do think things can be better than they are, and that each of us, in his or her own way, can have something to do with making it better. I also like blueberry ice cream, fluffy bunny rabbits, stuffed animals, especially teddy bears, and cute shoes, if they don't fit too tight."

"You silly ass," Florida said.

"Oh, one more thing. Earlier today, I found a dead body in a pond."

23.

We got back to the house late and took the bedroom Leonard had left us. He was asleep on the couch. We made love again and talked some more. I told Florida all I knew about Illium Moon, about how we found the body. She thought we should call the police. I did too. But Leonard had taken bullets because of me, the least I could do was give him some time.

"You never heard any of this," I said. "It comes up, except with Leonard, you don't know a thing."

"Oh, Hap."

"Not a thing, Florida."

"That poor man . . . down there."

"He don't know he's up or down. Another day isn't going to matter."

We finally snuggled and fell asleep, and I dreamed.

And in this dream I was under water. Down there in the bookmobile with Illium, but I could see clearly this time. It wasn't as dark as it had actually been. Uncle Chester was there too. They were swollen and spongy and their faces were no longer black. They were the color of damp oatmeal. Illium was sitting behind the wheel. He had a jar of coupons. Beside him, on the passenger side, reading a paperback copy of *Dracula*, was Uncle Chester. I was in the back, leaning between the seats, watching them. They didn't seem to notice I was there. I looked over Uncle Chester's shoulder. He was reading the part of *Dracula* about the "Bloofer Lady," the vampire child murderer. I could read it clearly, even though the words were gibberish, hieroglyphics at best.

Illium unscrewed the lid on the jar in his lap, and the jar filled with water and the coupons floated up and out, paraded before him like small, wafer-thin fish. He plucked one of them between his fingers and put it back in the jar. He grabbed another, and another, but as fast as he put them in the jar they floated out. Uncle Chester turned and looked at Illium. He shut the book and held it in one hand. With the other he reached over and clutched at the floating coupons. He helped put them in the jar, and still they floated out. The process was endless. Illium and Uncle Chester grabbing the coupons, putting them in the jar, and the coupons floating out.

I turned to the back and there was a trunk in the van, and the lid was up. It was Uncle Chester's trunk. I looked inside. There was a little black boy in there. Nude. His eyes wide open. His lips formed the words *Help me,* but I turned away.

On the opposite side of the van, mounted on the wall, was the painting Leonard had done of the old house amid the trees. The paint began to bead, then bubble. The bubbles filled with colors of the paint and streaked down its length as if crying Crayola tears.

I felt uncomfortable. Hot. I realized I was holding my breath. The back door of the van was shut. I tried to open it. It wouldn't budge. I turned and tried to walk to the front of the van, but now I was swimming. I tried to ease between Uncle Chester and Illium, make my way to the driver's window, but it was closed. I was growing weak, dizzy. I grabbed at the window crank and attempted to roll the window down, but the crank wouldn't work, and now Illium and Uncle Chester had hold of me and were yanking me back. I twisted and tried to fight them. Their faces were more puffed than before. Their eyes poked from their heads like peeled grapes. The little black boy was out of the trunk. He swam between them, took hold of my shirt. His eyes were pleading. His hand tugged at me. His arm came loose at the shoulder and floated up, but still his fingers held my shirt. Then his other arm came loose at his shoulder and floated to the top of the van. Then his legs. And finally his head. His torso came down to rest on my chest, and his body parts bobbed all around me, shedding flesh, leaving only the floating bones, the rib cage lying across me. I tried to pull the skeletal arm and fingers from my shirt, but I was too weak. The bony arm began to tug. Coupons swam by me. Illium and Chester Pine leaned over me and smiled. The water turned murky. I felt as if I were blacking out.

Then I woke up hot and mummy-wrapped in the covers. The moon was filling the room. Florida had rolled to the other side of the bed. The moonlight was mostly on her, and I was in shadow. I noted that the shadow made my skin dark as hers. I untwisted the sheets and sat on the edge of the bed and took in some deep breaths. After a while, I rolled back on the bed and took hold of the sheet and covered Florida and myself.

I thought about what I had dreamed. It seemed pretty silly now. There was a logical explanation for everything in the dream, but I felt my unconscious was also trying to tell me something I'd overlooked all this time. I still didn't know what it was, but I thought I had hold of the edges of it, and if I kept my grip, I might pull the rest of it into view.

I lay awake until the moon slipped away and the sun eased up, rose and gold and already hot.

Florida was still asleep, and so was Leonard, when I tiptoed into the kitchen and started coffee. By the time the coffee was beginning to perk, Leonard was awake. He came in wearing his gray robe and some grungy bunny-rabbit slippers. You know, those silly things with the ears on them, white cotton tails at the heels. Personally, I've always wanted a pair.

Leonard yawned, sat at the table. "Where's Florida?" he said.

"Still sleeping. We were up late."

"Contemplating the universe, of course. What's this?"

He was pointing at his painting. After I got the coffee going, I had brought it into the kitchen and propped it up in a chair. I had the copy of *Dracula* on the table. I had a pencil and paper there too. I had drawn on the paper.

"I been thinking stuff over, Leonard. I believe I've come up with some ideas."

"Like what?"

I poured him coffee, poured myself a cup, and said, "I'm looking at this now from your standpoint. Your uncle isn't guilty. Once I could get myself to think that way, I began to get some ideas. That's all they are, though, ideas."

"Let's hear them," Leonard said.

"Your uncle was a fan of mysteries. He wanted to be a cop. He was a security guard. He claimed to have information regarding child murders, and wanted to have his own personal investigation with assistance from the police, but he didn't want them in complete control. We know from what Hanson said that the child disappearances here on the East Side weren't exactly given top priority, and now, even if someone came in and wanted to pursue them, like Hanson, it's such an old case, it would still be a back-burner operation. We know too racial prejudice most likely affected the conclusions of previous investigators."

"Bottom line, my uncle didn't trust the police, but he saw himself as an investigator. It was his big chance to solve a real mystery."

"Let's say Illium, who was an ex-cop, met your uncle through one of his personal programs. Bookmobile, the recycling, whatever. They became friends, and they began to investigate this business. I don't know why they began to investigate. Some little pieces of evidence got them curious, and they were bored, and they went to it. Or they found the skeleton by accident, and your uncle brought it here because he wanted to examine it, try and figure what happened. Thing is, though, if he was investigating with Illium, and they were serious about what they were doing, they must have made notes. But where are they?"

"You're right," Leonard said. "Uncle Chester would have made notes."

"Let's hold our water there and back up. Your uncle began to lose it. Alzheimer's, not enough blood to the brain, whatever, but he began to experience problems. He got his will straight through Florida, left his stuff to you. But his thinking continued to muddle. Say he couldn't work on the case anymore, and that just left Illium. Your uncle wanted this business solved, but it was different now. His brain was melting. He couldn't hold his thoughts. I think that's why you have that bottle tree out there. A part of him knew there was something corrupt about, but he couldn't remember what."

"So he translated it as something supernatural?"

"Something evil. If he heard about bad spirits when he was a kid, it could have come back to him as real, his mind messed up the way it was. He might have thought he was actually doing something that could protect him. And in clear moments he wanted to tell you about it, or write it down, but he couldn't remember long enough, so the things that were important to the case became all the focus he had, and those things became symbols rather than thoughts."

"The coupons. The book. The painting."

"In a way, he was giving you a mystery to solve, not on purpose, but because those elements, those clues, were all that remained of his thinking on the matter. He might not even have known what those clues related to anymore, but they were important to him, and you were important, and he had enough savvy left to put those items together and have them stowed away in a safety-deposit box."

"It really is Agatha Christie shit?"

"Let's see what we got. The book, *Dracula*. I don't think it means anything particularly. I believe your uncle was thinking about Illium. Not directly, perhaps. But the book had to do with Illium, and it merely indicates a connection."

"Illium has, or had, the notes, is what you're saying?"

"Could be. If he did have them, I figure whoever left him the little present of the kiddie pornography and the clothes found them and destroyed them. The coupons, now. Both Illium and your uncle had them, and they seem important, but not so important Illium's killer took note of them. We certainly found them easy enough."

"Meaning, if they were important," Leonard said, "Illium's murderer didn't know they were."

"Yeah. Your uncle gave some coupons to Florida to give to you, and he put some in a safety-deposit box. Illium had coupons in jars. But what's it all mean? I haven't come up with a thing on that."

"The painting?"

"That one's up to you, Leonard. Tell me about it."

"I painted it when I was a kid, for my uncle. It's of the old Hampstead place."

"It's a real place?"

"Yeah. It's behind the house here, back in those woods. I used to go there now and then. The house was abandoned years ago. Hampsteads were white folks, and they owned all the woods back there. Used to be a couple hundred acres. The black community ended right behind the house here, where those woods begin. Guess it still ends there, but I don't know if all that land's still owned by the Hampsteads. They may have sold some of it. I really don't know anything about it anymore. Just that the house was once a fine house, there was some tragedy in the family, and they moved out, but kept the land and the house, but didn't attend to it. I been inside a couple of times. When I was a kid. Climbed through a window. It was a pretty spooky place. I don't even know it's still standing."

"Better and better. Look here." I picked up the pad and showed it to him. I had drawn a series of little rectangles within a series of lines.

"I don't get it," Leonard said.

"First day we came here, I saw a composition notebook on your uncle's desk. I glanced at it. It had a drawing, or chart, or whatever, like this on it. I didn't think much of it. I thought it was just doodling. For all I know, that's what it was, but I suspicion it might be a note that didn't end up with Illium. After the cops came, it disappeared. I guess they have it. Maybe they have more notes than we think, but I don't believe so."

Leonard studied the pad. I said, "I'm not sure I've remembered it exactly right, but that's close. Does it make you think of anything?"

"A floor plan with six rectangles in it."

"My thoughts exactly. What about the rectangles?"

"Furniture?"

"I don't think so. But leave that for a moment. If it is a floor plan, it's not to this house. Too many rooms. And the rectangles don't correspond with your uncle's furniture at all. Do you see what I'm getting at now?"

"If the coupons connect. If the book connects. Then the painting connects, or the location of it connects, and that location could go with this floor plan."

"Right. We just don't understand *how* they connect. Now, what comes in rectangles?"

"All kinds of things. A stick of gum. Books. He liked books, that could be it."

"Proportion throws that. The rectangles are too big to be books if this is a legitimate floor plan."

I hummed a few bars of the death march. Leonard's eyes widened. "Graves," he said.

"Ta-da!"

"You mean under the Hampstead place?"

"Could be."

"I'll be a sonofabitch."

"When Florida wakes up, she's going over to see her mother. When she does, you and I are going to go take a look at the Hampstead place."

24.

Late morning, a half-hour after Florida left, we entered the woods, Leonard carrying a shovel, me with a flashlight clipped to my belt, my remembrance of Uncle Chester's diagram folded up in my pants pocket.

At first the going was easy, as the woods were made up mostly of well-spaced pines and there were soft paths of straw to walk on, but soon the trees sloped uphill and there were hardwoods, vines and brambles, and the pines grew closer, and the going wasn't so good. It was humid too, and the smell from the pines and sweet gums became cloying, like being splashed with a bucket full of cheap perfume.

We scouted around until we found a little animal path and made our way down that. Traveling became easier. We startled birds and a deer. About an hour later the trail trickled out at the edge of a little dry creek bed. We didn't cross. Leonard led along the edge of the creek and deeper into the woods. We fought our way through the vines and brambles, and finally, thorn-torn, tired and hungry, we broke into the section of woods that held the house hostage.

Leonard leaned on the shovel, "I was set up right here when I painted it. It's in worse shape now. I don't remember a damn thing about the insides. There were fewer trees around it then."

The house was huge and had once been elegant. Two-story, with a porch that went all around, lots of windows and a railed upper deck, now sagging, like a dental plate hanging out of a drunk's mouth. There were some fallen-down outbuildings nearby and a tumbled-over rock well frame, and around the old well vines twisted and young saplings sprouted.

Trees were growing close to the house, and it appeared as if they were holding it up. An oak had erupted through rotten porch boards and was crawling up the front of the place, poking a limb through a glassless window frame, like a bully poking a big finger in a sissy's eye. The house's lumber had gone gray as cigarette ash. At one side, a persistent hickory had grown to the height of the house and was still growing, and in the process, one humongous limb was lifting a corner of the roof as if tipping a hat.

We carefully mounted the porch, watching our step as it protested our weight. A burst of birds exited a nearby window with a noisy flutter. I said, "Shit."

"Just yellow-bellied finches," Leonard said. "Not known man-eaters."

The front door was still intact, but when I took hold of the rusted doorknob, it budged only slightly before jamming. The hinges were rusted tight.

The window from which the birds had exploded was our next bet. Leonard kicked out the few remaining fragments of glass and broke apart the wood trim that had held the glass in the frame, and we climbed inside.

The room was large and decorated with vines and dust and a peeling, bubbled wallpaper that had a faded design on it that must have been colorful and jim-dandy about 1928. There was an old fireplace filled with trash from hunter and/or hobo camps. A chicken snake, big enough to play a starring role in a Tarzan movie, slithered quickly across the floor and disappeared in a gap in the wood.

The first-floor ceiling was mostly gone, and you could clearly see the roof was pocked with holes, and the shadowed sunlight through the gaps was like spoiled cheese oozing through the splits in a food grater. The flooring was also gapped, and there were sections where it was bowed up and the boards had popped and split from weathering.

We made it across and into the next room without falling through, and the flooring there was better because the ceiling was complete and less water had dampened it. The room was smaller and contained an old-fashioned chifforobe. The wood of the chifforobe had swollen and cracked. There was a bird's nest on top of it, and dried birdshit streaked its sides. The wallpaper here was good, and you could recognize the pattern as a series of pale green shamrocks.

In the next room, the kitchen, there was a black, dust-covered wood stove with white porcelain facing, and a long table shoved up against the wall. The table was weather faded but sound, with thick carved legs that terminated in lion's feet. Above the table, on the wall, the wallpaper—sick beige with no pattern—had water-stained itself in an interesting manner. The stain was dark and shaped like a face and there were darker dots on the face, like splash marks, and the shape of the face was familiar.

Leonard said, "The Wallpaper of Turin, or rather, of LaBorde, Texas."

"I read once about this Mexican gal saw Jesus's face on a tortilla," I said, "but I think we got her beat here."

"I don't know," Leonard said, "get tired of it, you can't eat it."

We went over to the table for a closer look. Leonard stepped back and glanced down, said, "Check out the floor."

I saw what he meant immediately. A large section of the floor we were standing on was newer wood. It was dark, as if weathered, but it was, in fact, treated lumber. About the size of a Ping-Pong table. You looked close enough, you could see it was all of one piece. You might not have noticed it, you weren't looking for something suspicious.

I got out the floor plan I had drawn from memory. I said, "According to this, if I recreated it right, and the basic design certainly fits this house, there are no graves at this spot."

"Yeah, but I think, good friend, we have just found the doorway to hell."

We got off the square of flooring, and Leonard worked the tip of the shovel into a corner of it and lifted. The square of wood creaked up. When it was high enough, I grabbed hold of it and helped raise it. It wasn't too heavy.

We pulled the section back and looked down. It was about three feet to the ground. You could smell the dampness of the earth. The ground was packed down there, as if it were well traveled.

I lay down on the floor, leaned over the edge of the gap, and looked underneath the flooring with my flashlight. There had been a lot of new wood put under there for support. About three feet to my left there was a metal container about the size of a personal safe, pushed back against the rotten wood skirting that went around the house. I flashed the light in the hole some more, looking for snakes. I didn't see any.

I climbed down there and got the metal box and handed it to Leonard. The box was made of tin. It was like an oversized breadbox. It rattled when I moved it. There was nothing but a slap-and-snap latch to keep you out of it.

I climbed out of the hole and watched Leonard open the box. Inside was a large Bowie knife, a small hacksaw, about a dozen child pornography magazines, a purple tablecloth, two candlesticks, and two new white candles.

I noted something was sticking out of one of the pornography magazines, an undersized page that didn't seem to belong. I pulled it out. It was a page from the Bible. The Psalms. I checked the other magazines. Each contained a page from the Psalms.

"I'll be damn," Leonard said. "Read a little Psalms, whack off to kiddie porn, read a little Psalms. That's some combination."

I unwrapped the purple tablecloth. It was stained in the center with something crusty, and at either end there were white stains that were obviously candle wax.

"Let's slide the lid back on the floor," I said.

"Aren't we going to look down there?" Leonard asked.

"Humor me. I need it to stand on."

We put the flooring back. We stood on it, and I ran a finger through the dust on the table. I said, "The dust here is a lot thinner than the dust everywhere else. Now, watch this. I think."

I pulled out the purple tablecloth and spread it on the table. It fit nicely. I took off my shirt and used it to pick up the candlesticks at their bases so as not to leave prints. I put one at either end of the table where the cloth had remnants of wax staining it. I shoved the candles into the sticks, tossed the porno magazines on the table for the hell of it.

I said, "Is a picture starting to form?"

Leonard let it cook a moment. "It's like an altar. And if that crusty stuff in the middle of the cloth is what I think it is, could be what we have here are sacrifices to a water stain of Jesus?"

"A water stain to some is but the face of God to others," I said. "Remember those idiots and the tortilla?"

"Well, it ain't a ritual we done much at our Baptist church."

"Not my church either, though I might have missed a couple of Sundays."

I put my shirt on, and Leonard shoveled the flooring up again. We pulled the section back, and I got down in the hole on my hands and knees with my flashlight and waved it around. I saw a number of termite mounds. I unfolded the floor plan and studied it with the flashlight. I felt certain I was close in memory to Uncle Chester's floor plan, if not dead on. When I thought I had the plan in my head, I folded it up and put it away. I stood up in the hole and said, "Give me the shovel and just hang tight a minute."

I took the shovel and started crawling toward what I remembered as a rectangle on the map. It was dark under there, but the trim around the house was rotten in spots and pencils of light came through like laser beams.

I got to about where I thought the map indicated a rectangle, and looked around. There wasn't a mound there, but there was a slight depression about two feet wide and four feet long. Water had run up under the house and filled it and the water had partially evaporated.

I put the light on the ground at an angle where it would shine in the depression, and got to work. It was so low I had a hard time managing the shovel, but I lay on my stomach and poked it in the depression and sort of rolled the handle in my hands and flipped mud and dirt to the side.

About the fourth time I flipped the dirt, a smell came out of there that filled my head and made me choke. It was so potent, I crawled back from it. I must have called out too, because Leonard said, "You all right?"

"Come down here."

A moment later Leonard crawled up beside me. "Shit, that's stout. It's something dead."

"Yeah."

We worked our shirts off and tied them over our faces, and while Leonard held the light, I crawled up to the depression and went back to work. I rolled a couple of shovelfuls out of there and came up with something. Leonard put the light on it. It was stuck to the tip of the shovel and I couldn't move it out of the hole.

Leonard's voice was muffled behind his shirt. "Chicken wire."

I edged the shovel beneath the wire and worked along the edge of the depression and picked up another shovelful and came up with more dirt-plugged wire.

Leonard said, "If I buried something and didn't want animals digging it out, I might put a little chicken wire over or around it. . . . Jesus, Hap. I don't think I can stand this stink for long."

It was strong, shirts over our noses or not. I was beginning to feel dizzy and ill. Another shovelful turned up some cloth, and the cloth ripped and snapped on the end of the shovel, and I pulled the shovel over closer and looked at the fragment. It was caked with mud and what I figured was lime. The lime had faded the cloth, and I couldn't tell much about it.

When I stuck the shovel in again and worked it back, I had a fragment of bone. It might have been a piece of a rib. There was something clinging to it. It looked like lardy chunks of flesh and cloth twisted up together. The smell from it was so intense I thought I was going to pass out.

"Maybe it's an animal bone?" I said.

"Yeah, and my dick's a water snake."

I dug around some more, and after a while I came up with what I knew I would. A hard round ball of mud. Except the mud came off the ball, and it wasn't a ball at all. It was the top part of a small, dirt-colored skull.

"Sonofabitch," I said.

I used the shovel to push all I had found back in the hole, then shoveled all the dirt back on top of it.

"We better look around some more," Leonard said.

We moved back a few paces, away from the smell, and I got my map out and Leonard held the light on it. We studied it, crawled around under there and found some likely locations, and I poked my shovel in them.

Once I came up with a chunk of damp cardboard box dripping doodle bugs. In another spot I came up with more chicken wire. Over near the front of the house, just up under the rotten front-porch steps, we found an open grave about four feet long and two and a half feet wide and two feet deep. It was empty. I pushed at the steps with the shovel. They moved. They weren't attached to the porch. I also noted that the steps were made of newer wood.

I thought about that. Whoever had made this graveyard had fixed it so they could get under here easy—through the trap in the kitchen or by sliding away the front porch steps. I thought too about this empty grave. Could this be where the skeleton in Uncle Chester's trunk originally belonged?

"You looked hard enough, sifted through the dirt under here," Leonard said, "I got a feeling you might turn up more of what we found in that first hole. In different degrees of disintegration."

"I've had enough," I said. "Let's get some air."

25.

We didn't eat any lunch that day. When we got back to the house we took turns showering. There didn't seem to be enough hot water and soap to make me feel clean. The smell from the grave was still with me. At least in my head.

While Leonard showered, I walked around the living room, nervous. I had put on jogging pants, a T-shirt, and tennis shoes, and I took advantage of the comfortable clothing to stretch and go through some Hapkido kicks in the living room. I shadowboxed at the air. I side-kicked the couch hard enough to slide it across the room.

After a while, Leonard came into the room. He had put on

gray sweatpants and tennis shoes without socks. He wasn't wearing a shirt. We looked at each other but didn't say a word. He got one end of the couch and I got the other and we moved it to the far wall. We moved some chairs around. We had a little room now.

We started to spar, lightly, just tagging one another with control. We did that until we were sweaty and tired and needed showers again. But we didn't shower. We got to work on the subflooring, and by late that afternoon we were finished. During that entire time, we hardly said a word, just something now and then about nails and boards and such.

When we finished, we sat on the subflooring for a while, sweating, letting time go by. I broke the silence.

"It's gone far enough, Leonard. I love you like a brother, man, you know that. But Illium didn't just drive off in that pond by accident. And under that house . . . no telling how many bodies there are. Your uncle's diagram is probably just for what he located. Or maybe he put them there."

"You're back to that," Leonard said, and he was angry.

"I'm not back to anything. I'm saying we don't know. We're not investigators. It's time we call in the law."

"The law has been on this case for years, Hap. We've found out more in a few days than they have in all that time. Or rather my uncle and Illium found it out and we picked up on it. We let Hanson in on this, he's still got to mess with the system. I don't even think it's purely a black-white thing anymore. It's more a thing makes the police force look stupid. Justice seldom overrides embarrassment.

"But black-white thing or not, white people run this town, and they're going to be a lot more rested they think a nigger did it, and did it to little niggers. That fits in with the general thinking and keeps it out of their backyard. They don't see anything black as being part of their immediate problem, even the liberals."

"Leonard, most likely, all things considered, a black man did do it. It sure points that way. A white guy would have to be pretty clever to cruise around over here and not get noticed."

"I'm not saying it isn't a black man. You're missing the point. Way it stands now, all we got to show the cops is certain proof my uncle killed those kids and hid their bodies at the Hampstead place, and that this Illium fellow was in on it. Shit, he's got kid's clothes and pornography setting on his couch, just waiting for the cops to eyeball it. Cops see that, they aren't going to look any farther, and Hanson isn't going to get the chance to look either. They'll have it all solved. Couple old dead niggers did it, or rather my uncle did it and Illium got in on the business late. Case closed. And I ain't having it. Uncle Chester's the one taught me about pride and honor. Taught me not to care about color, one way or the other. Not to hide behind it, not to use it to roll over nobody.

"I was growing up, you hear a crime newscast, read a newspaper, they were always quick to point out when the criminal was a black, but not when they were white. I got the impression it was blacks did everything. It was my uncle showed me things straight. That people were people and there were good and bad, and to just look at a thing head on, not try and dress it up any. And that's just a reverse way of saying it turns out to be a black man, it's a black man. That's no skin off my ass. I just want whoever it is nailed. But I don't want to give the cops the easy way out. Uncle Chester was a good man, Hap. He had honor. Me and him, we had our problems, but he wasn't a child killer. There's no reason you got to believe in him, but I believe in him, and I want to see he gets a fair shake."

"Thing is, Leonard, whoever killed these kids and did Illium in is still out there. Guys like that, they don't stop. You know that. While we're investigating, he could be planning to kill another child. That's who he's after. Kids. Illium only got aced because he got in the way, and somehow let on he knew something."

"I realize that."

"That first grave we dug into. That's fresh, Leonard. You know that. It doesn't take any time at all for a body to decompose. That one still had the stink on it. He'll kill again, and I don't want that on my head."

"And I don't want my uncle's reputation destroyed, and I don't think the cops are going to find who's doing this anyway. Like I said, they got their suspects. Uncle Chester and Illium. They'll close the book on this case so quick it'll make your head swim."

"I don't know what to say. I really don't."

"Don't say anything for a while. Don't tell anybody."

"Leonard, I already told Florida about Illium."

"Goddamn you, Hap!"

"She won't say anything. For a while."

"You shouldn't have done that. We had a deal. That goddamn pussy always did mess your thinking."

"Watch it, Leonard."

We sat there looking at each other like bad asses for a moment. Leonard smiled slowly. "Hell, Hap, I love you, man. We gonna fight?"

"'Course not."

"That would be some fight, you know?"

"I couldn't take you," I said.

"I don't know. I think you might. You hesitate now and then, you think you're gonna hurt someone bad. You ain't got that killer instinct, but you got mad enough, you'd be some bad business all right."

"I couldn't get that mad at you, buddy."

"Yeah, we're stuck with one another. . . . Shit, Hap. It's OK you told Florida. Hell, I know you got a head on you. She's all right. I mean, you're a dumb asshole, but what's done is done, and she's all right."

"It just slipped out. A thing like that, it's hard to keep under your hat."

"It's all right, bubba. It's just I don't know what to do exactly."

"Me either," I said.

26.

A few days went by. The recollection of those bodies burned my memories at night, found their way into my thoughts during the day. It was the same with Leonard. Not that he said much about it. But I could tell. I had known him long enough to see his feelings expressed in the way he moved or smiled or tried to laugh.

To flush the memories out we took to hard work. Manual labor has a way of sweating out impurities. Both physical and emotional.

We finished up the surface flooring late one afternoon and took what scraps of lumber were left over, and went to see

MeMaw, dumped the stuff in her yard and made a pledge to patch her porch.

She was agreeable and very grateful. She told us how much Jesus loved us and took us inside and showed us our snapshot. She had pinned it on the wall near the snapshot of her youngest son, Hiram, who she said Leonard reminded her of. She said her boy would soon be home for a visit. When she said it, her entire face brightened and she looked no older than seventy-five. OK, eighty-five.

I looked at the snapshot of her son and the one containing me and Leonard. Well, Leonard and her son were both black, that much was similar.

We had to eat some homemade bread and preserves before we were allowed to consider leaving. It wasn't a difficult task. We insisted she let us do a few chores for her as well, then we left out of the kitchen and shoved the lumber under her porch and vowed to be back to do the work in a day or two.

Back at Uncle Chester's, just as the sun faded, Leonard put some water in a pot of yesterday's pinto beans, dropped in a fresh strip of ham hock, and peppered it. While it stewed, I drove my pickup down Comanche Street to the East Side Grocery for a few supper items. It was a beautiful death to the day, and in the red and gray time before the dark, the East Side took on a sort of fairy brilliance. A lot of walkers had disappeared from the streets for supper, and those who had jobs were back from them and settled, so the streets were near empty and stained with the blood of the sun.

East Side Grocery was a center for more than commerce. It was where the old men gathered to rattle dominoes and cuss and tell about how they used to do this and used to do that. A bunch of them were sitting out front of the grocery, to the right of the door on the concrete walk, underneath an overhang with a tin-capped light that was already on and already swarmed with bugs. They were sitting on old metal lawn chairs playing dominoes on a fold-out table, laughing and drinking beer out of paper cups.

Behind them, stapled on the store wall, there were ads for great black blues musicians, like Bobby Blue Bland. Guys like that played the East Side often, and the white community never even knew it. There was also a colorful poster announcing East Side's Summer Carnival, August 27th, the "Only All Black Sponsored Major Carnival In East Texas," if one were to believe the poster. In addition, there were a variety of church and community project bulletins.

I nodded at the old men when I went in the store. They nodded and grinned amiably enough, but even though I had been here a lot of late, there was the usual suspicion on their faces, the unasked questions: Who's the white guy? What's he doin' here? Why's he keep hangin' around?

The store owner had been at the domino table, and he reluctantly followed in after me and got behind the counter and waited. I picked up some bread and eggs and cornmeal mix, a six-pack of beer for Leonard, and looked for some nonalcoholic beer for me but didn't find any. I got a six-pack of Diet Coke instead.

I took my stuff to the counter, plucked a couple of jerky sticks out of a box up front, threw them down with my purchase, and watched some hot links on metal pins turn and sweat and drip inside a humidity-beaded glass enclosure.

The owner had a lot of belly and a lot of gray hair and a sun roof that revealed a dark bald spot. He might have been five two. He appeared to have all his own teeth, and one of the front ones was gold as Rapunzel's hair. He said, "That do you?"

"Yeah. How's the dominoes?"

"I'm losing," he said.

He tallied up my goods on the adding machine, and I continued to look around. I examined a frame on the wall behind the register containing the first dollar the store had taken in, and noted the dollar was play money. Below that, on a shelf, I saw something that startled me. Next to a jar of pickled pig's feet was a larger jar stuffed with little slips of paper. It looked like one of the jars at Illium's.

I said, "That jar with the coupons in it? That is coupons, isn't it?"

He was bagging up my groceries; he stopped, glanced where I was indicating. "Yeah."

"I've seen that setup a couple times," I said. "The jars, I mean. There something to it besides you saving coupons?"

"That's the church's," he said.

"How's that?"

"Reverend Fitzgerald, he's got him a deal with all the businesses in town. We cut coupons, we see them. Folks bring them and donate 'em. Fitzgerald saves them coupons for his youth programs. You know, take the soccer, baseball team out to eat. He's got this deal with damn near everybody in the city. Even if the coupons expire, they let him use 'em. They gonna make money anyway, discount or not, him bringing in ten, twenty kids at a time, and often. He's got more coupons than he can use. Illium done told us he gonna stop picking up for a while, he gets this batch. He says they done gettin' yellow, they got so many. They could take soccer teams out for the next ten years and not run out of coupons. He done s'posed to got this here jar, but he ain't showed. I reckon he's been sick."

Yeah, I thought, real sick.

"Mr. Moon's the clearinghouse?" I asked.

"You know him?"

"Not really. Know who he is."

"Yeah, he runs all manner errands for the church. He's a real do gooder, that Illium. That sonsabitch dies, he's gone sit on the right side of Jesus, and Jesus gone give him a juice harp, personal like, let him play a few spirituals."

I figured Illium was probably twanging out a rendition of "The Old Rugged Cross" even as we spoke. I thanked the old man, paid up, and started back to the house, thinking about Il-lium, the church, Reverend Fitzgerald, and all those coupons, the connection right under our noses all the time.

Next day. A Saturday. Hot. Me and Leonard and Florida and Hanson, out at the lake near my old house, standing on the bank, shadowed by drooping willows, casting fishing lines in the water.

The fish weren't biting, but the mosquitoes were. They were bad here because of the low areas where the water ran out of the lake and gathered in pools and turned torpid be-neath the shades of the willows and gave the little bastards prime breeding grounds.

Florida, dressed in blue jean short-shorts, a short-sleeved blue sailor-style shirt, low-cut blue tennis shoes, and one of those stupid white fishing hats with a big brim that turns up in the front, was doing more slapping than casting.

"You should have worn long pants," I said. "I told you."

"Well, damnit, you were right," she said.

Hanson slapped a mosquito on the side of his face, hard. He looked at his palm. In the center of it was a bloody mess pro-truding broken insect legs. He wiped the palm on his pants.

"Boys," he said, "this is just peachy-keen fun, but you didn't invite me out here to fish. I can tell way you keep look-ing at each other, so don't fondle my balls—sorry, Florida."

"It's OK," Florida said. "I've heard of them."

"Get on with it," Hanson said. "And next time, skip this fishing shit and take me to a movie."

"I don't know you're gonna like this," Leonard said, " 'cause, you see, what we want to do is make some kind'a deal."

"I don't like deals," Hanson said. "It always means some guilty asshole gets off with less than he deserves."

"We're not guilty of anything," Leonard said.

"Except withholding evidence," I said.

"Yeah," Leonard said, "there's that."

"All right," Hanson said, reeling in his line, "that's enough bullshit. . . . You in on this Florida?"

"Nope," she said. "I'm just a humble fisher girl. And their lawyer, if they need me."

We all took a moment to slap at a black cloud of mosquitoes. Hanson said, "Let's go someplace we can talk without pain. Few more minutes of this, I'm gonna need a transfusion."

We walked back to Leonard's car, which was up the hill and in the sunlight. The mosquitoes weren't swarming there, there was just the occasional kamikaze. We took the rods and reels apart and put them in the trunk of the car with the fishing tackle. We poured the worms out so that they might breed and multiply. I watched them squirm around in the soft sand, making their way into the earth.

Florida climbed up on the hood of the car and stretched her legs and scratched at the knots the mosquitoes had made. On her, even the knots looked good. Hanson seemed to be taking note of that himself.

Hanson said, "I'm waiting. And not patiently."

"Once upon a time," Leonard said, "me and Hap found a dead guy in a pond."

"Yeah," I said, "in a bookmobile."

"Come again," Hanson said.

We explained about Illium but didn't give his name or say where his body was. We didn't tell him any more than we needed to. When we finished, Leonard said: "It's gonna look bad for the ole boy, things you're gonna find on his couch. A box of kid's clothes and some kiddie fuck books. But it's bullshit. He isn't guilty of anything. Neither's my uncle. You see, all this is connected to those missing kids, but it's not connected the way it looks."

"Another thing," I said, "me and Leonard got to talking last night, thinking about what we'd seen, and we came up with something else. In this guy's house—"

"The drowned guy?" Hanson said.

"Yeah," I said. "You'll find a dirty bathtub with pieces of hay in it. We figure he'd just finished mowing his field, was grabbed by whoever while he was in the bath, and drowned in his own tub. Then they put him in the van and ran it off in the pond. An autopsy will probably show the water in his lungs isn't the pond water."

We didn't say anything else. We leaned against the car and waited. Hanson looked at us for a while. "That's it?" he said. "You're not telling me any more than that?"

"We'll tell," Leonard said, "but we want something."

"You're not in any position to want shit," Hanson said. "It's best you talk your asses off."

"You know we haven't done anything," Leonard said. "We want to solve this crime, bad as you, but we want the deal you didn't give my uncle. You help us solve the case, but we lead."

"I can't do that," Hanson said. "Department wouldn't stand for it, a couple of amateurs. Why do you think they didn't let your uncle do it?"

"He was nuts?" Leonard said.

"Well," Hanson said, "that was part of it."

"We already got more leads than you on this missing child business," I said. "You might be amazed what we got."

Hanson studied the lake in the distance. A soft hot wind brought the smell of it to us. It stunk faintly of dead fish and stagnation. A large bird's shadow fell over us and coasted away.

Hanson said, "If I wanted to do it, I couldn't. I tell my superiors, they'll laugh their asses off, me suggesting you guys run an investigation. They'd be on you assholes like rash on a baby's butt. They got through with you, you wouldn't know if you wanted to shit or go blind. And they'd stick me writing parking tickets."

"We don't want you to ask them anything," I said. "Not yet. What we want is you to join up with us, and cheat a little. Show us the stuff you got on the case, we'll show you something. We think we know what's going on, but we want to set everything up, and the more we all know, the better. We see the files, we might recognize something there goes with what we already know."

"I've read those files," Hanson said. "There's not a whole lot of help there."

"Something that'll jump out at us," Leonard said, "won't necessarily jump at you 'cause you don't have the information we got."

"Sounds like some shit talk to me," Hanson said.

"This way," I said, "when we turn it over to you, and nod out like we never existed, no one's going to know we did anything, unless you want them to."

"Of course, *we'll* know," Leonard said, "and that's all that matters."

"You had all your ducks in a row on this," I said, "you could make those jackasses at the station stand up and notice, and you'd get the respect you deserve."

"Not to mention solving an important crime," Florida said.

Hanson turned and looked at her. "I thought you weren't in on this."

"Just a wee bit," she said. They held each other's eyes longer than made me comfortable.

"We're deadly serious," I said, drawing Hanson back to me. "We've got the guy that's been murdering these kids by the ying-yang, and now we're gonna put it in the wringer, crank it up a couple notches. You don't help us, we'll find some other way to get it done."

"I could just run your asses in for obstructing justice," Hanson said. "And ought to."

"You could," Leonard said, "but you don't want to."

"Say I don't?"

"You want this murderer bad as we do," I said, "and we can make things happen a lot quicker if you do it our way. You help us, we get the benefit of your experience, and you get to look like Supercop. Hell, aren't you tired of being neglected? You solve this, on your own, with our help, you might end up chief."

"And most important," Leonard said, "those kids will have justice. Well, some kind of justice."

"I don't know," Hanson said.

"We start with the body in the pond," I said. "Telling you who it is and where it is. It's not like we say, then to hell with it. It is, you play that one any way you want, then we feed you some more. Tell you what we know and how we know it and what we think it means. Then we'll stick the killer's dick in the wringer and put your hand on the crank."

Hanson crossed his arms, furrowed his brow, and looked into the distance. A minute ticked by like it was an hour on holiday.

"What'ya say?" Leonard said.

"I'm thinking," Hanson said. "Give me a minute to breathe here, will you? I'm thinking."

27.

Some mornings the beautiful face of my ex-wife, Trudy, hangs over me like a moon, but when I open my eyes there's only the sunlight as seen through tears. Some mornings the light itself is the color of her hair, and the smell of summer flowers is the smell of her skin.

Some mornings I awake and the bed is too huge and I cannot remember how I've come to where I am, cannot believe what happened to Trudy, or imagine that beautiful body and face of hers in the ground, withering, feeding the bugs and worms. I won't allow myself to look straight on at the memory of violence that took her and wounded me and Leonard.

She went wrong and I went after her, pulling my best friend behind. Gunpowder and bloodshed, sulfur and death were Trudy's final perfume. And me and Leonard, we've got the scars.

I awoke the next morning having dreamed that way about poor, pretty Trudy, awoke feeling old and blue and not much for coffee. All this the consequence of Florida not being in my bed. She had not invited herself to stay and I hadn't the guts to push it.

Her absence between the sheets had been part of why the old dreams of Trudy came back; part of the feeling behind my bones and viscera that violence was oncoming direct in my path, like bright lights on my side of the highway on a dark, wet night; the feeling I was about to meet wet grillwork head-on, followed by two hot tons of speeding steel.

I got dressed and went outside without waking Leonard and sat on the porch steps in the cool of the morning and watched the sunlight brighten. Long about the time you could call the morning golden, Hanson pulled up at the curb in a car I had not seen before, a beige Buick with a dent in the rear fender. He got out of the car with something under his arm and looked at me. He managed his cigar out of the inside of his coat and put it in his mouth and came up to the porch and sat on the step beside me. He looked tired. He rolled the cigar with his tongue and put what was under his arm on the steps between us. It was a thick manila folder.

"Glad you're up," Hanson said. "I was gonna wake you."

"Thanks for giving Florida a ride home last night," I said.

"Yeah, sure," he said.

"That was damn nice of you."

"No problem."

"I like the idea of an officer of the law seeing her home safe."

"Part of the job."

We sat in silence for a while. Hanson shifted on the step so that he could pick up the folder and open it. He looked at the contents for a few moments, then put the folder on the porch. He said, "All right. We got a deal. I want you to know, 'cause of you and Leonard, I almost lit this damn cigar last night. Haven't smoked in years, just sucked on it now and then, but I almost lit it."

"Thanks for the folder," I said, and meant it. "And the world thanks you for not lighting that damn cigar."

"I photocopied all this shit last night, on the sly, and it gets out, well, my job is gone, and I just might be sleeping behind bars. And you and Leonard will be there too. You can bet on that. Here's how it's gonna work. I'm gonna leave you this, you give me the name of this guy in the pond, tell me where the pond is. I got some lies ready to use for leads. I find him there, we're in business. I don't, you are not only gonna give me this stuff back, I'm gonna punch both of you in the mouth and see to it you're out of town."

"Before sundown?"

"Just as quick as the toe of my shoe in your asses will move you."

I told him Illium's name and where to find him. I didn't tell him any more than that.

"OK, son. Let's see how we play the game."

He got up, leaving the folder on the porch. He started down the walk. About halfway to his car I said, "Marvin."

He turned.

"I really like Florida," I said. "A lot."

"I know, son, but sometimes things don't work out the way a man wants them to. Ask me about that sometime."

He finished off the distance to his car. He drove away.

I fixed coffee and breakfast and woke Leonard and showed him the folder. We ate and cleared the dishes and spread the contents of the folder on the table. There were a couple of photocopied snapshots of missing kids. Just a couple. Both boys, and both staring at the camera, the way young kids do, like startled deer.

One of them had his head shaved close and had ears that if he could have moved them would have given him lift-off. He was the first reported to disappear. It occurred to me that had he lived, he'd be a young man now.

The other boy was a nice-looking kid with a couple of front teeth missing. I looked at those photographs hard. I wanted those kids to be real, not just reflections on colored paper. I thought about the other kids. No photographs available. While they were living, no one had bothered. It was as if their existence was of no importance, no need for a matter of record.

We studied the material for a while. There was a lot of it, but it didn't say much. There were notes from the cops and detectives. Hanson had a few notes of his own. The obvious thing was that one child a year had come up missing from the East Side for the past eight years and had not been accounted for.

I said, "See any patterns?"

"All boys," Leonard said. "All about nine or ten. All of them noted as not having the best of home life, and in some cases, not being reported missing until some time after their initial disappearance. Part of that might have been the parents and part of it may have been the sorry attitude of the police force."

"What about when they were killed?"

Leonard studied the contents of the folder. After a while he said, "I'll be damned. Every one but one came up missing in August. Corey Williams was reported last September."

"Before you woke up, I did some figuring on that," I said. "Taking in the fact a lot of the reports came in late, they were probably all kidnapped sometime in the early part of the las week of August. Personally, I think that's a little too big a co-incidence."

"This is August," Leonard said.

"Yep. And week after next is the last week of the month."

"So what's with the last week of August?"

"I don't know. It sounds like a pattern, but I also got to thinking about the smell that was in that grave. That's fresh, or seems to be. So maybe all this late-August stuff is just co-incidence and he got started a little early this year, but I don't think so. Stink could be due to slow disintegration. Soil like that, sometimes it happens, something gets buried just right.

"Another thing that jumps out at me is all the children were illegitimate. No fathers. The mothers were all teenagers. Couple of the kids had been shuffled around to foster homes, had been in some kind of trouble almost before they were out of diapers. Little robberies. Drugs. Stuff kids ought not to even be thinking about. See the pattern?"

"I don't know that's a pattern," Leonard said. "Not the way you mean, anyway. Just shows they're the type of kids to be at risk."

"Well, we've already got our good Reverend in mind here, due to the church connections, coupons, recycling—which explains all those goddamn newspapers Uncle Chester had. And if you remember, Fitzgerald really had a hard-on for il-legitimate children. Do you recall anything he said that stuck with you?"

"It all stuck with me. . . . Yeah, when he was talking about the mothers of illegitimate children, he said the mothers had produced baby boys. He didn't say girls, or children. He said baby boys without fathers. Something like that."

"It didn't mean anything to me then," I said, "not really, but I caught it. What I think is, we got a religious nut serial killer. He's somehow tied his religion in with his sex and power urges. I don't know, maybe something that happened to him in his childhood."

"Shit, Hap, I don't give a damn what happened to him in his childhood. I mean, he got fucked by his next-door neighbor who was a scout leader, I'm sorry for the kid he was, but for the man he is, I don't give a shit. He made his own choice."

"I don't know some people have a choice, if certain things happen to them."

"Cancer does what it does because it's got no choice, but I get a cancer, I'm not going to psychoanalyze the little bastard. I want it cut out. This guy's a cancer."

"Even so, if we understand what drives him, we got a better chance of nailing his ass. Obviously, he doesn't care for illegitimacy. Gets him worked up."

"OK, Hap, I'll play. He's got a thing for boys, so he was maybe nine, ten, when he was raped by a man. Good guess?"

"Probably a person of authority."

"A preacher like himself? That what you're driving at? Something that links God, religion, sex, and abuse together."

"If Fitzgerald was illegitimate, I wonder if he knew who his father was and what his father did for a living? Preach, maybe? And think about the position Fitzgerald's in. It's perfect. He's trusted. He has access to children. He has all these youth programs. Kids like the ones in this file, neglected, probably not wanted, they'd be raw meat for this wolf. And I think this guy's a psychotic, not a sociopath. Or he's both. He gets off on the power of controlling the kids, and he thinks he's doing God's will. He controls them to some extent through positive services. Baseball, soccer, what have you, but—"

"It's not enough."

"For certain illegitimate children, it isn't enough. The ones that maybe remind him of himself at that age. If he can control them, destroy them, he can control his past, destroy it. At least for a year at a time."

"But why a year? We're talking a pretty perfect pattern here."

"I don't know."

"OK, Hap. When he was nine or ten, he was raped by a man, his father maybe, who was a preacher. Or he was raped by a preacher. If not a preacher, someone in authority he trusted. It warped him. And he's a religious nut. That your track?"

"Yep."

"OK. He's tied fanaticism in with his deviance. That's why there's a page of Psalms stuck in each of the porno mags we found. The two are linked with him. Or maybe a part of him knows what he's doing is evil, and somehow the Psalms consecrate it in his mind. Say he's a psychotic. That he's killing for God. Any of that's true, it doesn't take us one whit closer to nailing the bastard. Let's just try and put together the hard evidence, and you can play Freud on your own time. Come on. What have we got?"

"That's the problem," I said. "I don't know it's such hard evidence. But here's what I think we've got, and what I speculate. Your Uncle Chester and Illium were friends. Illium worked with the church. That's why Uncle Chester's poor addled mind thought the coupons were important. He was trying to point a finger at the church. The painting led us to the Hampstead place, and what's under it. We've already established what the book's connection was."

"Illium," Leonard said. "And maybe with the title of the book, he was trying to give us the nature of our criminal. Dracula ain't nothing compared to this guy."

"I think your uncle and Illium, probably because of something Illium saw at the church, got onto Fitzgerald. Perhaps the way he dealt with the boys in the programs there, the illegitimate ones especially. And somehow Chester and Illium connected him to the Hampstead place. Could be the good Reverend makes a pilgrimage up there to worship the water stain or something. Illium followed, watched from hiding. Fitzgerald went home to memorize his sermon, and Uncle Chester and Illium poked around and found the bodies. Six of them anyway. I bet the other two are up there."

"So my uncle took one of the bodies and hid it here while he and Illium did their own investigation. Probably in case the old boy moved the remains."

"That's where they screwed up. They should have gone to the cops."

"Yeah," Leonard said, "and by not going, the body being found here, it just helped give the Reverend a way out."

"That's right," I said. "Your uncle loses his memory, dies, so he's out of the picture. Add Illium into the equation, dead at the bottom of his pond with porno mags and kid's clothes on the couch, and the Reverend isn't going to look as ripe for the part as he might have back then. So we have a lot of circumstantial evidence. Is it enough?"

"Have you thought about this?" Leonard said. "Could be we just don't like the bastard, and we're tying all this together the way my uncle got tied. It looks bad, but are we seeing smoke or fog? Just because it all leads back to the church doesn't mean it leads to Fitzgerald."

"I've thought about that," I said. "I've also thought about the last week of August coming up. I've thought too, we play our hand before we have the evidence, the bastard could get off. He did, he wouldn't quit doing what he's doing, but he might get more cautious doing it."

"It's not like he's been sloppy so far," Leonard said. "This has been going on for years."

"Kids like this, to some extent, they're like prostitutes when they're victims. They're considered expendable. Illegitimate black kids with no hope and no future and no one to care. It's easy to waste someone like that and not get caught. And consider that the murderer started wasting them during a period of police administration when views toward the ethnic community were less than considerate, and are maybe still that way—"

"He could go on indefinitely."

"Exactly."

"Got a next step, Mr. Sherlock Freud?"

"We wait until Hanson finds Illium, then we tell him what we suspect. Tell him about the Hampstead place and show him what we found, and see what he has to say."

"And in the meantime?"

"I guess we fix MeMaw's porch."

Leonard poured us another cup of coffee. He said, "Something else is wrong, isn't there?"

"Why do you say that?"

"I can just tell. Florida?"

"Yeah."

"She went home with Hanson last night, didn't she?"

I looked at him. "You could see something too?"

"They had eyes for each other. You could kind of smell it too. His musk, her in heat."

"Thanks for being delicate."

"Well. Did she?"

"I think she did."

"I'm sorry, man."

"She's a grown woman. She does what she wants."

"Hey, she's the one messing up here. You're good people, Hap. It's her loss. Even if Hanson probably has a bigger dick."

"Thanks, Leonard, that perked me right up."

"Hey. We friends, or what?"

28.

It's hard to deal with knowledge like that. Dead kids under a house, a killer on the loose, and his prime time for new murder fast approaching, and then there was the matter of my woman done gone off and left me for an older man, and me and Leonard were building a porch.

Fortunately, the work we were doing was soothing. I had begun to like the lumber, the feel and smell of it in the hot open air. I liked the sensation of taking something weak and insubstantial and turning it into something solid and pleasing. I liked helping MeMaw.

MeMaw looked rough that day, but she gave us a dentured

smile and invited us in for late-morning coffee. We drank it, even though we were already floating in our own. We finished that up, she asked us to help her to bed, said she felt weaker than usual and wanted to be perked for when her baby boy showed up. We helped her out of the walker and onto the bed and Leonard covered her with a light blanket and turned a fan on to circulate the warm air.

"Won't our hammering bother you?" I asked her.

"Tired as I am, only one can wake me up is the Lord. And he gonna have to shout today."

"Rest, MeMaw."

She looked so ancient lying there. Not like a person, but like a praying mantis. All bone and tight-stretched skin. She was asleep before we could leave the room.

We worked as quietly as possible, and long about noon, Leonard decided he wanted hamburgers and fries and was going to use one of Uncle Chester's coupons to get it. I stayed to crawl beneath the house and pull out some old lumber that was under there so we could take it to the dump. It had fallen out from beneath the porch ages ago and was wet and rotten and an invitation to termites.

I was doing that when the porch above me squeaked like a sick rat. I figured it was Leonard. I crawled back to the front of the house and out from under the porch and stood up, ready for a burger. But it wasn't Leonard. It was a black man about my size and age, and I knew who he was immediately, though we had never met. He has wearing a cheap blue suit and was looking at me like I was a snake that had crawled out from under the house.

"Who are you?" he said, and he had the look of someone ready to fight.

"Hap Collins," I said. "You're Hiram, right?"

He eyed me for a second. "How'd you know that?"

"I've seen your picture. I'm a friend of MeMaw's. Me and my buddy Leonard are fixing her porch."

"Where'd she get the money for that?"

"Doesn't need any. She paid in pie."

He grinned slowly, and when he grinned, damned if he didn't have that confident air Leonard's got, like he's immortal and knows it. MeMaw was right. They did favor.

I stuck out my hand. "Good to meet you."

"You too," he said, and we shook.

"She's sleeping. Said she was resting up for you. I didn't know she meant you were coming today."

"She didn't know exactly, but I called and told her it was likely. I always come around this time of year. It's my vacation time from work."

He nodded toward his white van in the drive. I saw on the driver's door the stenciled words EASTEX SCHOOL SUPPLIES.

"That's right," I said, "you're a salesman."

"I can sell socks to a legless man, Hap."

He certainly sounded as if he could. I said, "But you don't sell socks to schools."

"Nope."

"Pencils? Notebooks?"

"Nothing like that. They get that stuff at the drugstore. I carry stuff like American and Texas flags, sell those on the spot. Take orders for flagpoles, podiums, sweatshirts, senior rings. That kind of thing. Mostly it's riding around and talking and showing my teeth a lot."

Across the street, Leonard pulled into the drive and got out with a greasy white burger bag. He crossed over and nodded at Hiram. He said, "MeMaw's baby boy."

Hiram grinned. "That's me. You Hap's friend?"

"Gosh," Leonard said, "I hate getting put on the spot like that."

Hiram laughed like that was really funny. You could certainly see the salesman in him, but he seemed like an all-right kind of cuss too.

"We can split this stuff with you," I said.

"Naw, thanks. I reckon Mama's got something in the box in there."

"Just stuff that tastes like ambrosia of the gods," Leonard said. "Can't figure why you'd want to eat that and not share our burger."

"I got a strong character," Hiram said. "I'm gonna tiptoe in here and check on Mama. You boys take it easy. And thanks for doing this work. I wasn't so damn tired right now, I'd help you. I been driving all over. Come in from El Paso today."

"That's on the other side of the world," I said.

"Yeah."

"Say, Hiram," Leonard said. "We're gonna work a little more, then clean up some of this lumber and stuff, then we're gonna knock off a bit. We gotta run in and get some nails, a few things to finish out."

"Need money for it?" Hiram said.

"It's on us," Leonard said.

Hiram smiled at us and thanked us, and quietly went inside and closed the door.

Way the world was, the things I knew about, it was good to see everything wasn't crazy. Good to be reminded sons still loved their mamas and came home to see them. Not everyone had dead children under their house.

About two that afternoon, right after we'd come back from the lumber yard with nails and stuff, Hanson pulled up in Uncle Chester's driveway and got out. He had the white cop Charlie with him. Charlie was wearing the same sheen-green Kmart suit he'd had on last time, but he'd added a porkpie hat to his outfit. Maybe to keep that pesky fly off his head.

Charlie stayed by the car, and Hanson walked across to MeMaw's where we were working.

"You boys got a moment?" he said.

We put up our materials and crossed the street and went into the house with them. Before we could get seated at the kitchen table, Hanson said, "Charlie's in on it, boys. I had to have some help."

I looked at Charlie. He looked the way he always looked. Calm, a little bored, old-looking for his age, disinterested, dumb. I figured he was about as dumb and disinterested as the proverbial fox. When we were seated, I said, "OK. How'd it go?"

"Well, he was down there," Hanson said.

"Identify him?" Leonard said.

"It's Illium Moon. Looks like a suicide. Providing you accept the old bookmobile in the pond method."

"That's unusual, all right," I said.

"I've seen weirder," Hanson said. "I seen a guy that had frayed a lamp cord, plugged the good end into a socket, put the frayed end in a cup of water, along with his dick. Barbecued that fucker."

"His dick?" Leonard said.

"The rest of him too," Hanson said.

"About Illium," I said. "Find the goods on the couch?"

"Yep."

"And?"

"I think it's like you guys think," Hanson said. "A setup. It's too goddamned cute."

"Yeah," Charlie said. "Some of those kids' clothes were new. Could be of recent victims, but we don't think so."

Hanson said, "Whoever did Moon in wanted to make him look like he killed some kids and had some souvenirs from the killings, but he didn't want to give up his own souvenirs, 'cause I'm sure he's got 'em. A killer like this has always got 'em. A few magazines he's willing to lose, but the actual clothes his victims wore, that's much too special for a dick like this."

"Couldn't part with the stuff," Charlie said, "so he went and bought some at Kmart. I checked myself. Kmart is where I like to shop."

"They got some deals all right," I said.

"Yeah, and they take shit back easy, it don't fit right," Charlie said.

"I know a man likes Wal-Mart for that same reason," I said.

"Yeah, well," Charlie said, "Wal-Mart's all right."

"You guys through shopping?" Hanson said.

"He's always business," Charlie said. "He don't get any recreation."

Hanson ignored him. He got out his sloppy-ended cigar and put it in his mouth and did the side-to-side routine with it. He said, "Some of the jeans are brands and styles not made until this year. There might be one authentic piece in there, something belonged to one of the dead boys, but that's it. And I'd stake my career on it."

"Actually, way this is going," Charlie said, "you're staking my career on it too."

"Wouldn't that be a loss?" Hanson said. He turned to us. "Newspapers are gonna be bad to Moon, I think. I can't do anything about that. We can hold off what we found a little while, but not long. Best thing we can do is prove the truth here, show he's been set up. You boys look at the files?"

"Sure." I said.

"Anything?"

"Maybe," I said.

"Don't be coy," he said, "we had a deal."

"Still do," Leonard said. "The deal is we let you in on what we know when we want you to know it."

Hanson took the cigar out of his mouth and put it in his coat pocket and took a deep breath like his chest hurt. I hurt with him. I wasn't sure we were right in holding anything back. I was still going by Leonard's rules, but I wasn't certain how much longer I could do that. I was getting scared.

"Listen," Hanson said. "I'm playing with you guys 'cause I think you got something and I want it and I don't want to climb mountains to get it. But you start thinking we're too cozy, start thinking this is all play, I'll wring your fuckin' necks for you. I'll throw you so far under the goddamn jail you'll be wearing a coolie hat."

"Damn," Leonard said, "I think my pulse just jumped a little."

Hanson seemed to swell. "Fuck with me, you smart-ass motherfucker, just fuck with me, see where it gets you."

"I wouldn't fuck you with Hap's dick," Leonard said. "Hell, I wouldn't fuck you with Charlie's dick."

Hanson moved toward Leonard, and Charlie caught him, and I put an arm across Leonard's chest. I said, "Boys, let's ease off, now."

Hanson took a deep breath. He tried to smile but made a face like a man that had just found a dog turd in his mouth. "All right," he said. "All right, I'm OK. I'll play your way. But only for a little while. A very goddamn little while."

29.

A night of heat lightning. A giant bed.

Leonard had found that the couch was more to his liking for some reason, so the bed had stayed mine. That had been all right when Florida was around, but now I felt I ought to try and get him to trade. I decided that would be an important topic of conversation tomorrow. Why I should have the fold-out couch and he should have the bed. It was the time of night when stuff like that seemed significant.

I lay there and counted sheep, tried to remember the name of every dog I had ever owned, attempted to let my mind go blank, all the stuff you do when you're restless, but I still couldn't sleep. I thought about Florida. The way she smiled and talked, the nights we had spent together. That special first night we had made love, that night out at the overlook when I thought our relationship was cementing.

I thought about Hanson. I wanted to be mad at him, but he hadn't done anything but respond to what was there to respond to. Hell, I liked the big bastard. Really. He was a swell guy. I just hoped his dick would fall off.

I got up and sat by the window awhile and watched the heat lightning leap around. When that bored me, I watched the drug sellers and their clients. The clients came and went as brisk as patrons at a drive-through hamburger joint. I attempted to listen in on conversations, but all I could hear was talking that sounded like bees buzzing, that and occasional bursts of laughter and the sound of their music, which from where I sat was mostly the throb of the bass line; I felt it more than I heard it.

When I tired of that, I put on my sweatpants and did a few Hapkido moves, shadowboxed a bit, then turned on the end-table light, stretched out on the bed, and tried to get back into reading *The Hereafter Gang*.

I was managing to do that when along about midnight I heard a noise, like whimpering. Then there was a slight banging under the house, followed by silence.

I listened a moment, and it didn't repeat itself. I figured a dog had gotten up under there, bumped its head, and moved on, but I was too nervous to let it be. Lately, with the stuff we'd found and the assholes next door, a bird chirped, Leonard cut a fart, I was ready to leap.

I turned off the reading light, got out of bed, put on my shoes, got my .38, and went out into the living room.

Leonard was up and putting on his shoes. I wasn't the only one hearing things. There was enough moonlight in the room I could see his face. He nodded at me. He went over to the closet and opened it quietly and got the twelve-gauge pump. "Front or back?" he said.

"Front."

"Get the door, count twenty-five slowly. That'll time us close."

I went to the door and quietly as possible freed the locks. I was up to fifteen on my counting when I heard Leonard open the back door and slip out. The shitass was counting too fast. I opened the front door and darted onto the front porch, bending low.

The outside was lit with starlight and the clean silver rays of the moon, and off in the east was the heat lightning. I could see quite well, but there wasn't anything to see.

I held my position and listened, felt a little silly. All I could hear were the assholes next door. Their voices. Their music. I looked over there. The porch light had been turned off, but I could see a couple of people on the porch. I could hear them talking. They weren't looking in my direction. I eased down the porch steps and stopped to listen again. And heard something this time.

The whimpering. It reminded me a bit of a dog I'd had when I was a kid. It had been fed glass in raw hamburger meat by our next-door neighbor who didn't like it digging in his flowerbeds. The dog died. When my dad found out what happened, he worked the neighbor over with his fists and tried to feed him about three feet of a garden rake handle. He finished up by using the neighbor's head to plow the man's flowers up. My dad liked animals. For petunias, he didn't give a damn.

I eased toward the sound, which was consistent now and had turned to a moaning. I went around the side of the house and saw Leonard down on his hands and knees. He had put the shotgun on the ground and was crawling through a gap in the skirting around the house.

By the time I got over there, Leonard was backing out and pulling something out with him. It was a kid. He had the boy by the pants, and when he had him tugged out from under there, I recognized him in the moonlight. It was the boy who had gotten the shot of horse on Uncle Chester's front porch, the boy who'd ended up with a beeper.

The boy was shaking and his eyes were rolled up in his head and he was making the sound that had reminded me of the dog. He was in a bad way and didn't seem to know where he was. He'd crawled under the house like a wounded animal, seeking the dark, the cool pressure of the ground. I thought it odd that the gap in the siding, the place he'd chosen to hide and try and ride out his pain, was beneath the flooring Leonard and I had built. He had been lying not far from where Leonard had discovered the trunk with the pathetic little bones inside. I realized now in my dream, when I had visualized the child in the trunk, the bones dressed in flesh, it had been the face of this boy I had seen.

"He don't seem to be injured," Leonard said. "I don't see any blood."

"Overdose," I said. "He's riding the merry-go-round, hard."

"Goddamn them," Leonard said. "He's just a baby."

I gave the revolver to Leonard and picked up the boy. "I'm calling an ambulance."

I started across the street to MeMaw's. I heard an asshole yell from the crack house, "Hey, whatcha got there?"

The sound of that guy's voice was like sandpaper on my brain. Later, I would think back and know that voice had been the snapping point, the catalyst for what was to follow. I heard that voice and was reminded of what was going on next door, and thought: here Leonard and I were trying to stop some whacko from torturing and killing kids, and in quite a different way, next door to us, operating against the law, but not restrained or bothered by it, a whole houseful of ball sweats were doing a similar thing, and we weren't stopping them, weren't making any effort to. Kids were being tortured to death by addiction, and the drug dealers were taking in big money and making friends with the bail bondsmen, and were practically being treated like businessmen.

I went up on the porch and kicked the bottom of the door, yelled, "MeMaw. Hiram. Emergency. It's me, Hap."

A few minutes later the door opened. It was Hiram. He stood looking at us through the screen. He was dressed in his bathrobe and the expression on his face was odd. You'd have thought I was bringing him a take-out order.

"Wha . . . ?" he said.

"Wake up, man. Got an emergency here."

I could feel the boy shivering in my arms. I glanced down at him. Saliva was running out of the corner of his mouth and his body was trying to bend into a fetal position.

"Yeah . . . yeah," Hiram said, and opened the screen.

I slid inside, said, "I need to call an ambulance. We found him by the house. Drug overdose, I think."

"I'll take him," Hiram said. "No need to wake Mama. She's sick."

I handed the boy to Hiram, and he held him and looked at him, then took him around the table and into the back room. I used the phone to call the ambulance. I'd no sooner done that when I heard a shotgun blast.

I ran outside, keeping low. I saw Leonard standing in the yard of the crack dealers. He had a shotgun. He fired another shot into the side of the house. He yelled: "Out, ever'body out!"

"Leonard," I yelled, and I started running across the street. I wasn't fast enough. He'd reached the porch over there, and there was one guy still standing on it, standing between Leonard and the front door. Not because he was brave, because he was petrified.

Leonard reached out and shoved him aside. The guy went over the edge of the porch and rolled on the grass and got up and started running.

Leonard tried to open the front door, but someone had locked it. I got up on the front porch about the time Leonard screamed, "Stand back, motherfuckers," and shot a hole through the door big enough to poke your head through.

I grabbed Leonard by the shoulder, "Hold up, man."

Leonard looked back at me, and I saw in his eyes what I had felt moments ago. Anger. Frustration.

"You can't kill them, Leonard."

"I can kill the house."

I took my hand off his shoulder and stood back, and he kicked the door where the blast had torn a hole, and the hole got wider, and he kicked again, and an entire panel of the door collapsed, and swift as a summer cloud blowing across the face of the sun, Leonard hit the door and it went to pieces and he was inside.

And I was in after him.

The house was poorly lit, and when we came through the door, Mohawk and the one I called Parade Float came out of the dark. They leaped and grabbed Leonard, one on either side, Mohawk trapping the shotgun against Leonard's body.

Mohawk yelled, "Now, baby."

Over Leonard's shoulder I saw a stringy white woman with greasy hair, dressed in nothing but a pair of shorts, stick a little automatic in Leonard's face and pull the trigger.

Nothing happened. The gun had jammed. A rush of adrenaline shot through me like a gusher of crude oil blasting to the surface.

I stepped in and hit Mohawk in the side of the head with a right and he loosened up on Leonard just as Leonard kicked the woman in front of him in the stomach and sent her tumbling down the hallway.

I reached out and clawed my fingers across Mohawk's face, raking him in the eyes, and then I turned sideways and kicked him in the side of the knee. The kick was off, and the knee didn't break, but he yelped and let go of Leonard and fell backward through an open doorway.

Leonard was using the shotgun stock to do some dental work on Parade Float when I went by him and grabbed the woman. She was obviously fucked up on something and feeling no pain, and she'd gotten up on her knees and grabbed the gun again. She pointed it at my groin, and I reached down and scooped it aside with my palm and jumped in close and grabbed her head with both my hands and gave her a knee in the face, hard as I could. I figured I'd be hearing from the Southern Club for Manhood after that, but I didn't give a shit, you try and hurt me, I'm going hurt you back. She went backward with her nose flat and blood flying and the gun went off and plaster puffed out of the wall. I kneed her again, and the automatic went sailing away from her, down the hall, and now there were guys coming out of nowhere, all over, a half-dozen of them, and one of them came up behind me and grabbed me in a full nelson. I dropped to a wide stance and punched forward with both hands, and that loosened the guy's grip. I wheeled and hit him in the side of the head with my elbow, and followed on around with my body and scooped my arm around behind his head and pulled him down and kneed him in the groin and kicked the inside of one of his knees and then the other, and the second one broke with a sound like a drumstick snapping.

I took a punch in the side of the head and one in the kidney and I yelled and turned and hit a guy with a forearm and saw another guy fly by me on the end of Leonard's foot, and then I saw the stock of Leonard's shotgun catch another one in the side of the head, and after that I saw less of Leonard because I was busy.

I threw some punches and kicks, but mostly punches and knees and elbows, because the working conditions were tight. Guys started running past me and Leonard, darting for the door. Back of the house I heard a woman scream, and some guys yell, and the back door slammed, and I knew a fistful of folks who'd been on the buy were out of there and making tracks.

I checked the woman. She was still out.

I looked behind me. Parade Float was on his ass, unconscious, leaning against the wall, dribbling blood-soaked teeth down his chest. He was still wearing his shower cap. Those things were really worth the money.

Another guy, the one whose knee I'd broke, was on the floor screaming so loud I thought my brain would turn to mush. Leonard walked over and kicked the guy in the face, hard, and I grabbed him to keep him from doing it again.

Leonard turned away from me and went into the room where Mohawk had gone, and I ran over there and entered just behind him. And there was Mohawk, on the bed, on his knees, holding a revolver, pointing it at Leonard. The gun vibrated like a guitar string. Mohawk said, "Don't! Don't now. I'll shoot your goddamn dick off. Get away from me, you crazy nigger."

And Leonard, truly crazy, crazed as if he had a hot soldering iron rammed up his ass, walked right up to him. Mohawk didn't fire because he was too scared to fire, afraid the bullets would bounce off Leonard's chest.

Leonard tossed the shotgun on the bed, reached out and grabbed the barrel of Mohawk's gun and twisted it away from him and grabbed him by the throat with the other hand. He tossed the gun aside and whipped Mohawk around and put his forearm under Mohawk's chin and applied a judo choke. One of those that doesn't cut the wind, just cuts the blood off to the brain, and because of that, I knew Leonard had gotten himself together.

Mohawk thrashed a little, then got still.

I put a hand on Leonard's shoulder. "Let him go, man."

Leonard let him go, and Mohawk fell off the bed and onto the floor. He was out. With that choke, it only takes a few seconds.

Leonard got Mohawk by the feet and dragged him out of the bedroom, and I watched from the hallway as Leonard pulled him onto the front porch, and down the steps, Mohawk's head thumping the steps like bongos. Leonard laid Mohawk out in the yard and came back in the house. He reached down and got Parade Float by the shirtfront and boosted him to his feet and put the big bastard over his shoulder and turned to me.

"Drag 'em out," he said.

I went over and picked the woman up. She was very light. A temporary feeling of guilt went over me, hitting her like that, but then I thought of the gun pointing at my balls and her firing it, and I wanted to hit her again. I took her out in the yard and laid her between Mohawk and Parade Float. I went back inside and got hold of the guy with the broken knee and pulled him onto the porch and shoved him off. He screamed all the way and really screamed when he hit the ground.

In the distance, we could hear the ambulance sirens.

"Inside," Leonard said.

We went inside and into the bedroom where Mohawk had been. Leonard pulled the mattress off the bed and started dragging it through the doorway. He piled it in the hallway, and I followed after him as if I were a strand of toilet paper stuck to his shoe.

We went into the kitchen, and Leonard rumbled around and found a box of kitchen matches. He tried to open the box but was so wired he dropped them on the floor. I picked up the box and opened it and got a match out and struck it on the side of the box and handed it to him.

He grinned at me. The devil was behind that grin. He took the match and carefully lit a curtain over the kitchen window. The curtain began to blaze. I got a match out, went over to a sack of overflowing garbage, struck the match on the counter and looked at the flame. I saw the overdosed child in it, saw the dead bodies beneath the house, the bones in the trunk, the shadowy shape of Illium.

I dropped the match on top of a grease-splattered Hamburger Helper box. A moment later the sack was flaming. I kicked the fiery sack under the kitchen table and the flames licked up and caught the plastic table cloth. The table itself was littered with garbage. It caught fire pretty quick.

We moved down the hallway, and Leonard took out his pocketknife and cut the mattress open. I lit the stuffing inside, and the mattress blazed mightily.

We did the same sort of thing in the bedroom with the curtains and the sheets. Leonard rescued his shotgun, and we went over to the bathroom and found some bottles of alcohol in the medicine cabinet. We sloshed that around the place and lit it. Flames raced up the walls.

By the time we walked out the front door our matches were used up and the house was seriously on fire. There were ambulance attendants in the yard, looking at Mohawk and the others. There was an ambulance at the curb.

"Not those assholes," Leonard said, pointing across the street. "There's a boy over there."

One of the attendants looked at us, let his eyes rest on the shotgun cradled in Leonard's arms. "Easy, fellow. We're on it."

I looked at MeMaw's house. I was sure she was up now, sick or not. Lights were on all over. There was an ambulance out front. Attendants were sliding a stretcher into the back of it. Hiram was on the front porch. He looked over at me and Leonard. The red-and-blue lights from the ambulance strobed across him, blended with the yellow-white porch light. He didn't lift his hand toward us.

I turned back to the crack house. I could see flames behind the windows, like the light inside a jack-o'-lantern. One of the windows exploded suddenly, and a thick coil of black smoke rolled out into the night. It carried a stench with it. Burning plastic perhaps. Or just all the badness in that house on fire.

"Those old wood-frame houses certainly do catch quick," Leonard said.

"Yeah," I said. "Lumber's mellow when it gets that old."

Me and Leonard walked back to Uncle Chester's house. Leonard had tossed my .38 onto the porch, and he showed me where it was, and I got it.

We went inside and waited for the inevitable.

30.

Holding cells are very small and short on comfort. And this one smelled like a dog kennel. Me and Leonard were sitting on the floor with about ten other guys, and the floor was cold and hard and not a single throw pillow was in sight. A drunk kept trying to put his head in my lap and wanted to call me Cheryl.

There was one toilet in the place, but you sat down on it to take a dump, everyone was going to be looking at you. I can take about anything, but I like private toilet space. In my book, defecation is not a spectator sport. It wasn't that I needed to go, but I was worried about the situation if the necessity arose. Of course, the bars and the back wall of the cell were painted a very comfortable blue, and that's supposed to be a relaxing color if you're trying to make with a bowel movement. If memory serves me, however, green is better. Perhaps I could suggest that to the jailer. Get an audience with the mayor.

Another bad thing about a holding cell is you don't exactly meet a great crowd of people. A lot of them are criminals.

The people we'd had our row with weren't around. I figured Parade Float was visiting an oral surgeon, and the rest were at the hospital. But we had some real cuties nonetheless. One of them, a greasy white guy with the physique of an industrial meat freezer and a swastika tattooed on his forehead in red ink, got his dick out and pissed between the bars on a jailer's leg. A cop came over and yelled at him, and the guy pissed on the cop. The cop hit the bars with his nightstick and cussed, and the big guy laughed and turned around and shook the dew off his dick.

"Fucking assholes," the big guy said, then he quit grinning and looked all of us in the holding cell over. "You're assholes too," he said.

None of us assholes argued with him. Me and Leonard, we were tired and sore assholes. The big guy, without putting his dick up, wandered over to the far edge of the cell and intimidated a sad-looking little Mexican guy by giving him the hairy eyeball. Also, a guy staring at you with his dick out will make a person nervous.

Hanson came up to the bars and stood looking inside. He was dressed in a black T-shirt and jeans and what looked like house slippers. His stomach bulged inside the T-shirt, but it looked hard, like a washpot. The wet end of a chewed cigar stuck out of the T-shirt pocket. I gave him a little wave. He smiled insincerely and spread his arms wide. "My boys! How are you?"

"We're a little tired, Lieutenant," Leonard said.

"Arson and assault, trespassing," Hanson said. "These things wear on you. Jailer. Open up."

The jailer opened up. Hanson stood in the open doorway and said, "My boys, come to me."

We got up and started out. The big guy with his dick out came over and tried to follow after us. "Not you," Hanson said, and after we passed Hanson pushed the guy back inside.

"Piss on you," the big guy said and thrust his hips forward like he was going to piss on Hanson. Hanson reached very quickly and grabbed the guy's crank and yanked it as if he were popping a whip. The guy made a noise like a sudden hole in a helium balloon and went down to his knees.

Hanson said, "Put that thing away, or I'll have it mounted on a board."

Hanson came out of the cell, the jailer closed the door, and Hanson gave us a soft shove down the corridor.

We came to a door and Hanson reached between us and opened it. "Gentlemen," he said.

We went inside. It was an office full of smoke. Charlie was sitting behind the only desk in the room with his feet propped on it. He had thin soles on his shoes. He had a copy of a trash rag and was reading it. He had his suit coat slung over the back of the chair, and he was wearing a green pajama shirt stuck in his slacks, and he had his porkpie hat tilted back on his head.

Mohawk was sitting in a fold-out metal chair on the left side of the room. Just sitting there smoking a cigarette. There was an ashtray on the floor in front of him and it was filled with cigarettes. There were stomped out cigarettes all around the ashtray.

Charlie wasn't paying Mohawk the least bit of attention. He didn't look at us when we entered the room. He was deep into his rag.

On the right hand side of the room, wreathed in Charlie's smoke, was Florida. She was leaning against the wall next to a fold-out chair. She was dressed in jeans and a tight white T-shirt; she was a knockout. Just what I needed to see at a time like this. Then again, I knew she'd be here. She was mine and Leonard's lawyer, and when I got my one call, I'd called her.

"Hap," she said.

"Florida," I said. "Thanks."

Leonard nodded at her.

Hanson said, "Charlie, watch 'em. I got to wash my hands. I been pullin' a guy's dick."

Charlie didn't look up from his rag. He just lifted a hand over it. Hanson went out and shut the door.

I glanced at Mohawk and Mohawk glanced at me. He'd looked better. His mohawk was leaning a bit to the left, and there wasn't one ounce of cockiness about him. There was a knot on the side of his head where I'd hit him. He looked away from me and took in Leonard.

Leonard smiled at him. It was one of those smiles Leonard can give that you'd really prefer not to see. Mohawk's Adam's apple bobbed up and fell back down. He dropped his eyes to the floor. The cigarette between his fingers was almost burned down to his skin. He sucked it once and dropped it. It nearly hit the ashtray. He said, "Where the hell's my motherfuckin' lawyer? They got their lawyer here, I want mine."

"Got to call him first," Charlie said, and turned a page on his rag.

"You ain't let me call shit, man," Mohawk said. "That ain't legal."

"Hey," Charlie said, "we're busy, we'll get to it."

"You look busy," said Mohawk.

"The work of the mind is subtle," Charlie said.

During this exchange, Charlie hadn't once looked away from his paper. He kept reading. After a few moments, without taking his face out of the paper, he said, "You know, there's some strange things in the world. They found a picture of Elvis in an Egyptian tomb." He put the paper down and looked at me. "You know that, Hap?"

"No shit?" I said.

"No shit. Painted right there on the fucking wall. Had his hair slicked back and stuff. Had on a white jump suit and aviator glasses. It's right here in the article. They got a picture."

"Yeah?" I said.

"Yeah," Charlie said. "They hunt around the tomb some more, they expect to find a mummy with the facial structure of Elvis."

"You're certainly on top of things," I said.

"You'd be surprised the stuff I know," Charlie said. "I keep up with current events. I'm real current. Most current is I had to get out of bed 'cause I heard about a fire tonight, and I heard it was you two assholes set it."

"We looked out our window and saw a fire," Leonard said. "We went over to help pull the victims to safety. We're goddamn heroes."

"That motherfucker's lying!" Mohawk said.

"Keep your seat, Melton," Charlie said.

"Don't say anything else," Florida said to Leonard. "You and Hap be quiet. You'll do better being quiet."

"Ah hell," Charlie said, "Hap and Leonard, they like to talk."

"That's true," Leonard said. "We can't shut up."

Hanson opened the door and came in. He went over to the desk. "You mind I have my chair?" he said to Charlie.

"Naw," Charlie said, "it's all right."

Charlie got up and went over to Mohawk. He said, "Get up, Melton."

Mohawk looked at Charlie. Charlie grinned. Mohawk got up and leaned against the wall. Charlie sat down and used his foot to move the ashtray and the ill-aimed cigarette butts aside. He scooted the chair forward and put his feet on the edge of the desk and rocked back so the chair was against the wall. He looked pretty precarious.

Hanson sat behind his desk and studied me and Leonard. "First time I seen you guys, I liked you. I don't like you so much now."

"That hurts," Leonard said. "Shit, man, we like you."

"I been eating Rolaids like they're candy," Hanson said. "I almost lit my cigar again. And you guys know why? I'm tired of the bullshit. Arson, that's a serious crime."

"So's selling drugs," I said. "That boy under our house might even think using them's a bad idea."

"He don't think nothing," Hanson said. "He died before he got to the hospital."

Silence reigned for a moment. Leonard said, "I think the whole goddamn police force has got some gall, that's what I think. These fuckers," he jabbed a finger at Melton, "they been in that house for ages, selling drugs. They fed that boy dope. That boy is dead, man, and I'm not supposed to have a right to get pissed? I know they're selling drugs. Everyone here knows it, but now you got us on arson, and you're saying we'll do time?"

"Could be," Hanson said. "I ain't got shit to do with the way the law works, just with doing what it says."

"Some law that lets people like this creep do what they're doing," I said. "What happened to justice?"

"We get enough evidence, we pick 'em up," Hanson said.

"And let them go," Charlie said.

Hanson looked at Charlie. "You quittin' the force? You with them?"

"I'm a cop 'cause I want to lock bad guys up," Charlie said. "I don't want to pick 'em up so they can come down here to use the phone and toilet. And I certainly don't want to arrest no citizens on a misunderstanding."

"Misunderstanding?" Hanson said.

Charlie took his feet off the desk and let the chair rock forward. "Couple of citizens see a fire, go in and rescue some people, I don't see that's a crime."

"They kneed a woman in the face!" Mohawk said. "They knocked out my main man's teeth."

"That woman's a crack head," Charlie said, "and she got that way 'cause of you. She's a hooker. She stabbed a girl friend near to death three years ago. She's got a record longer than a basketball player's leg. And your main man, hell, he's fixed up good now. All them teeth missing. You ought to be grateful. He can suck your dick like a vacuum cleaner."

"Just the thought of that gets me excited," Leonard said.

"I'd also like to mention the woman got kneed in the face stuck a gun in my balls," I said.

"Let's cool our language," Hanson said. "We got a lady present."

"Why all of a sudden?" Charlie said. "And besides, she ain't a lady now. She's a lawyer."

Florida smiled. She said, "Marvin, my clients just saw a fire and went to help."

"Oh, God," Hanson said, "not you too."

"I'm sure the owner of the dwelling, Mr. Otis—"

"Some fat cat honkie, I reckon," Leonard said.

"One of the fattest," Florida said. "Mr. Otis, who I know is an upstanding citizen, and a friend of the police chief, would be upset to discover the house he's renting out is being used to sell drugs."

"Naw," Charlie said. "Old fart gets a slice of the action."

"We don't know that," Hanson said.

"We can't prove it," Charlie said. "Ain't the same thing."

"I'm sure he would be upset," Florida persisted. "But I know he'd be happy to hear of the bravery of men like Hap Collins and Leonard Pine, who selflessly went to the rescue of the inhabitants."

"We see our duty," Leonard said, "we do it. We can't help it. It's the way we were raised."

"Yeah," Hanson said, "and in the process of doing your duty y'all knocked a man's teeth out, broke another's knee, and busted up a woman's nose."

"Hey," Leonard said. "My knuckles hurt. They're all scraped up. Show him your head, Hap." I turned the side of my head toward Hanson. Leonard pointed to it. "See there, he's got a bruise."

"Christ," Hanson said.

"Sometimes, in the heat of the moment," Florida said, "even when you're trying to do a good deed, you can make mistakes. They were rough, but they saved lives."

"They set the fire!" Mohawk said.

"I been in that place," Charlie said. "Knocked the door down and come to visit a number of times. Joint's a shit hole, a fire hazard. Fire could have started any kind of way."

"You have a shotgun with you to shoot the fire out," Hanson said to Leonard. "EMTs said you were carrying a shotgun."

"I was cleaning it. We heard the boy under the house, didn't know what it was, and we'd seen the fire out the window, so I rushed out with it in my hand. I was so excited I forgot I had it."

"Shut up!" Hanson said. "Every one of you, shut up. Charlie, take Melton here to the restroom."

"I don't need to go," Mohawk said.

Charlie stood up and took Mohawk by the elbow. "Sure you do. Come on, I'll show you how to fold the toilet paper."

Charlie and Mohawk started past us. I said, "Thanks, Charlie."

"Us Kmart shoppers got to stick together," he said, and he and Mohawk went away.

Hanson said, "All right, let's cut the bullshit. Here's the deal. I don't give a damn about that house or Melton and his asshole buddies. I want them nailed bad as you do. I don't want any more drugged-out dead kids. But I've had all the cat-and-mouse I'm gonna do on this child murder thing. I don't want any more dead kids that way either. You jerks are gonna come clean, or I'm gonna use this arson thing to nail you, and don't think I won't."

"And don't think I won't give your case a hard time in court," Florida said. "Melton wouldn't exactly make a sympathetic witness. Neither would the rest of the house's occupants."

"You'd do that to me?" Hanson said.

"Business," Florida said, and smiled at Hanson.

Hanson smiled back. "Yeah, guess you would. All right, here's how it's coming down. You two saw a fire, went to help, couple of occupants panicked, didn't know you were trying to rescue 'em, so they got rough, and you got rough, but you saved them. OK?"

Leonard and I agreed.

"I'll call Melton back," Hanson said, "explain to him he wants to fight it, he can fight it, but it's just gonna be shit for him. He'll talk tough a couple of minutes and let it slide. He don't want any court trouble, I'll promise that."

"He hasn't seen court trouble till I get on his ass," Florida said.

I looked at Florida and smiled. She smiled back. For a moment it seemed like we were together again.

"In return for me being the generous fella I am," Hanson said, "for not dragging your asses through court and sending you upriver, you're gonna be sweet as sugar to me. You're gonna tell me some things you know that I don't know. Got me?"

I glanced at Leonard. He nodded. He said, "I guess we've played detective enough."

He told Hanson about the Hampstead place and what we found. But I noticed he conspicuously left out the sweet Reverend Fitzgerald.

31.

Hanson let us go, charge free. Florida took me and Leonard home. When she pulled into the driveway and we got out, she got out too. The smell of burnt lumber from next door was strong in the air. Florida said, "Hap, can we talk a moment?"

"Sure," I said.

Florida looked at Leonard.

"I'm worn out," Leonard said. "I'm just going to take a cheerful look of what's left of next door, then go to sleep."

We walked around to the bottle tree and stood there looking at the smoky, blackened shell of the house.

"Mucho mojo," Florida said.

"What?" I said.

"Much bad magic," she said. "Next door was mucho mojo. Something my grandmother used to say. *Mojo* is African for magic."

"I thought it was sex," I said.

"That's because you listen to blues records," she said. "It is sex, or even the sex organs. But that's bastardized. Meaning sex is like magic. *Mojo* means magic. My grandmother knew some Spanish, and when things were bad, she'd say 'mucho mojo.' Spanish *mucho* for much, African *mojo* for magic. But what she meant when she said it was much bad magic. To her, mojo was always bad."

"Well, they're a little less bad next door," Leonard said.

"Yeah," I said. "And we can feel good looking out our windows, but they'll just move to some other street. They're not really gone, they're merely inconvenienced."

"I'd rather inconvenience them than just let them go," Leonard said. "Scum like that get inconvenienced often enough, they might think the career they got isn't worth it. It's the good folks of the world that are supposed to be in charge, not the assholes. Though, in my darker moments, I sometimes fear the assholes outnumber us. By the way, Florida, who's this Otis guy?"

"White guy who owned the house, and a lot of houses here on the East Side," Florida said. "I've heard he openly refers to these as his nigger rent houses. And it's pretty well known he gets a cut of the drug pie over here."

"And he's a friend of the police chief's," Leonard said.

"Yes," Florida said. "And he'll just build the house back. Cheaply, of course."

"Well, that's for another discussion," Leonard said. "Good night, Florida. Hap, don't you stay up late, now. I don't want you fussin' when I get you out of bed tomorrow."

Leonard went in the house and Florida and I sat on the porch in the glider. I remembered that the glider was where our romance had begun.

I said, "This is sort of the Dear-John talk, right?"

"I've wanted to talk to you, I just haven't had the guts, because I really don't know what to say."

"I guess 'Bye-bye, Hap, and don't forget your hat' would be OK."

"It's not like that."

"How is it?"

"I'm going over to Marve's tonight."

"I'd rather you just said, 'Bye-bye, don't forget your hat.' "

"He's a good man, Hap."

"That's what pisses me off. It's hard for me to feel self-righteous. I like the big bastard. But I still don't like hearing it. Not that I didn't already know."

"I wanted you to hear it from me. I just didn't have the courage to do it right away. I should have said something soon as I knew. Hap, it wasn't like you and me were a hundred percent anyway. I never said our relationship was forever."

"Hurts just the same."

"You'll get over it."

"Yeah, but I'd rather it have worked out."

"Me too. Really. I do care for you. I maybe even love you a little."

"Please."

"It just happened, Hap. I don't know what to tell you. It happened, and it happened fast. It was good between you and me, and you taught me some things about myself, but—"

"Hanson's black."

"I suppose, if I'm honest with myself, I'll admit that makes it easier."

"You never took me to that movie, Florida. You know, I never even been to your place. I bet Hanson has. Hasn't he?"

"Yes. But I knew the night I saw him over here he was the one. I don't know why. I'd seen him before, but that night was the first time I was really close enough to feel the heat."

"Maybe it was just a hot night."

She smiled. "No. It wasn't just a sexual thing. There was that, but it's not that he's the prettiest thing I've ever seen."

"He's not the prettiest thing anyone's ever seen."

"But I saw him, and somehow I knew. And the other night, when he took me home, we didn't go to bed or anything like that. I wanted you to know that. We didn't just jump in the sack. We talked, and talked, and talked. There was a connection between us that goes deeper than the one you and I've got. It's that simple. Maybe being black does give us a kind of history, but what I feel for Marve isn't merely because he's black."

"Of course, you two don't just talk now."

"First time we made love was tonight. Charlie called for him at my place when they got the news about the fire and about you and Leonard. After Marve left, you called and told me where you were. But of course, I already knew. I was about to be on my way. I figured you and Leonard could use a lawyer."

"Did Charlie calling interrupt anything?"

"That's juvenile, Hap."

"Sorry."

"We were lying in bed talking. Talking about you."

"Comparing dick sizes?"

She got up briskly and started to leave. I caught her wrist and she jerked it away from me. "Let go of me, damnit!"

"Florida," I said. "I'm sorry. Really. But this isn't easy for me."

"It's not easy for me, Hap. I don't want to hurt you."

"But you want us to be friends, right? Isn't that the thrust of this talk?"

"I know you're hurt, but I didn't plan this. It happened, damnit. It just happened."

I turned my head and looked toward the pile of blackened rubble that had been the crack house. Smoke was drifting up into the starlight. I turned back and looked at Florida.

"There really isn't anything I can say to that," I said.

She slowly and carefully sat down beside me. She sat close. I could smell her perfume. It was the same perfume I often smelled on my pillows. She took my hand.

I said, "You really sounded like someone who was more than an ambulance chaser tonight."

"I did, didn't I?"

"Hanson knew you got our case in court, personal feelings or not, you'd have given him hell."

"And I'd have beat him too. Even if you did burn the house down. And on purpose."

"You'll do all right," I said. "Maybe you just needed a little rest. Sounds to me, you got your ambition back."

"Can we be friends?" she said. "I know it sounds cliché. But I really and truly want to be friends."

I spent a minute thinking about it. "Give me some time on it. Right now I look at you, I don't see you that way. I don't know how I see you."

She leaned over and kissed me on the cheek. "You're a good find for the right person, Hap. I'm just not the right person."

"That's what they all say."

She stood up and touched my shoulder. "I'll see you, soon?"

"Soon as I can handle it," I said.

She drove away. I watched her taillights till they were out of sight. The wind picked up and turned cool and hooted in the bottle tree.

32.

When I awoke it was early morning and I was lying on the glider and my back ached. Where I'd caught those punches hurt too. My wrist ached from the shock of the blow I'd dealt Mohawk on the side of the head.

There was a blanket over me and a pillow under my head. Leonard, the one constant in my life, had been out to check on me. I hadn't even felt him move my head or cover me. Bless him.

I sat up slowly, feeling the stiffness. The air was intense with the charred aroma of next door. The sunlight was beautiful. It was still cool. I missed Florida.

Before we left the station last night, Leonard told Hanson about the Hampstead place and what was under it. Today, late morning, Hanson and a hand-picked crew would be out. He was also bringing in a friend from Houston, a retired coroner.

In spite of his talk, Hanson wasn't ready to turn what he knew over to the police chief after all. He wanted to make sure everything we told him was as we said, wanted to make sure we'd translated the evidence properly.

I think he knew too, if he told the police chief what he had discovered, told how Illium was linked, the chief would take the case away from him for not coming forward sooner. But if Leonard and I were right, if Hanson could get all his ducks in a row and solve this case, no matter what the chief thought, things were going to turn out OK. It'd be pretty hard for the chief to fire Hanson for solving a multiple child-murder case, considering the publicity that would surround it.

And I was pretty certain Hanson knew we were still holding out on him. That we had an important part of the puzzle we weren't showing.

So, Hanson was going to get a court order, quickly and quietly, not hide it from the chief, but not announce it either, and he and his crew were coming out.

His crew was going to be Charlie, the retired Houston coroner, me and Leonard, and a couple other folks he thought he could trust. It wasn't a morning I looked forward to.

I stood up and stretched and checked out the remains of the crack house, felt a rush of adrenaline from last night. I also felt a rush of shame.

Violence and anger against another human being always made me feel that way, no matter what my justification. I lost it, I always feel somewhat diminished. But I would have felt even more diminished to have done nothing. That little boy, dying up under the house like a dog with a belly full of glass. . . . It's hard to figure why it has to be that way.

But had it been just that? Had I done what I did, followed Leonard because I wanted vengeance for that child, all the children they infected with their slick talk and drugs? Or had my willingness to lose it also been part of my problem with Florida? Was I finding a way to self-righteously vent my disappointment and rage? I didn't like to think about that kind of snake inside me, crawling around, waiting to strike.

Across the street I heard a screen door slam, and looked to see Hiram out on MeMaw's porch. He had a cup of coffee and was wearing blue jogging pants, a blue T-shirt, and dirt-tinted white tennis shoes. He walked to the edge of the porch and hacked up a big wad of phlegm and spat into the yard: He looked up and saw me.

"Hap," he called.

I walked out to the curb, talked across the street. "Thanks for last night," I said. "I didn't know where else to go."

"What else could I do? How's the boy?"

"Dead."

Hiram nodded. "I'm not surprised. He didn't look none too good. He had that look about him, like he wasn't long for this world."

The screen door opened and MeMaw started working her walker outside. Hiram grabbed the screen and held it open. "You don't need to come out here," he said.

"But I want to," she said. After a full minute, she was in the center of the porch, leaning on her walker. She said, "I'm glad you did it. I'd been younger, I'd did it. Lenny up?"

"No, ma'am," I said. "I don't think so."

"Well, you come on over," she said. "I've got breakfast cooking."

"Ma'am," I said. "I don't want to intrude."

"Biscuits, eggs, and bacon," she said. She turned her walker slightly, then slightly again, until she was facing the screen. Hiram opened the screen for her. She worked her way inside, called over her shoulder, "Don't let it get cold."

Hiram smiled at me. He said, "I think you better come on to breakfast."

MeMaw looked extremely frail that morning, but she was radiant just the same. Happy about the crack house being turned to smoke, happier yet her baby boy Hiram was home. The breakfast was great. The bacon was thick. She'd gotten the meat from one of her sons who raised hogs, and we spread real artery-jamming butter on the biscuits and dipped them in the sun-yellow yolks of farm-fresh eggs acquired from a friend of hers who had his own chickens.

After breakfast, MeMaw entertained me and embarrassed Hiram with stories about when he was a child, told some cute incidents, explained what a good Christian child Hiram had always been, and when Hiram had had all of that talk he could take, he said, "Hey, what're your plans today, Hap?"

"Not much," I said, not prepared to mention that I was going to exhume bodies.

"You ought to work out with me."

"After last night, I'm pretty bushed. What kind of workout?"

"Boxing."

"I hate that boxing," MeMaw said. "Two grown men hitting one another in the head for fun. You'd think Hiram and Reverend Fitzgerald would be old enough to know better."

"Reverend Fitzgerald?" I said.

"Yeah. I come in once a year, we get together, do a little boxing, talk old times. Play chess. I do it mostly to please MeMaw. She thinks I ought to know the right hand of the Lord. Not that we didn't get drilled with religion all the time we were growing up."

"When I was able," MeMaw said, "I saw that this family lived in the church."

"You know Reverend Fitzgerald pretty good then?" I said.

"Didn't you meet him the other day?" MeMaw asked.

"Yes, ma'am," I said, "just briefly."

I gave Hiram the *Reader's Digest* version of that, leaving out all the tense stuff between him and Leonard. I was getting to be a pretty good liar.

"I've known Fitz for years," Hiram said. "We used to go to his daddy's church. Me and him played together. His daddy taught the both of us how to box. Fitz is a little older than me, but I'm a scrapper. 'Course, he still beats hell out me. Or has in the past. I'm kind of hoping age will catch up with him."

"It hasn't so far," I said. "I saw him working a bag. He's in shape. He can still hit hard. He drags his back foot in the bucket a little when he moves, but that could just be the way he works a bag."

"You know something about boxing then?" Hiram said.

"A little."

"Another man likes to get hit in the head," MeMaw said. "I can't figure it. . . . By the way, how's that little boy?"

It took me a moment to shift gears and know who she was talking about. Then it came to me. I said, "He died, MeMaw. We found him too late. The drugs snuffed him out."

"Oh," she said. "I'm so sorry. A child like that, in that den of wolves, he ain't got no chance. What I'd like to know was where his mother was."

I'd found out a little about the boy last night from Charlie and Hanson, and I told MeMaw what I knew. "He was a street kid, MeMaw. Name of Ivan Lee."

"I heard of the Lees," MeMaw said, "but I can't say I knew nothing about them."

"Ivan lived with an aunt," I said, "but apparently there wasn't much going on there in a family way. He was on his own. Wasn't even going to school, hung out on the streets most of the time. He'd been picked up for little crimes here and there. He fell through the cracks."

"Over here," MeMaw said, "lots fall through the cracks. There's always somethin' pushin' in on a person here. Bad people and bad things from all sides. A baby has got to have a shield from the world. Got to learn how to shield themselves. I'm lucky I raised all my chil'ren without none of them gettin' messed up."

"Don't fret, Mama," Hiram said. "That little boy was a goner from the start. Ain't that right, Hap?"

"I don't know anyone's a goner, you get to them in time," I said. "But there's a line you can step across that puts you on a path of no return. In little Ivan's case, I don't know he stepped across so much as got shoved over it."

"Maybe so," Hiram said. "But if he runs with the dogs, he, well . . . 'becomes like them that go down into the pit.' "

"I presume that's biblical," I said.

"Yeah, I guess it's a way of saying birds of a feather stick together. Or if you lie down with dogs you get up with fleas. Whatever . . . whatcha say, Hap? You gonna work out with me? We won't be there long."

I considered a moment. There really wasn't any clear evidence, other than circumstantial, that Fitzgerald had done the things Leonard and I thought he had. There was still the possibility that Chester Pine and Illium Moon were what we thought they were being framed to be. Another look at the Reverend might be of interest.

"Yeah," I said. "I'm game."

33.

We took Hiram's van. It was a cluttered thing, and I had to move a small box of folded Texas flags off the seat to sit down. I sat them on a box of American flags in the back. Strewn on the floorboard, front and back, were booklets containing designs for senior rings and samples of paper to choose from for high school yearbooks and bulletins, and there were pamphlets advertising photocopying machines, typewriters, and the like.

"Yeah, I know," Hiram said. "I'm messy."

When we backed out of the drive and hit the street and the merchandise stopped shifting, Hiram said, "I didn't want to say anything in front of MeMaw, but actually, going over to see Fitz isn't always that wonderful. He's a little quirky."

"I thought as much when I met him. I mean, he was nice enough, just a little fanatic."

"That's not all bad. I mean, he's a good guy. But that's why I was hoping you'd come along. I'm not saying I mind boxing him or playing a game of chess now and then, but he can be a little much sometimes."

"I understand."

"MeMaw is just crazy for church and religion though, bless her sweet heart, so she always sort of invites me to go over there, I want to or not. She thought Fitz's old man was something special. Had the hot line to God."

"But you didn't think so?"

"Actually, the old man could put up a good front for someone when he wanted to. I was around Fitz a lot when I was a kid, spent the night over there now and then, and I saw the old man was kind of a bully. Never let the kid really enjoy his childhood. Always had some kind of complaint. And he was very much a hands-on person. He was hard on Fitz 'cause Fitz wasn't his child."

"A former marriage?" I asked.

Hiram shifted gears and shook his head. "I can't figure why the old man married Fitz's mother. Didn't seem a preacher's type. She'd been a kind of sportin' woman before they met. I guess he liked the idea of transforming her from a Jezebel to a woman of God. Though I don't know she changed all that much. There were stories went around, and enough of them, so I figure where there was smoke, there was fire."

"What about Fitz's real father?"

"Don't know nothing about him. Neither does Fitz. He was some guy who bought Fitz's mother and did his job and left. Probably never even knew he'd made a baby."

We cruised by the East Side Market. The old man who owned the place was sitting outside at the domino table, watching the street, perhaps planning his strategy for when the rest of the players showed up.

I said, "So the Reverend is actually illegitimate?"

"Well, he got his stepfather's name, of course. But strictly speaking, yeah. I figure that's what makes Fitz such a hard-nose. He's trying to live up to something. The old man never let either Fitz or his mama forget where they come from and what a big deed he was doin' for them."

I thought about the profile I had put together on the Reverend Fitzgerald. I was beginning to think I should pursue a career in psychology. Of course, when it came to putting together a profile on women, I'd have to pass. I understood the secret life of the hummingbird better than I understood women.

I said, "The mom still around?"

"Fitz's mama disappeared. Probably ran off. The old man got some kind of cancer or something. Died slow. Lot of people thought God was paying him back for the kind of man he was. As for Fitz, well, he's got his good points. He's developed things to keep kids off the street. He's real antidrug. He's introduced soccer and boxing and baseball and the carnival."

"Carnival?"

"Yeah, I like the carnival myself. I go every year 'cause I'm here at just the right time. There's something about seeing black kids who can't even afford to get across town being able to walk over to the fairgrounds and have a good time. And Fitz has a bus so he can pick up kids might not be able to make it, or might have to walk through a bad section of town. He takes them over there, and they haven't got the money, he sees they get in and get some rides."

At mention of the carnival, something had shifted inside my head. I said, "Saw a sign on the carnival. It's next week, isn't it?"

"Yeah."

"Does it always take place sometime during the last week of August?"

"Yeah, it's just for one night. One night is all can be afforded. Fitz gets the local merchants to sponsor it, throw in donations. He raises money for it other ways too. The carnival owners sell tickets to get in and for the rides, but they're cheap, so most anyone can afford it. It's a little operation. Black owned. Goes around to black communities. Fitz heard about it and made the deal with them, so the carnival comes back every year. Wasn't for Fitz, lot of the kids here wouldn't have anything going for them."

I felt a sickness in the pit of my stomach. "How long ago was it Reverend Fitzgerald set this carnival business up?"

"Let's see. Nine, ten years ago."

"That's real benevolent of him."

"He's got his good points. Like the way he protects his brother, T.J."

"Brother?"

"Half-brother, actually. He's retarded and about the size of a small army tank."

I thought of the big man Leonard and I had seen working in the yard outside of the church.

"Rumor has it," Hiram continued, "the boy wasn't really the old man's son either, but that the wife had been slipping around again. I don't know. Maybe the Reverend wanted to believe she was slipping around. Man like him, it might have been easier to believe that than believe his seed could be tainted, could produce something like T.J. A giant with the mind of a poodle. Fitz, though, he always treated T.J. special. Real special. T.J. didn't have Fitz, he wouldn't last long. They got a serious bond."

When we were close to the church and Reverend Fitzgerald's house, Hiram said, "This might be the last year I see Fitz. When MeMaw passes, I know I'm through. Me and Fitz were kind of close when we were kids, but the older I get, harder it is for me to connect with the guy."

We parked in the church lot, and before we got out of the van, I said, "I got a confession. Me and Leonard were over here the other day, like I said, but it didn't go that well. We came looking for someone Leonard's uncle knew that Reverend Fitzgerald was supposed to know, and well, Leonard and him didn't hit it off."

"How bad did they not hit it off?"

"Hard to say. Fitzgerald was polite. No one came to blows, but it was a little tense."

"It was a point of religion?"

"That, and the fact that Leonard's homosexual."

Hiram was quiet for a time. "He's queer?"

"That's not a word he prefers."

"Well, I didn't mean nothing by it . . . I guess I didn't. You queer?"

"No, I'm a Democrat when they've got the right people to vote for. Listen, Hiram, Leonard's a good guy. I don't know what your deal is concerning homosexuals, and frankly, I don't care, but I wanted you to know what happened."

"Leonard seems all right."

"He is. Gay guys come in all shades and types. Leonard's one of the good guys."

"It's just a surprise."

"I know."

"He's not like I thought a queer was. He's like us, you know. I mean . . . hell, I don't know what I mean."

"Nothing to know. I took you up on your offer to box so I could apologize to the Reverend. Things could be a little awkward is what I'm saying. I figured I ought to tell you now. You're uncomfortable, you can drive me back."

"No. No. I know how Fitz is. We'll get through it."

"Thanks," I said.

We got out of the van and walked around to the back of the church.

T.J., dressed in gray sweatpants and T-shirt and tennis shoes, was standing at the back door and it startled me. He was just standing there, not moving. His arms hung limp by his sides. He seemed to be waiting on something, or considering some deep, forgotten secret that wouldn't quite come to him. He looked like a black golem. He lifted his huge arms slightly and his hands flopped forward like catcher's mitts on pegs.

Hiram said, "Fitz in, T.J.?"

"Uh-huh."

"You remember me, T.J.?"

T.J. thought about it for a moment, and shook his head.

"That's OK," Hiram said. "Would you tell Fitz I'm here? Just say Hiram's here. He's expecting me."

The giant nodded, turned and opened the door, and disappeared inside. Hiram turned to me, said, "Every year T.J. forgets who I am. He can only hold certain kinds of thoughts for so long. Remembering me from year to year isn't one of them."

A moment later T.J. came back, and Fitzgerald was with him. T.J. let Fitzgerald go outside, then took his place in the doorway, filling it, substituting for a door. Fitzgerald was wearing a white T-shirt and white shorts and tennis shoes. He was grinning until he saw me. He looked at me, then Hiram, then back to me. Slowly the grin came back.

"You decide I was right?" the Reverend said. "About wanting to hand your life over to God?"

"Not exactly," I said. "I conned Hiram to get a ride over here. I wanted to apologize for the other day. I'm sorry about how it went with you and my friend."

"Ah, yes. Him. Well, it didn't go so bad. Apologies were made all around. It's over with."

"I didn't apologize," I said, "and I wanted to. For me and him. We just got sideways. It wasn't our intent to step on your beliefs."

"You didn't. They're too solid for that. And I don't need an apology. I was merely trying to do what it's my mission to do. Point out how God sees things. Then let you, and your friend, take your own path. If you're going to owe anyone an apology, it's God."

"Maybe I'll drop him a card," I said, then immediately wished I hadn't. I was getting as bad as Leonard.

The Reverend, however, hadn't lost his grin. He said, "You can laugh about anything in this life, my friend, but in the next—"

"Hap boxes," Hiram said. "He's a friend. That's why I brought him. To box. Why don't we just do that?"

"All right," Fitzgerald said, "we can do that. T.J., move aside. You fellas come on in."

34.

The only light in the gym was the sunlight that came through high shutter windows, and it was bright to the center of the gym, but there its reach played out and the shadow took over, grew darker toward the far wall.

The Reverend took off his T-shirt and showed us a hard body, and said, "Hiram, you and me. We'll start easy, get warm."

Hiram nodded, picked up some blue boxing gloves lying against the wall, and put them on. They were the slip-on kind. No strings.

The Reverend pulled on a pair of red gloves, and he and Hiram moved toward the center of the gym, and the line of light and shadow split them down the middle, putting one side of their bodies in the light, the other in the dark, but then they began to move, to bob and weave, to shuffle and dance, and they were one moment in brightness, the next in shadow.

Back and forth, around and around, reaching out with the gloves, slow at first, touching, jabbing, and then they came together and the blows were smooth and soft and not too quick, and on the sidelines T.J. watched like an attack dog, ready for the word.

They slugged and dodged and bobbed and weaved, and Hiram was, as he said, a scrapper, not a boxer but a scrapper. He threw his punches wide and dropped his hands, but he was fast and game and landed shots because of it. Fitzgerald was somewhere between a boxer and a brawler. It was obvious he was holding back. He could easily have been a retired heavyweight, a guy that might have been a contender.

They eventually came together in the center of the gym, locked arms, and began moving around and around in a circle, light and shadow, their foreheads pushed together as if they were Siamese twins connected by flesh and brain tissue. Around and around. T.J. carefully watching.

Finally Fitzgerald pushed Hiram away and smiled at him. "You're a little better, my man."

"I been working out at a gym," Hiram said when he got his breath. "But I've had all I want."

"You tire too easily," Fitzgerald said.

"That's the truth," Hiram said.

Fitzgerald looked at me. "You want to go?"

"Sure," I said.

Fitzgerald turned to T.J. "Take it easy, T.J. It's just fun."

T.J. nodded, but there wasn't anything on his face that showed he thought any fun was going on. He didn't relax a bit. Tiny rivers of sweat rolled down his face, and he stood partially crouched.

"Kinda takes the thrill out of it with him at my back," I said.

"He's all right," Fitzgerald said. "He's just overly protective."

I got the gloves from Hiram and pulled them on. They were sweaty inside, and hot. It was starting to warm up in the gym, as the air-conditioning was off and the air came from the same place as the light—the outside.

"You should go to church," Fitzgerald said to me. "Everyone should go to church."

"How do you know I don't?" I said. "I might preach somewhere. God might have sent me here to whip your butt."

"No," he said, smiling. "I don't think so. Your friend, he went to church, he might realize the perversion of his homosexuality. He could change his ways. There might be forgiveness from the Lord."

"Might be?" I said.

I took up a southpaw position and we moved and threw some jabs, but there was no real connection. Fitzgerald said, "There's no true home in the House of the Lord for the sodomite, young man."

"Let it be, Fitz," Hiram said from the sidelines. "Just box."

I threw a quick jab and hit the Reverend on the forehead, and we started shuffling about, looking for openings. I said, "You make homosexuality sound like a true sin. Right up there with murderers, child molesters, false prophets. You might as well include unmarried mothers and illegitimate children."

Fitzgerald studied me curiously. He jabbed and right-crossed and hooked. Lightly. I blocked and countered with a weak combination.

We moved apart, he said, "There are some who are lost to the joys of heaven. They have to be put aside."

"Aside?" I said, and hooked him with a left to the gut, hooked him hard. He covered and slid back. "What's 'aside' mean, Reverend? You sound as if you're out to punish souls instead of save them."

His face turned into a black Kabuki mask, and he came with a jab and a crossing combination. I took it on the side of my face and rolled it, but it still hurt. We weren't playing tag now. I got my focus. I let myself settle. I tried not to concentrate too much. I tried to relax and let the reflexes take over. I thought too much, I was going to get hit while putting together a combination. I had to react, not plan, and I had to remember not to kick. We were boxing.

I threw a jab and tried a hook, and Fitzgerald leaned away from the jab and moved outside of the hook and came over my hand and hit me with a right cross over the left eye.

I bobbed and weaved and let a couple of shots ricochet off me while I got it together, then we were close and the fists were flying and I was distantly aware of the sound of the gloves as they slapped on our sweaty flesh, and I was aware of moving in and out of light and shadow, and finally, when he stood in shadow and I stood in light, with the sun at my back, I decided to hold him. I wasn't going to move. He wasn't coming into the light. He was going to take what I had to give in shadow. Take it and like it.

I took a few myself and had to like it, but I had moved beyond pain. It was going to take a damn good shot for me to feel it now. We weren't playing. We were hitting. Hiram said, "Hey, men, too much," but we didn't stop, we kept slinging and the sound of the gloves became sweet, like a backbeat to good music, and Fitzgerald tried to press hard, to move around me, to move into the light, to push against me and bring himself to my side of the gym, but I wouldn't let him. He tied me up, I shoved him off and jabbed him. He tried to circle, I hooked and crossed.

Hiram was calling something from the side, but I wasn't aware of it anymore, I couldn't make sense of his words. There was a copper taste in my mouth. And then there was a great shadow, like a cloud moving before the sun, and I knew T.J. had slid up behind me, eclipsing my light, and I sensed him close to me, ready to grab me, and I thought of those children, like rag dolls in his hands.

Fitzgerald tried to bob and explode, like Smokin' Joe Frazier, but when he bobbed, I uppercut him solid enough to bring him on his toes, and I hooked him on the jaw and was driving him back farther into shadow, going with him, deeper into shadow, and he was in trouble, but holding up, and then I felt a vise fasten around my body, trapping my arms to my sides, and I could smell anxiety sweat as T.J. crushed me to him and the gym began to spin. I struggled in his grasp, thought about stomping back and down to break his kneecaps, or driving the back of my head into his face, but this was a friendly situation, nothing serious here—a little out of hand, but friendly. Any second T.J. would let go. He'd realize his brother was in no real trouble here. He'd drop me. Someone would stop him.

The walls of the gym turned to hot liquid and flowed over me and the ceiling fell down and light and shadow scrambled and there were bongos in my head and I realized I had waited too late, because T.J. wasn't going to put me down, and I was too weak now to do anything about it.

Bright and dark, bending in upon themselves, whirling around and around to the tune of blood pounding in my skull, and I had a flash of that dream where I was underwater in the bookmobile with Illium and Chester and the dead boy with the flesh floating away from his bones. . . .

When I awoke, I was on the floor of the gym. First thing I saw was Hiram. He was leaning over me. He looked concerned. He said, "Hap, you OK?"

"Yeah," I said.

Fitzgerald came into view. "Sorry about T.J. Normally, he stays in check. He got the feeling we were really into it. He squeezed your air out."

"I know," I said. "And we *were* into it."

I sat up slowly. The gym was only moving a little. My ribs were mildly sore. I figured that would balance out the knot on my head I'd gotten the night before. I'd certainly had an interesting two days, and it wasn't even lunch yet.

T.J. was standing against the far wall with his hands by his sides and his head hung. He looked as passive as a puppet. I thought: *Klaatu barada nikto.*

"Yeah," Fitzgerald said, "we were into it. It's my turn to apologize again. For T.J. And for going so hard, keeping up with the rhetoric. I guess I do bear a little animosity for the other day, and I just can't help but be a preacher. By the way, you were putting it on me pretty good. But I'd have come back."

"Now we'll never know, will we?"

"Maybe we'll do it again sometime."

I got up slowly with Hiram's assistance. "It could happen," I said.

On the way home, Hiram was quiet until we turned onto Comanche Street. He said, "Man, there's more than stuff between him and Leonard. What's the deal with you two, that's what I want to know?"

"Bad chemistry," I said.

35.

When we got back and I was out of the van telling Hiram 'bye, apologizing for going in the first place and letting things escalate the way they did, I began to feel a strange sensation.

It was partially due to the fact that Hanson's car was parked at the curb along with a pickup I didn't recognize, and of course, I knew what that meant. But there was something else, and I didn't understand it until I was on Uncle Chester's porch about to open the door. Then it hit me.

The sensation was fear. Because now I knew what I thought I'd known all along. Fitzgerald was a killer.

I had been with him and his giant brother, and I had been unconscious on the floor of Fitzgerald's gym. I had pushed certain buttons inside Fitzgerald and inside myself, and it was possible I had fucked things up. I had let the Reverend know I knew something was going on with him and the kids.

Perhaps all that had saved me and Hiram was the fact that Fitzgerald assumed someone, like MeMaw, knew where we were going. Then again, had he been inclined, he could have taken his chances, put us unconscious in Hiram's van and taken us for a little drive that ended at the bottom of some pond somewhere—an exit like Illium's. Maybe kiddie porn would be found in our possession. And when the good Reverend was questioned, all he had to say was we never arrived. Or that we came and went.

Then again, that might have been too complicated in broad daylight, or Fitzgerald may have figured me for nothing more than a belligerent sinner and not worthy of action.

I felt like a fool attempting to beard the lion in his own den, but I felt another thing now. An absolute certainty Fitzgerald, with the help of his poor brother, was our killer. It all fit together too damn neat to be otherwise.

I was trembling by the time I discovered the front door was locked. I realized Leonard and the others had gone on up to the Hampstead place.

I got a shovel off the back porch and went up there too, along the creek bed and through the woods.

When I arrived at the Hampstead place, Hanson was there, along with his crew. Unexpectedly, the retired coroner from Houston had brought his own crew. They were dressed in white paper suits and gas masks with charcoal filters. The front steps had been removed and a number of boards had been taken off the porch. White suits were crawling under there, busy as grubs in shit.

Inside the house, down in the open trapdoor, Leonard and Charlie, wearing paper suits and gas masks, were bringing out buckets containing dirt and worms and dirty lard. The worms were long and red and very busy. Leonard put his flashlight on the bucket, and I watched them squirm, like dancers under spotlights. The odor that came from the bucket and from the dank dark below was stronger than sun-hot road-kill.

"Where you been?" Leonard said through his mask. He sounded like Darth Vader.

"Visiting a friend."

"Good time for it, asshole."

"Sorry."

"Hi, Hap," Charlie said.

"Hi, Charlie. See you're wearing those Kmart shoes."

"Won't leave home without 'em."

"You see Mohawk . . . Melton, tell him Hap says hey, will you?"

"Absolutely."

Hanson introduced me to the retired coroner, Doc Warren, an old wizened white-haired guy who looked as if he might have been dug up himself. He had on a paper suit and gloves. He was sitting on the floor by the trapdoor taking a rest. He was sweaty and tired looking. His filtered mask was in his lap. There were fragments of bone on a plastic drop-cloth beside him. Very small bones. He didn't bother to get up or shake my hand.

He said, "You and your friend have found quite a mess."

"Tell me about it," I said.

Turned out they had located four bodies. One of them, the one that smelled, the one I had first discovered, had been there about a year. As I had suspected, something in the soil down there, the way the water flooded in, had caused it to decay slowly, in spite of the East Texas heat. That lard in the bucket was not lard at all. It had once been flesh. It was now the result of decay and putrefaction. With the lard were bones. A child's bones.

The rest of the bodies were not bodies at all, but bones, skeletal remains. Warren estimated the other bones had been there some time. They were all the bones of children. There was enough evidence to suggest the bodies had been cut up and wrapped in cloth and put in cardboard boxes and wrapped in chicken wire, then buried carefully.

"I believe you'll find enough bones to make up for the missing kids from the East Side," I said. "Maybe more."

"I believe you're right," Doc Warren said.

Leonard popped out of the hole. He said, "Hey, Hap, you gonna supervise, or what?"

"Is the job open?"

"Ha," Leonard said, and disappeared back into the trapdoor hole.

"You'll need to slip on one of these paper suits, get a gas mask," Hanson said.

"You got to watch infection," Warren said, "case there's any more bodies with meat on them. Streptococci likes to get in your lungs and into cuts. It can fuck you up big time."

I put on a paper suit and gas mask and went to work. It's not a day I'll forget. Sometimes, even now, I awake from a dream where I'm crawling on my belly beneath that old, rotten house, turning my shovel awkwardly in the dirt, and the smell of that child, the one that was lard and bone, still seems strong in my nostrils.

By nightfall we'd found the remains of nine children. And one large skeleton—well, what was left of a large skeleton. Warren said it was a woman. He estimated she had been there a long time. Thirty years or longer. Warren concluded her skull had been cracked, and she had most likely been cut up the same way as the kids. There were no immediate signs of cloth, but around her remains was a coil of chicken wire.

Later, paper suits disposed of, back at Uncle Chester's, we sat around and drank coffee. The crew that had come along with Doc Warren had parked on the far side of the woods, and when they finished for the day, they left that way. I never saw them again. Hanson's crew, a black man and woman who worked for the fire department, departed in the pickup in the yard. I never saw them again either. That left me and Leonard, Hanson, Warren, and Charlie.

We were sitting around the kitchen table drinking coffee, and I was thinking about those big fat red worms, wondering how long it would take them to work their way into my coffin when I was dead, and trying to tell myself it didn't matter, when Hanson said, "Something licks the bag here. That woman's body being that old, the killer would have to have started when he was a kid. Unless he's a geriatric fucker."

"Watch your mouth," Warren said.

"No offense," Hanson said.

"Yeah, well," Warren said, "I get my feelings hurt easy."

"But that's right, ain't it?" Hanson said. "Same M.O."

"It's passed down," Warren said. "Just a fucking minute." Warren put his fingers in his mouth and plucked out his false teeth and put them on the table by his coffee cup. "Sonofabitches are a bad fit," he said, and his lips flapped like flags in the wind.

"Goddamn," Leonard said, "put 'em back. I'm trying to drink my coffee here."

Warren ignored him. When he talked, he could be understood, but it sounded as if he had a rag in his mouth.

"You see, I think the original murder, the woman, was done by someone who had a child helping. Took him up there, showed him how to do it. Sanctified it somehow in the child's mind—"

"And he's repeating it," Hanson said.

"Yep," Warren said. "Good ole Freudian stuff. 'Course, nothing says the murderer has to be a man, or that it was a boy that saw him do it, but I'd bet you money. I'd say too, who-ever did this is some kind of religious nut, and he's got that and this ritual, this murder he saw take place as a child, all twisted up in his head. That water stain up there looking like it does, and his first impression of it coming to him as a child, well, it could have had quite an impact."

"I think I understood all that," Hanson said. "But . . . Christ, I'm with Leonard, put your teeth back in."

Doc Warren ignored him, sipped his coffee. He sounded like a pig at the trough, way his loose lips flopped.

"Hap gets an *A* in Psychology 101," Charlie said, "but so what?"

"Yeah, well," Warren said, "lots of folks think Freud was full of shit. Not everyone who's seen bad stuff as a child re-sponds by becoming bad. Maybe this psychology stuff is all horseshit, and whoever is doing this just likes doing it. Which brings us to the fearful question that there may in fact be real evil in the world. No one likes that idea. Everything has to have cause and effect, and maybe it does. But why do some people respond to evil with evil, while others do not?"

"Personally," Leonard said, "I don't give a shit. I've always believed in evil, and I don't need religion to believe it. I just want this guy. And I want you to put your fuckin' teeth in, Doc."

Warren sipped more coffee.

Hanson looked at Leonard, said, "I'm with you. On the teeth and this guy too. You say you want him, so isn't it about time you tell the rest of it? I know there's more. I've stood for all the dicking around I'm gonna take."

"Yeah," Leonard said, "there's more."

I said, "Allow me, Leonard. I got something to add you don't know about."

"This have to do with where you were this morning?" Leonard said.

"Yeah," I said. "OK, Doc. I think you see it the way it is. Let me run over your territory and fill it in some more. Say there's this preacher, a real do-gooder in some ways, but you see, he comes from a background where his father was a religious nut too. Say the father wasn't actually the father, but a stepfather. The stepfather married this woman with a child, and this woman's child was a bastard. She was a prostitute, or at least a loose woman. The preacher, the stepfather, he thinks he can do right by her, show her the way of God. And perhaps, down deep, a whore is exactly what he's looking for. With me so far?"

"We're with you," Hanson said.

"So he marries the woman, but he can't reconcile the shame. He treats her badly. He treats the boy badly. He never lets them forget that she's a slut and the boy's a bastard, and that he's doing them special as the right hand of the Lord. The woman gets pregnant again. The child is retarded. The preacher can't stand it. He can't accept his seed would produce such a child. Now he has two bastards, and one of them has the sense of a cement block. He gets it in his mind the woman's gone back to her old ways, that she'd been with another man. Maybe she has, maybe she hasn't. It doesn't matter. The preacher broods, and one night something sets him off, and in a moment of anger he strikes and kills the woman."

"And the stepson sees it," Doc Warren said.

"Yeah. And let's say the preacher knows the boy saw it, but instead of killing the boy, who's already warped enough to think his father is God incarnate, he forces the child, or the child is willing, psychologically browbeat, however you want to put it . . . But say the boy goes along with the father to help get rid of the body. The father makes a religious ritual out of it. Perhaps to cover his guilt to the boy, to himself, both, or maybe he really believes that he's done the righteous will of the Lord.

252

"Out of brutality, or convenience, the preacher cuts the woman up to fit in a cardboard box, wraps her body parts in a cloth and takes her to this abandoned house he knows about, wraps the body in chicken wire, to keep the animals out of it, probably in cloth too, like the others, buries her under the house. Later, she comes up missing, he says she ran off. She's got a reputation to go with this possibility. What he was ashamed of before, now protects him. She was just a whore. She used a good man. She ran off and left him with two sons to raise, one of them retarded. See where I'm going?"

"This is guesswork, right?" Hanson said.

"Some of it," I said. "And now it takes up where you left off, Doc. The boy is continuing to do that work in his own way, copying his stepfather's pattern."

"Why isn't he killing women then?" Hanson said. "Me and Doc here, we dealt with a guy in Houston once, called himself the Houston Hacker. He had a thing against women, and women were all he killed, 'less someone got in the way. This kid sees his father kill a woman, why's he killing kids? Wouldn't he have a thing against women because his stepfather did, even if it was his mother?"

"That's easy," Doc Warren said. "He's killing himself. He's killing the nine- or ten-year-old fatherless, unwanted child that he was. Killing him in the righteous manner his stepfather killed his mother. He's not associating the crime with women, he's associating it with the evil of what she produced. A bastard. Himself. And somewhere, deep inside, he's maybe killing himself because his existence is what turned the stepfather against the woman in the first place."

"It has a nice ring to it," Charlie said. "It sounds like bullshit to me, but it rings nicely. It'd sound better you had them teeth in, though, Doc."

"What about the page of Psalms in the kid porn mags?" Doc Warren said. "You're suggesting this isn't a sex crime, but one of religious psychosis, so what's with that?"

"I really don't know," I said. "Maybe the whole thing has turned sexual for him. Somehow he's cleansing himself of that sinful preoccupation by getting rid of his magazines and destroying their power with a page of the Psalms. Like a cross in a vampire's grave. I really don't know. But here's another piece of the puzzle. The retarded child grew up to be only slightly smaller than the Empire State Building. He does what his brother tells him. He helps him do this thing he does. And they do it every summer, last week of August. Which is, probably, about the same time of year the first murder occurred, the mother's murder, and coincidently it's a great time of opportunity for our man. It's the week the East Side carnival comes to town, something our man helps sponsor."

"I'll be damned," Leonard said.

"Now for the sixty-four-thousand-dollar question," Hanson said. "Who the hell is it?"

"A fella I went to visit this morning," I said. "The guy who killed Illium Moon, and would have tried to kill Chester Pine if Chester hadn't died first. A preacher's son. *The* preacher's son. A preacher himself. Reverend Fitzgerald of the First Primitive Baptist Church."

36.

Space suits in daylight. Red worms in flashlight, writhing and twisting in dark, odoriferous lard. . . .

That night I lay in bed and remembered all that. It was not conducive to sleep.

I got up and went into the kitchen for a drink and saw Leonard had not made the couch into a bed. He was sitting on it watching television. The screen jumped with snow and rattled with static.

The movie he was watching was coming from a long ways, and the cheap rabbit ears weren't picking it up too well. I could see it clear enough to make out noble German shepherds crawling on their bellies toward some nasty space aliens. I recognized the movie. *I Married a Monster from Outer Space.* It had scared me when I was a kid. I doubted any monster movie would scare me again.

I forgot the drink of water and went over to the couch and sat down by Leonard. He didn't look at me. I saw in the reflected light of the television screen that he had tears in his eyes.

I turned my attention to the TV set. The aliens were catching hell now, both from German shepherds and good-old American citizens who weren't going to stand for no space aliens messin' with their women.

I said, "You all right?"

"Yeah."

"Uncle Chester?"

"Yeah."

We sat until the end of the movie and then another one started up. This one was about a guy that got some kind of radiation on him and grew incredibly big and had to wear a loincloth.

Leonard said, "What about you and Florida?"

"What about us?"

"That bad?"

"She just wants to be friends. I don't know how you fags work, but a gal wants to be your friend after you've been fucking her, it usually means she doesn't want to be anything to you but gone."

"I'm usually the one wants to be friends. I used to want a relationship. These days, the shit I've been through, except when I have a hard-on, celibacy seems acceptable and preferable. You, on the other hand, don't feel that way. If ever there was a guy wanted to be married and have two kids and a dog in the yard, it's you."

"Call me transparent."

The big guy on the screen was starting to have some serious trouble with the U.S. Army. They were blasting the shit out of him.

"This murder case," Leonard said, "how do you think we did?"

"It's not over, but I think we did all right. Hanson believes he solves this case he'll be in for a promotion. Him and Charlie both."

"Charlie don't think that. Told me he's put in applications at burger joints, claims he's one hell of a cook."

"What Charlie is, is full of shit."

"Hap, what if we're wrong, and it ain't Fitzgerald?"

"It's him. And his brother too, though I don't know you can count T.J. as knowing what he's doing. He's like a fuckin' golem. Just does what he's told."

"We got so much circumstantial evidence, Hanson could get a warrant. Look around the church and Fitzgerald's house. That might be better than this plan of nabbing the Reverend at the carnival with a kid in hand. Whatcha want to bet Hanson gets a warrant, looks hard enough, he'll find some dead kid's underwear with the Reverend's cum in 'em?"

"But if he doesn't, then the motherfucker's tipped off and he can get real careful. Hanson plays it his way, he just might nab him. Fitzgerald puts his hands on a kid, kidnaps him, then Hanson's got something to work with, a righteous reason to bring the bastard in. Then, with a little luck, the rest of it will come out."

"We're out of this now, right?"

"You betcha."

"Hap, not that I'm petty or anything, but I told you Uncle Chester wasn't the one."

"I shouldn't have doubted you."

"I'm a good judge of character."

"I'm proof of that."

Leonard was silent for a moment. "Well, even I fuck up now and then."

The All Black Carnival came to the East Side on a hot morning that threatened storm. The storm lay in the west, dark as an army boot, and the heavens rattled with poisonous thunder.

Our fear was the storm blew in, the carnival might be canceled, and if that happened, Hanson's plan was gone with the wind, and the Reverend would have to wait for another night. Strike somewhere unexpected.

Me and Leonard were out of it, but we couldn't resist the temptation to drive over to the fairgrounds early that morning and watch the carnival trucks pull in behind the tall chain-link fence, observe the machineries of fun going up: the Tilt-a-Whirl, the coaster rides, the Slingshot, as well as rides I couldn't put a name to.

I kept wondering how Fitzgerald was nabbing those kids and getting them away from there to commit murder. He was a high-profile individual. People on the East Side knew him well and weren't likely to forget him walking off with some kid, but somehow, every year, he was grabbing a kid and taking him up to that death house.

How was he choosing his victim? Was the kid someone Fitzgerald had been watching, someone who'd been attending church activities? Someone Fitzgerald knew would be going to the carnival? Someone whose home life was a disaster, or someone who had no home life at all? Someone whose past would indicate anything could have happened? Someone like the little boy under Uncle Chester's floor?

I tried to tell myself it wasn't my problem now. It was Hanson's. We drove back home.

About two in the afternoon, Leonard and I went over to MeMaw's, and Hiram helped us finish up the porch. There wasn't a lot left to do. About an hour's work. It was very hot.

The sky was clear and blue except in the west, and from those brooding clouds there came a kind of mugginess that was almost overwhelming, and I couldn't get my mind off the oncoming night and the carnival and what might happen. I hit my thumb with the hammer three or four times, dropped boards and nails, and cussed enough Hiram had to ask me to stop.

"No offense, Hap," Hiram said. "But I don't talk that way, and don't want that kind of talk around Mama. She might hear you."

I apologized, truly embarrassed for making Hiram uncomfortable. I hoped MeMaw hadn't heard me.

When we had driven the last nail, Hiram said, "Come on in. Mama'll want y'all to have some ice tea."

"I need it," I said.

Hiram went inside, and Leonard and I promised to follow, after picking up a few nails and boards. When Hiram was out of sight, Leonard said, "I'm fucking ashamed of you, all that cussing."

"Yeah, well, you can eat shit."

Then we heard Hiram yell for us from inside the house.

"Hap! Leonard! Oh, God! Come here, quick!"

We rushed inside. MeMaw was slumped in a kitchen chair, almost falling off of it. There was a pool of urine in the seat of the chair, dripping on the floor. Her walker was turned over, as if she had let go of it in the act of trying to rise.

The stroke had come swift and silent, lethal as a black mamba. She was alive, but comatose. We stretched her out on the floor and packed a pillow behind her head and called the ambulance. They came quick, hauled her off to Memorial Hospital. We followed after, Hiram in his van, me and Leonard in my truck.

At the hospital, we sat with Hiram in the waiting room while the doctors did their work. Which wasn't much. The bottom line was MeMaw was old and it didn't look good. All they could do—all we could do—was wait.

When we got the word, me and Leonard went into ICU with Hiram and looked at MeMaw. She was wired up like a spaceman and seemed to be smaller and frailer than was humanly possible. I was somehow reminded of those pictures you see of Mexican mummies, the ones that have been exhumed and put on display because the relatives couldn't afford to maintain the burial plot. I noted the liver spots on her hands. Why hadn't I noticed them before? They looked like old pennies viewed through weak coffee.

We stayed for a while, then Leonard said, "Hiram, we'll check back. You need anything, just ask."

"Yeah," Hiram said. "Thanks. Man, I can't believe this. I mean, I can. Her being old and all, but I can't believe it either."

"I know," Leonard said.

"Need us to call relatives?" I asked.

"No," Hiram said. "A few minutes, I'll do that."

We left Hiram sitting by MeMaw's bedside, holding her hand.

37.

Late that afternoon, the storm in the west really started to boil, turned darker, and moved our way. We were sitting on the porch glider, watching it, when Hanson drove up.

He walked up on the porch with his cigar in his mouth. The end of it was dead, but I could tell it had recently been lit. There were ashes all over his cheap sports coat.

I said, "I thought you quit smoking."

"I did," he said, "and I just did again. Listen here, I wanted to tell you it's going down. You deserve that much. It's all over, I'll tell you how it went."

"We'd appreciate that," Leonard said.

261

He nodded, turned, and looked toward the storm clouds. "Man," he said.

"It's moving slow," Leonard said. "Things could still go all right, he makes his move soon enough."

"Yeah, well," Hanson said, "see you."

He went out to his car, and I watched as he lit the cigar and took up smoking again before he drove away.

"Nice guy," Leonard said.

"Yeah," I said. "Thing I like best about him is he took my woman and he sucks on a nasty old cigar. Asshole."

We watched the storm some more, then got in Leonard's car and drove over to the First Primitive Baptist Church, telling each other all the way over we were just going to have a look.

We didn't pull up out front of the place but parked a block down. There wasn't much to see from there, but before we parked, we drove by once, and I was able to see that the bus and the Chevy were still in the yard. I also noted that a block up from the church, parked on the opposite side of the street, facing the wrong way, was what looked like an unmarked police car. I didn't recognize the balding white guy behind the wheel, but he looked like a cop and he had his eyes on the church. I thought it was a good thing Fitzgerald wasn't expecting anything. This guy was about as inconspicuous as a pink pig in overalls.

We drove on by and went around the block and came back the other way and parked. From where we sat we could see the church and we could see the cop car. Gradually we saw less of both. It turned dark and the storm clouds from the west turned it darker yet.

After a while, lights came on inside the church, then outside of it, lighting up the driveway. An hour passed and cars began to pull up at the curb, and one, a tan Volkswagen, drove around back. Men and women and kids got out of the cars and walked up to the church, around the side of it, and out of sight.

Another fifteen minutes went by, and men and women came away from the church without their kids, got in their cars, and drove away. I thought about that. Parents bringing their kids to a safe place, the church. Leaving them with someone safe, the Reverend, assured in their hearts that their kids were off to have a good time.

And most likely they were. It wasn't the loved kids the Reverend wanted, so just exactly what was the Reverend's game? Figuring what he did want made my head hurt.

A minute or two later, the short bus came out from behind the church with its lights on. I could see the Reverend driving, glimpsed the shadowed forms of kids through the windows. The bus turned left and drove past the cop car and on down the street.

The cop car fired up quick and pulled around in the center of the street and went after the bus. Mr. Sneak. He might as well have been standing on a bucket, jerking his dick and singing a song.

Leonard cranked up and we followed after. Actually, neither we nor the cop had to be sneaky. The bus did what we expected it to do. It drove straight to the carnival, paused at the gate and went on into the fairgrounds. So far, things were going as expected.

Not having a special pass, we, along with the cop, parked outside of the fence, and walked up to the gate. When we got there, we were standing behind the cop. The guy at the gate, a black guy with a physique like the Pillsbury Dough Boy and black glasses with white tape on the nose bar, wouldn't let the cop in because he didn't have a dollar. The cop, a hard-boiled guy wearing what was once called a leisure suit, a style of clothing that went out of favor and production not long after the demise of the seventy-five-cent paperback, wanted to show him his badge and let that do.

"I don't need a badge," said the fat gatekeeper. "I need a dollar."

"Listen, this is police business," the cop said.

"You're shittin' me," the gatekeeper said. "The carnival's police business?"

"Here," I said, handing the gatekeeper a dollar. "Let him in for heaven's sake. You're holding up the line."

The gatekeeper took the dollar. The cop eyed us the way cops do, said thanks like he didn't mean it, and went inside. The gatekeeper said to me, "Man, look at this, two white guys back to back, ain't that some kind of lucky omen or something?"

"Two white guys, one in an ugly leisure suit, means it's going to rain," I said.

"I can believe that," the gatekeeper said, "That guy, I don't think he's on cop business at all. I think he's too used to free meals and shit. That might work uptown, but not here. And where'd he get that suit? What the hell color was that anyway?"

"Orange or rust or dirty gold," Leonard said. "Take your pick."

We paid and went inside. We saw the cop walking toward the lot where the permitted vehicles were parked. He walked wide of the lot and onto the pea gravel, went over and leaned against the fence where the carnival lights were weak, got a cigarette out, lit it, and tried not to act as if he was looking at the bus. He wasn't very good at it.

The bus door opened and Fitzgerald got off the bus, and a line of loud, excited kids came out behind him, followed by a pretty, middle-aged black woman. I assumed she was one of the kid's mothers, helping the Reverend out.

The kids, mostly six to ten years in age, evenly split between girls and boys, bounced on their toes and stood in a line that gyrated like a garter snake on a hot rock. The woman and Reverend Fitzgerald chatted amiably. He smiled. She smiled.

The Reverend went back to the bus and leaned inside, then leaned out. I thought maybe he had said something to someone inside. T.J. perhaps. From where we stood, no one was visible, but the plywood window replacements in the back and on the side could have hidden them.

The Reverend smiled at the woman again. They spoke. Half the kids went with her, the other half with the Reverend. Mr. Leisure Suit followed after the Reverend and his charges. T.J., the walking eclipse, did not make an appearance.

Me and Leonard were trying to decide what we were going to do next, when Hanson walked up and surprised us. "You assholes," he said. We turned and got a look at him. He was his usual pleasant-looking self, but he no longer had his cigar. I presumed it was in his pocket. I hoped he remembered to put it out before he put it up. "Didn't I just see you fucks? I said I'd let you know."

"I'll say this," Leonard said, "you walk light for a big dude."

"It's my fuckin' Indian blood. What you two doin' here? I said you were out. You done more than you're supposed to already."

"And very well, I might add," said Leonard.

"Don't let your dicks get too hard," Hanson said. "You did all right, but you had some luck."

"So did you," I said. "We came along."

"You didn't even know for sure you had a case before we showed up," Leonard said.

"I still don't know I got anything," Hanson said.

"Bullshit," I said.

"All right," Hanson said, "you're goddamn wizards of detection. Now go home or take in the carnival. I want you out of my way. I mean it now. I got men on the job, and they even know what they're doin'. Well, they got an idea, anyway."

We left Hanson and walked around the carnival. It was bright with lights and the sounds of voices and the cranking of machinery and the blasting of music, presumably conceived by ears of tin and played on matching instruments. There was the smell of sweat from excited children and tired adults, the butter-rich aroma of popcorn and the sugar-sick sweetness of cotton candy, the burning stench of fresh animal shit from the petting zoo.

We were over by the petting zoo when we came across Hiram. He was standing there with his hands in his pockets, looking forlorn as a man who'd just prematurely ejaculated. He was looking at a spotted goat.

We walked up beside him. I said, "Hiram."

He turned and looked at me, but it took him a moment to know I was there.

"Oh, hi," he said.

"Surprised to see you here," Leonard said.

"Mama's with my sister. She drove down."

"How is MeMaw?" I asked.

He shook his head. "Same. Doctor said she could stay like that awhile. A day, six months."

"I'm sorry," I said.

"Me too," Leonard said.

"I had to get out, you know?" he said.

"Sure," I said. "Nothing wrong with that. There's not a lot you can do."

"I just needed a break," he said. "Even if I just end up watching a goat."

Hiram turned back to watch the goat, and a little boy came up and started petting it. We stood there in awkward silence for a time, then said good-bye and slipped away.

"Too bad," Leonard said as we bought cotton candy. "I like MeMaw and Hiram."

"Yeah," I said, "but she lived a full life. We all got to check out sometime."

"It's not dying I hate for her," Leonard said. "It's lingering. I think we embarrassed Hiram."

"Yeah, he feels guilty. Like he ought to be with her, but there's just so much of the deathwatch a person can take."

"You know what?"

"What?"

"This cotton candy is making me sick."

I guess we wandered around for a couple of hours. We saw the Reverend and his kids and their leisure-suited shadow a few times, but the Reverend didn't see us. We saw Melton, aka Mohawk, walking with a young black girl who looked as if she had not long back abandoned her training bra and dolls. They went around behind a hot dog stand and we lost sight of them. We saw Hanson a few times. He looked as sullen as ever, as if the sight of us was causing his nuts to shrink.

As we strolled, a lot of blacks looked at me like I was an exotic animal, maybe belonged in the petting zoo. And in a way, I suppose I was exotic, least here and on this night. There were only a handful of white people at the carnival, and some of them were cops.

Another hour passed, and you could smell the storm on the warm night wind. It mixed with the other aromas and became a heady cocktail. You could taste electricity in the air. The machinery that wound around and around and took the children up into the sky and back down again, creaked and whined and groaned and squeaked and rattled bolts in its metal joints and made me nervous. Off in the distance, amid that swirling darkness, was the occasional flash of lightning, like a liquid tuning fork thrown against the sky.

Not long after the lightning flashes, the machineries stopped and the rides got canceled. All that was left was the petting zoo and the booths where you lost your money trying to throw softballs into bushel baskets or baseballs through hoops.

A half-hour later they canceled the whole thing and disgruntled patrons were moving toward the gate. Before we got out of there, the rain blew in, came faster and harder than anyone would have expected. Through the sheets of aluminum-colored rain, the lights of the carnival were like winking gold coins at the bottom of a fountain, and now there was nothing to smell but the rain, and the rain was cold, and within seconds Leonard and I were soaking wet.

We made our way through the crowd and out to the car. We sat there and watched as people rushed out and cars pulled away. We watched as the short church bus came through the gate and drove off. We drove off after it.

The deluge was intense, and the bus drove slowly, and so did we, and so did Leisure Suit. He was following behind us. After a little bit, we decided to beat the bus back to the church, get our parking place. As we passed, Leonard said, "Hap, the Reverend ain't driving. It's that woman. I don't see him at all."

I drove on around, tires sloshing and tossing water. "Don't mean he isn't there. I didn't see the woman when they left the church. He could be in back."

"Yeah, but . . . I don't know. Something sucks the big ole donkey dick here."

We beat the bus, got our parking place, turned off the lights, and sat there and ate from a box of M&Ms Leonard had left in the glove box. They had melted into a colorful mess, but we ate them anyway. We were licking our fingers when the bus drove up to the church and stopped in the driveway.

"Reckon they're staying close to the curb to help the parents out," Leonard said. "Kids are already soaked to the bone."

Leisure Suit drove over to the curb opposite the church and parked facing the wrong way.

"Cop is less smart now than he was earlier," Leonard said. "I don't think he's even made us yet, ain't figured we been riding around behind him and paying his way into the carnival. Mr. Sneaky, he don't see any connection between us and him and the bus."

"As the day wears on," I said, "a cop's brain settles. It's kind of like sediment."

"And he ain't fueled by the magic of melted M&Ms."

"There's that too."

"Ain't the green M&Ms supposed to do something to you?" Leonard said. "I always heard you had to watch the green ones."

"The guy at the factory, he jacks off in the juice makes the green ones, that's what I heard."

"No," Leonard said, "that's the mayonnaise at McDonald's, or Burger King, or one of those places. It's supposed to be a black man does it. That way it scares the shit out of the peckerwoods, 'cause the black customers, they're in on it, it's a conspiracy-type thing. They know to hold the mayonnaise. The white folks, they don't all know about it, so some of 'em eat it. Oh, and the black guy, he's got AIDS."

"No shit?"

"No shit. Ain't that awful, a nigger with AIDS jacking off in the poor honkie folks' mayonnaise?"

"A queer nigger, of course?"

"Without question. And he's ugly too."

38.

We sat there until our asses and the seatcovers seemed one and the same, then the cars started to arrive and park at the curb, beating their wipers against the rain.

It was hard to see with the rain the way it was, but we could see kids come off the bus and rush into cars, and those cars would go away, then more would show up, and a new flock of kids would come off the bus, and pretty soon all the cars were gone, and no more came. The bus cranked up, turned on its lights, drove to the back of the church.

"What now?" Leonard said.

Before I could answer, the tan Volkswagen, which I had

forgotten about, came out from behind the church and turned left. The church lights gave me enough of a view to tell the driver was the woman who had been driving the bus, and she had a little girl with her. Mom, having done her duty, was on her way home with her own child.

"You're right," I said. "I don't think the Reverend was on the bus when it came back. He could have got off out back just now, but I don't think so. I think he stayed at the carnival."

"We've been hoodwinked, and not on purpose," Leonard said. "I can't figure how Fitzgerald did it exactly, but he had prearranged plans with the woman. I don't mean she was in on it—"

"I know what you mean. He had her drive the kids back, but he had a kid in mind wasn't on the bus."

"Someone won't be missed. Some kid he gave a free pass to. And he had another way of leaving the carnival other than the bus."

"If we're right," I said, "where does that leave us?"

"With the clock ticking," Leonard said.

We sat silent for a moment, then almost in unison said: "The Hampstead place."

Leonard drove us by the cop in the leisure suit. He was still watching the church. He didn't even blink as we went by.

We made our way to the Hampstead place from Uncle Chester's. Up through the woods on foot. The rain hadn't slacked, and it was slow going. The wind had picked up and turned surprisingly cool, and it tossed the rain hard as gravel. Tree branches whipped and cut us, and our single flashlight did little to punch a hole in the darkness. We hadn't taken the time to get rain slickers, so we were soaked to the skin. I wished now we'd bothered to get guns. But all we'd brought were ourselves and the flashlight in Leonard's car.

When we got to the Hampstead place, we were exhausted. We didn't want Fitzgerald and his brother to see us coming, so I turned off the flashlight just before we broke out of the woods, into the partial clearing.

Out there, with no light, pitch dark without moon or starlight, the rain hammering us like ball bearings, we only had our instincts to guide us. It was rough going. We could hear the boards in the old house creaking, begging the wind to leave it alone, and we linked arms and let those sounds guide us. I barked a shin on a porch step, and Leonard followed suit. We climbed onto the porch, trying to be as quiet as possible, which was difficult when you felt like your leg was broken. We found our way along the porch to the busted-out window we had used before, cautiously crawled inside.

Rain was driving into the house from the hole in the ceiling and the hole in the roof above. It was so dark inside we couldn't see the rain, but we could hear it and feel it. We listened for other sounds, the sounds of movement, but there was only the wind and the expected creaking of lumber.

We had no recourse but to turn on the flash, and we used it to avoid the breaks in the boards, but still they squeaked as we walked. We went through the room with the chifforobe and into the kitchen, and it was dry there, and I realized suddenly that my nerves were starting to settle. The pounding rain had been like a severe case of Chinese water torture.

But as soon as we were both inside the kitchen, not really expecting to find anyone since we'd heard neither movement or seen illumination, my flashlight caught a shadow on my left, and I whipped the light that way, and the shadow came at me. I swung the flashlight, and there was a grunt and a shattering of bulb, and the light went out. Then I felt hands on me. I shifted my body and jabbed with an elbow and then there was light on the right of me and I saw Leonard out of the corner of my eye, and he was planting a side kick in a man's midsection, and in that same instant my hands felt their way around my injured attacker's body, and I hip-threw him hard against the floor. Then a light shot up at me from the floor, and behind the light the shadow shape said, "Goddamn you, Hap."

It was Charlie.

The cop Leonard kicked was named Gleason. I had seen him the day they tore Uncle Chester's flooring up. He was the fat cop with the bad toupee Mohawk had yelled at. He wasn't any slimmer, and now his bad toupee was wet and in the light of his and Charlie's flashlight, it looked like some kind of strange tribal skullcap.

Leonard had really planted that kick. Gleason took a long time to start breathing naturally, but the guy had enough fat nothing got broken. Charlie wasn't feeling that good either. He had a knot on the side of his head where I had connected with the flashlight.

"Man, that flashlight hurt," Charlie said.

"Sorry," I said.

"Goddamn, you motherfuckers are quick."

"How's the head?" I said.

"It hurts, what'ya think?" Charlie rubbed the knot on his head. "Goddamn."

"Sorry, Charlie. If it's any consolation, I think you broke Leonard's flashlight."

"Yeah, well, buy another. My head, I just got this one. What the fuck you two doing here?"

We told him.

"You think Hanson didn't think of covering this place?" Charlie said. "Jesus, we may not be the incredibly clever sleuths you boys are, but we think of a few things. We even brought along a lunch."

"Charlie forgot the chips, though," Gleason said. "I told him twicet about the chips, and he still forgot 'em. A sandwich without chips ain't no good."

"Would you lose the chips, Gleason?" Charlie said.

"I just said you forgot is all," Gleason said.

"The point here is not that I forgot the chips out of our lunch," Charlie said, "it's that you two morons are screwing stuff up."

"I told you we're sorry," I said. "Jesus, what you want us to do, shoot ourselves?"

"You could have fucked up an investigation."

"Considering Fitzgerald hasn't showed yet," Leonard said, "I think things are already fucked."

"Man," Gleason said, "I think this guy busted something inside."

Charlie put the light on Gleason. "You're all right. Lose some fuckin' weight. And take off that stupid toup."

"He ought to leave it," Leonard said. "The bad guys show up, he can scare 'em with it."

"Yeah, well, you guys laugh," Gleason said. "I had this special fitted."

"Fitted for what?" Leonard said. "A fence post? You got more head than you got hair there. You need to shoot and field-dress another mop, pal."

"Right, you're Vidal Sassoon," Gleason said.

And that's when we heard someone coming through the woods from the back of the house.

"The lights," Charlie said, and he killed the flash and Gleason killed his. We listened as the tromping came closer.

Charlie whispered, "Spread out, here's you guys' chance to use that karate shit on someone deserves it."

We spread out. I took position by the door that led into the kitchen. I knew Charlie was somewhere to the left of me, and Leonard and Gleason were across the way.

We waited and the tromping went on around the side of the house and onto the front porch, then we heard the porch boards squeak, and not long after, the inside boards squeaked louder. The squeaking came our way. I felt the hair on the back of my neck bristle and there was a tightening of the groin and a loosening of the bowels. A light came from the room with the chifforobe, and the light bobbed into the kitchen, and a man came after it. Then the light swung to the right and its beam fell square and solid on Gleason, standing there like a stuffed bear, his toupee dangling off his skull like an otter clinging to a rock.

"Hey," the startled man with the light said, and it was Fitzgerald's voice, and for a moment, time was suspended. Then time came loose and from behind Fitzgerald a monstrous shadow charged into the room, and I moved, and everyone else moved, and I realized then that someone was running away from the chifforobe room, someone who had been with Fitzgerald and his brother, someone who had panicked.

I started to go after him, but I couldn't get past the Reverend, so I stepped in and hit him with a right cross to the jaw and he dropped the flashlight and staggered across the room and Gleason grabbed him. When I hit him, the flash hit the floor and went around and around, showing Gleason and the Reverend, then shadow, then light, then the flash quit rolling and pinned them.

The big shadow was T.J., of course, and when Gleason grabbed Fitzgerald, T.J. grabbed Gleason, got him by the head with his huge hands, held it like it was a basketball he was about to shoot.

I heard the one who got away fall through some boards in the front room, heard him grunt and scramble, then Gleason let go of Fitzgerald, and Fitzgerald spun and hit Gleason in the stomach with a hook, and though I was already moving, and so were the others, it was all too fast. T.J. had Gleason good. He twisted Gleason's head like he was screwing the lid off a stubborn pickle jar. Gleason's sad toupee popped loose, soared above the light of the flash, then came back to it like a hairy UFO and slapped the floor. Behind it all, you could hear Gleason's neck crack like a plastic swizzle stick.

"Stop them!" Fitzgerald yelled to T.J., and Charlie was on Fitzgerald, and Leonard stepped in and kicked T.J. flush in the groin and drove his palm up into the giant's chin, and the giant grunted and reached for Leonard, and Leonard moved away into shadow.

Charlie flew into me unconscious, courtesy of Fitzgerald's left hook. I eased Charlie aside, and me and Fitzgerald came together.

The rhythm of our punches and the constant kicking of Leonard against T.J.'s body filled the room. I hit Fitzgerald with a jab and he hooked me to the body and I felt a rib crack, but I'd had that before. It wasn't poking through the skin, so it was a pain I could isolate. I bobbed in and jabbed again and threw an overhand right, but Fitzgerald had moved out of the moon of light the flashlight provided, and I threw my punch at movement instead of substance. He leaned away and landed another in my ribs, same spot; it hurt like a knife had gone there.

But I had something Fitzgerald didn't have: a four-wheel drive. I kicked him hard in the side of the leg, just above the knee, and he wobbled into the light, and I could see him good now, and I hit him with a right in the face and kicked with a left roundhouse to his ribs. He faded back into the darkness and ran.

I turned to look at Leonard, just as Leonard scoop-kicked the inside of T.J.'s knee, then side-snap-kicked to the front of it. T.J. went down with a yell, hit the floorboards hard, rolled over and screamed, tried to get up, but the shattered knee wouldn't hold him.

I heard Fitzgerald break through glass and kick out window struttings, then I heard him drop to the ground outside. I grabbed the flashlight and went after him, my ribs throbbing. When I got to the window and started through, I heard Fitzgerald scream like a man with a stick in his eye, then the scream turned to an echo, then a flat, soul-breaking whine.

I dropped to the ground and shone the light around. The rain was still pounding, and even with the light it was hard to see. I could hear him, though: "Yea, though I walk through the valley of the shadow of death . . . Oh, Jesus, not this way."

I went toward the sound, and it was coming from the old well. Fitzgerald had tumbled down there in the darkness. I cautiously slid up to the pile of rubble that had been the well's rock foundation, bent over, and shone the light down.

Fitzgerald wasn't saying anything now, he wasn't making any kind of sound, but he was alive. I could see his eyes blinking at the rain. The well was not wide, and the fall had been hard, and there was all manner of rubble down there—rocks from the curbing, limbs and brush, stagnant water—and he had hit in such a way that his waist was twisted and his legs were turned at an angle only pipe cleaners should make.

"I'll get you out," I said.

But he wasn't listening. He bent his head toward his chest, and his ruined body shifted and his chin went to his knees, which were too high up for anyone but an acrobat, then he was still. He eased slowly into the water, then hung on some kind of debris.

I didn't need an M.D. to tell me the Reverend Fitzgerald had passed into darkness. I held the light on him for a time, watched the rain beat him, realized that the way he was now, he looked like nothing more than a peaceful embryo waiting for birth.

I went back to the house by the porch and window. I didn't see anyone lurking about. I found where the one who had gotten away had fallen through the boards, and down there I found something else too. Lying on his side on the ground, a black bag over his head, hands bound behind his back, ankles tied, was a child.

I got the boy out of there and pulled the bag off his head. He had a bandanna around his mouth, and under that something stuffed in his mouth, and he was having a hard time breathing. I got the thing out of his mouth and saw that it was a sock. I sat him on the side of the floor where the boards had given away, let his legs dangle. He looked at me. He was shaking.

"Please," he said.

"It's OK, son. I'm not one of them."

"Please."

I saw there was something else down in the hole, and got back down in there and grabbed it. It was a large piece of cloth, and under it was a book of the Psalms. I wrapped the book up in the cloth, which wasn't just a cloth at all, and picked the boy up and made my way around the gap in the boards and carried him into the kitchen. He was stiff and frightened. I sat him on the floor with his back against the wall. He saw T.J. twisting on the floor, and he started to struggle, but the ties on his hands and feet prevented any real movement. He merely fell over and lay still.

"Easy," I said. "You're OK now."

I glanced over and saw that Leonard had gotten Charlie's handcuffs and was putting them on T.J. T.J. kept yelling over and over, "Bubba. Bubba."

When Leonard had T.J.'s arms cuffed behind his back, he limped over to where me and the boy were.

"The runner lost the prizes," I said, and lay the cloth and the Psalm book on the floor.

Leonard got out his pocket knife, and the boy flinched and made a sound like something dying.

"It's OK," Leonard said, and he cut the boy's hands and feet free. "We got 'em for you, boy."

Free, the child lay on the floor with his knees drawn to his chest. "They hurt you?" Leonard asked him.

The boy didn't answer. He stared at Leonard. Leonard stroked the boy's head. "Gonna be all right."

I checked on Gleason. It didn't take much of an examination to determine he wouldn't be coming around. His head was twisted at such an angle it made my throat hurt. I found his toupee and stuck it on his head as best I could.

I went over then and looked at Charlie. He was lying on his back, conscious, but weak. "Where's it hurt?" I asked.

"My head," Charlie said. "Jesus, what a lick. The world's spinning. I'd rather you hit me with the flashlight again."

"Left hook," I said. "He had a good one. He hasn't got anything now."

"You kill him?"

"The old well took care of him." I worked Charlie's coat off of him, folded it up and put it under his head. "Man, you going to have to go shopping. This suit coat is ruined. Pocket's ripped clean the hell off of it."

"Got his hand caught in it," Charlie said. "Think Kmart'll take it back?"

"Even they got to draw a line somewhere."

"Gleason?"

"Afraid not. Take it easy, now. You might have a concussion. I'll get some help."

"Hanson don't hear from us in a while, he'll be up here."

"I'm not going to wait that long, Charlie."

I went back to Leonard. He said, "My ankle's bad twisted. I've got down here now and can't get up. It's swollen from me kicking that big devil. I must have hit wrong. I think I'll have to cut off the shoe."

"Leonard, it's not over yet."

"I know. You'll get him, won't you? For me and you, and Uncle Chester?"

"You know it."

"And Hanson for that matter. Boy is he gonna be pissed."

"That's how I like him best. Pissed . . . You'll be all right?"

"Get him, Hap. Get him now."

I folded the cloth around the Psalmbook and went away.

* * *

It took me a while to get from the Hampstead place back down to Uncle Chester's, but not as long as it had taken us to go up there. I wasn't trying to sneak and the rain had subsided. I thought all the way down. I thought about how stupid I'd been. I was so mad my ribs didn't even hurt.

When I got to Uncle Chester's, I went on past and across the street to MeMaw's. The porch light was on, and Hiram's muddy van was in the driveway. The porch overhang was dripping water like rain off the bill of a cap. I climbed on the porch and knocked on the door. A full minute passed before Hiram answered. He was wearing a different set of clothes than I had seen him wearing at the carnival. His hair was wet and his face was flushed and sweaty. He was a little out of breath. He had his van keys in his hand.

I said, "How's MeMaw?"

"The same," he said. "I'm going up there."

"Can I come in?"

"Man, I don't mean to be rude, but I got to run. I was just going out."

"I just need a minute," I said and pushed my way inside, and he closed the door. The house had the faint and pleasant aroma of home cooking. I looked at the photographs on the wall, the picture of Jesus behind the stove. The cheap, yellowed curtains. The place seemed a lot less clean than when I had seen it last, and smaller, and darker.

Hiram said, "You look like hell."

"I been busy. I bet you're fixing to light out, aren't you?"

"What I was saying. I got to get back to the hospital. I need to get on back right now, spell my sister."

"I think you think the Reverend's going to do some talking. I don't think you're going to the hospital. I think you're going to run like a goddamn deer."

He looked at me, trying to think of something to say. "The Reverend?" he said.

"Did you know you and I just missed each other?" I said.

"How's that?"

"I got something for you that'll explain."

I went over to the kitchen table, took the cloth out from under my arm, and shook the book of Psalms out of it. I took the American flag, popped it wide, let it float down over the table and the book.

"I believe you dropped this," I said. "At least it wasn't the Texas flag. . . . You were going to wrap a child's body in it, weren't you, Hiram. Stick a sheet from the Psalms in one of the magazines hidden up there. That day I was over here, you quoted part of a Bible verse. That was from the Psalms, wasn't it? MeMaw saw you got religious training."

"Hap—"

"You didn't know I was at the house, Hiram. You thought the Reverend was caught and going to talk, and you were just about to make a run for it. You know what? Fitzgerald's dead. And T.J., hell, he wouldn't remember you an hour from now. Not so it'd cause you any trouble anyway. But you panicked, and that's what nails you."

"Hap—"

"Oh yeah, there is someone who'll remember you. You dropped the kid too. The one you were watching at the petting zoo. I bet he got a good look at you, seeing how it wouldn't have mattered had things gone according to plan. Simple plan, huh? Fitzgerald loaded the kids back in the bus, said he had to stay for some reason, would catch a ride, whatever, then you helped him grab the boy. Or rather you helped trick the boy. He was someone Fitzgerald knew from the church, someone he gave a frcc pass to, someone he was acting like a father to, one of the lost ones. And T.J., he was on the bus, but he got off too, to help. He'd do anything for his brother."

"You got to understand, Hap. I didn't start any of this."

"I don't need to understand anything. All I understand is you and Fitz and T.J., every year, killed a young boy, cut him up and buried him under that house. That's all I need to understand. The why of it doesn't mean a thing to me."

"I was going to stop. Really."

"No. I don't think so. And it doesn't matter anyway."

Hiram seemed to consider a moment, then whirled and snatched up one of the kitchen chairs and came for me. He brought it around and hit me on the side, and my injured ribs exploded with pain, but I moved into him as he swung, and cut the force of the blow. I grabbed his face with both my hands and slammed my forehead forward, into his nose, and he jerked back, spewing blood. He dropped the chair, fell leaning against the stove. The impact shook the wall, and the picture of Jesus rocked on its nail and came loose and fell on top of the stove and the glass shattered.

He came at me again, but I moved in with a right to the stomach, hooked a left to his head. It wasn't a good left. My ribs hurt too bad to put the torque into it. He hit me high above the ear, not a good shot, but all those blows I'd taken from Fitzgerald were wearing on me. I could feel my legs going rubber. I covered my face with my arms and fist and let him chunk a while. He wasn't any better a boxer than he had been before, just a scrapper, and his wind wasn't any better either. The blows stung a little, but Leonard gave me worse when we sparred.

After a few hits Hiram began to breathe hard through his mouth, gulping air like a whale gulping plankton. I broke my cover and hooked between his hands with a solid right and took out what breath he had left, then put him down with a swinging elbow. That last technique made my injured rib move a way it wasn't supposed to move, and I felt it stab against my side. The damn thing had been cracked, and now it had broken loose. I couldn't help but lean against the sink and feel sick, and when I turned to look at Hiram, he was up. He'd gotten a butcher knife off the cabinet, and he lunged at me with it. He wasn't any better a knife fighter than he was a boxer.

I parried the lunge to the outside with my arm and grabbed his wrist and pulled him off balance and tugged him against the sink counter and used my free hand to strike him behind the head with my forearm, driving him down into the porcelain sink. His head made a sound like a clay jar breaking and he went out, would have hit the floor if his chin hadn't hung on the edge of the sink. I kicked his feet out from under him and he went down, sprawled on the floor with blood running out of his mouth. His hand opened slowly, like a flower blooming, and the knife lay free in his palm. I kicked it away. I stood over him a moment, feeling something I couldn't put a name to.

Finally, I leaned against the sink and tried to get my breath. I was starting to lose it. MeMaw's kitchen was spinning like a Disney World ride. I turned on the faucet and ran some cold water into my hands and splashed it on my face and rubbed it through my hair. That didn't help much. I held my head low in the sink beneath the faucet and let the water run over my neck and the back of my skull. A few minutes later the spinning stopped and my rib really began to ache.

I eased my way over to the phone and called the law, asked them to patch me through to Lieutenant Hanson, and to tell him his good buddy Hap Collins was on the line with a murderer in tow.

39.

Four nights after Hiram went down, MeMaw died, and two months later I was still thinking about her. I was glad she never woke up. Never knew. Hiram had lied about his sister being with MeMaw. He'd never called anyone. The need to kill had been so strong inside him, he'd left his dying mother's side to do what he felt he had to do. The whole thing haunted me like a ghost.

I was thinking about this one warm but pleasant afternoon while me and Leonard were out on the lake fishing, not catching anything, of course, just drifting around in the boat, untangling moss from our lines and watching birds fly over.

At least most of the mosquitoes had called it a season. It was still warm enough that a few of them came out on scouting missions, looking for a place to land, a place to refuel, a place that generally seemed to be located somewhere on the back of my neck, but an occasional quick slap took care of that matter.

"Get your mind off of it," Leonard said.

"What?"

"You just took the bait off your hook and cast the empty hook back in the water. I'd say you're thinking about Florida or Hiram."

I had been thinking about Florida earlier. And Hanson. They were going to get married. Florida had invited me to the wedding. By mail. She said she hoped I'd come. Word from Charlie, who still shopped at Kmart, was that Hanson was hoping I'd stay home. I kept thinking I ought to wish Florida and Hanson well and be happy for them. That was the right thing to do, but I kept hoping she'd miscalculate and get her period on her wedding night. It was the least fate could do for me.

"It's Hiram," I said. "The whole mess."

I reeled the line in, gingerly. My ribs were a lot better, but I still found simple things painful. The doctor had wanted to put a body cast around me, but I'd had broken ribs before. After he helped me get them set, I'd insisted on an Ace bandage, wrapped tight. I figured another month from now I could put on a Chubby Checker record and do the twist. Leonard had recovered just fine; the sprain had gone away within a week.

"You know," I said, "I kinda liked Hiram. He had a good side."

"You kinda liked his bullshit. There's no balance in having a good side when you got the other side he had. Hell, you don't know he had a good side. He had a good front, man. That guy had more masks than a gaggle of trick-or-treaters.

Look the way he went off and left his mother so he could kill that kid."

"I guess. You think he'll get life, or a needle full of shit?"

"I pray for the needle. I'd like to be there to push the plunger in the fucker, or maybe just forget the dope and jab him to death with the needle."

"The thing that worries me about you, Leonard, is you have such a hard time getting in touch with your true feelings."

"Yeah, I'm gonna get me an analyst can help me out on that. Tell me why I'm queer, too. They like stuff like that. He'll want to know if I dream about my daddy's dick. Hell, maybe I'm lucky, shrink'll be some blond stud that's queer himself."

"Hope springs eternal."

"Listen, man, you worry too much about the psychology of things. That stuff's just head voodoo. It don't mean a thing. You took all the psychiatric and psychology degrees in the world, balanced that paper against the truth, there wouldn't be enough there to wipe a baby's ass on."

"Maybe. But it figures with Fitzgerald, if the stuff Hiram says was true, and I think it was, but Hiram, I don't know."

"You want everything to come up neat, Hap. That's bullshit. What Hiram said about Fitzgerald is probably true, what he said about himself is probably bullshit. What you're doing, is still blaming yourself for not figuring Hiram sooner."

"I should have seen it. Shit, everything was there. Boxes of flags in Hiram's van, and each of the bodies had been wrapped in cloth, and he had quoted that piece out of Psalms. Add to that the fact he was here every year at the time of the murders, knew the Reverend and had a history with him. Toss in the religious connection, the way he'd acted that night I handed him Ivan, all drugged and dying, the way he looked at the kid like I'd given him a gift from God. The thought of that, knowing what I know now, gives me chills."

"Monday morning quarterbacking. I've heard it all, Hap, and frankly, I'm tired of it. Look, amigo, I don't blame myself. You shouldn't blame yourself. Hiram was cool, and Fitzgerald, hell, he was ripe for the part and was guilty too. We had our eyes on him and couldn't see the whole of it. That flag shit, hell, who would have thought of that? Only way it would come together is the way it did. You found the flag and the kid. But the thing is, another kid didn't go down. We got 'em all. I'm gonna feel sorry for anyone, it's T.J., rotting away in some state institution. Not that I'd want the fucker on the street, but in his case, I got a tear or two for him."

"I don't see any."

"I cry on the inside. And I hope every day the poor bastard will die in his sleep. He ain't nothing for this world. Shit, Fitzgerald told T.J. his own dick was a snake, he'd have believed it. Cut it off and tied it in a knot had Fitzgerald wanted him to."

"No doubt about that."

"Actually, thing that cheers me at night is thinking of that motherfucker falling down that well. I wish I could have been close enough to hear his bones break."

"Your humanity overwhelms me, Leonard."

"Now forget Hiram, the whole mess. Set your hook. Personally, I put my next bait on the hook, I'm gonna pretend I'm putting the needle in Hiram's eye. . . . Come on man, let's catch at least a couple perch. I'd like fish for dinner."

"You know what it is, Leonard?"

"No, but I'm gonna find out."

"It's the fact they were the same, and yet, they were different."

"Hiram and Fitzgerald?"

"Yeah. I mean, Hiram says they were the same, but what do you think?"

"Same thing I thought yesterday. They're both better off dead, and when Hiram goes and makes it a duo, I'll buy a party hat and a noisemaker. But since you just got to talk about it, let me give you my last word, brother. Fitzgerald, if Hiram can be believed—and like you, I believe this part—got jacked around early on, right? What did you call him?"

"Psychotic."

"Right. And Hiram, he was a psychopath. No matter what story he tells about how he and Fitzgerald were turned into what they were. I don't buy it. Least not in Hiram's case."

I remembered the story Hiram told, or at least I remembered it as best Hanson would tell it to me later. Hiram told the law and the psychiatrists he couldn't help himself; he'd been made that way. Said when he was a boy he spent time with Fitz, and Fitz's father raped not only his son, but him as well. This, he said, was why the old man killed his wife. Not that he thought she might be sleeping around. That was just the bullshit he told me to distance himself from Fitzgerald. The old man's wife caught the elder Fitzgerald in the act with him and Fitz. Hiram said they watched the old man murder her and wrap her in a flag from the church. Then he made them help load the body in his car, go to the Hampstead house with him, watch him dispose of her by candlelight, all the while telling them it was the will of God. Words confirmed by the image on the wall, the water-spot face of Christ.

Hiram said the old man told him he ever said a word, he'd do the same to MeMaw, so Hiram had been quiet all those years. But the memory wouldn't go away, and he'd wake up at night and see the blood and think of it oozing through that flag. He'd envision the water spot on the wall and smell the fresh dirt beneath the house, and he'd feel angry. He developed an urge to light fires and make little animals suffer. He did both on the sly.

When he was a grown man, animals weren't enough. And he and Fitzgerald, scarred by the same crime at the same time, found a linking between them. The murders began. They felt they were doing the will of God, getting rid of those sad cases, those admonitions. Or so said Hiram.

"You see, man," Leonard said, "Hiram was lying. He understood the reasons Fitzgerald was the way he was too well to be operating by them himself. It had been Fitzgerald who had believed in what he was doing; he was the one with the psychotic delusions that he was doing God's work as given him to do by his daddy. But you can't let Fitzgerald off the hook either. He made a choice. And there was something else, man. He had those porno mags same as Hiram, and the sex with the kids, they can say that was part of the pattern, but it all sounds like a power trip to me, plain and simple. But let's give Fitzgerald a little room and say it isn't all his fault. Not much room, but enough to turn around in, and then let's go on to Hiram.

"Hiram, he got a bad break for a kid too, but hell, that wasn't his environment. He'd got over it in time, dealt with it, told eventually, he'd wanted to. But he liked the killing from the start, was born with a wire twisted and a piston loose. I bet he was doing them animals in before he ever got butt-fucked and in on that murder. With Hiram, it was like dropping ole Br'er Rabbit in the briar patch. He was born and bred for it, same as some dogs come out bad and others come out good, and they come from the same stock. MeMaw was good people, but that didn't mean the genes didn't come together in Hiram crooked somewhere. Got the wrong combination."

"Then in a way," I said, "that means he couldn't help it."

"Bad dogs can't help but bite either. I've seen 'em born vicious and just get worse as they got older, no matter how good you treated 'em. They can't help it, but I couldn't help putting a bullet through their heads either. You don't bite me, or try to bite me but once. . . . Shit, Hap, some things just are. Hiram was a predator from birth, and he enjoyed feeding Fitzgerald's religious frenzy, so in turn he could feed his own needs. Think about what they found in Tyler."

When Hiram's home was checked into, the police in Tyler found souvenirs, more souvenirs than could have come from those dead boys under the Hampstead place. It looked as if once a year in LaBorde hadn't been enough for Hiram. In time, if he talked more, the Tyler police felt certain they'd clear up a lot of local cases involving missing children.

"No telling how many kids Hiram's nailed," Leonard said. "Here, in Tyler, on his route. He had the perfect job for his little hobby. And he'd kept right on doing it until he was stopped or the grave got him."

"I know," I said. "I guess there's a part of me thinks somewhere along the line everyone could have been saved. Maybe not come out perfect, but not come out a monster either."

"Hap, my man, there is evil in the world. True evil. It doesn't twirl its mustache and it doesn't wear black and it doesn't slink and it doesn't come in any one color or sex. Sometimes evil comes from good places, like MeMaw, and sometimes it can wear all kinds of good faces and talk good as anyone can talk, but it's just a face and it's just talk. Evil's real, man. Same as good."

"And what about T.J.? How does he fit into your theory?"

"I don't care if he fits at all, Hap. Now shut up and fish."

I baited my hook and did just that, but I never could get my mind right. I kept thinking about it all, wondering if the kid we'd saved would have a chance now, or if he'd just go right back to the street. I wondered if at this very moment he might be sticking a shot of horse into his arm.

We didn't catch any fish. Leonard was pissed. His mouth was set for a finny friend. We stopped off at Kroger's on the way home and went in there to buy a fish to fry. They were all out. We got some fish sticks and took them home and baked them in the oven.

Later that month, on a cool night with the sky black and the stars bright, I moved away from Uncle Chester's. The work on the house was completed, except for painting, and Leonard decided to live there at least until spring. At that time, I was supposed to move back and help paint the place, then he'd put it up for sale.

But for me, for now, I wanted away from there and the remains of the drug house next door, MeMaw's house, the woods out back, and the Hampstead place. I felt it all closing in on me at night, as if the houses, the remains of the drug house, were living things that could reach out and touch me.

I suppose, believing that way in some primitive part of my mind, I should have believed Uncle Chester's bottle tree could protect me, but it had become easier to believe the evil than the good.

Me and Leonard had a big dinner that night, and after dinner I shook hands with him, put my stuff in the back of the pickup, and we stood around outside and listened to the wind in the bottle tree. It was a cool wind. It was an agreeable night.

"You be true, Hap."

"Don't be surprised you don't hear from me for a week," I said.

"All right."

"Don't be surprised you hear from me tomorrow."

He smiled at me. "Drive careful, man."

I hugged him and drove away from there, started home, but didn't make it. I went out Highway 7 instead. I drove on out to the scenic overlook and went up there and parked. I got out and lay on the hood of the truck with my back to the windshield and looked at the sky. It was a beautiful night and the stars were as clear and bright as a young girl's eyes. Beautiful like that time Florida and I had come up here. It was hard remembering exactly who I had been then. I felt older now and the world seemed sadder, and it was as if everything I had ever learned was ultimately pointless. When I had lain here with Florida beside me that night, not so long ago—but in another way, a million years past—she told me we could see Forever. And we could. But Forever then was a wonderful place, full of mystery and hope and eternity.

Tonight, I could still see Forever, but Forever was nothing to see.